ACCLAIM FOR JAMES PATTERSON'S HOTTEST SERIES!

THE GAMES

"FAST PACED...THERE IS NO DOUBT YOU CAN FINISH THIS BOOK IN ONE SITTING."
—Blograma.com

PRIVATE PARIS

"THERE'S NO FLUFF OR DEAD WEIGHT, AND REVELATIONS COME FAST AND HARD...This story is drenched in realism and really strikes a chord, proving to be a worthwhile read."
—matthewrbel.blogspot.com

PRIVATE VEGAS

"NEVER A DULL MOMENT IN THIS ACTION-PACKED PAGE-TURNER." —Writerswrite.co.za

PRIVATE INDIA: CITY ON FIRE

"IT IS UNPUTDOWNABLE AND DEFINITELY A PAGE-TURNER...ONE IS FORCED TO KEEP READING TIL THE END, THOUGH THE END IS OVER 450 PAGES AWAY."
—Winnowed.blogspot.com

THE GAMES

Books by James Patterson
THE PRIVATE NOVELS

Private Paris (with Mark Sullivan)

Private Vegas (with Maxine Paetro)

Private India: City on Fire (with Ashwin Sanghi)

Private Down Under (with Michael White)

Private L.A. (with Mark Sullivan)

Private Berlin (with Mark Sullivan)

Private London (with Mark Pearson)

Private Games (with Mark Sullivan)

Private: #1 Suspect (with Maxine Paetro)

Private (with Maxine Paetro)

A complete list of books by James Patterson is at the back of this book. For previews of upcoming books and information about the author, visit JamesPatterson.com or find him on Facebook.

The Games

James Patterson
AND
Mark Sullivan

GRAND CENTRAL
PUBLISHING

New York   Boston

Copyright © 2016 by James Patterson

Hachette Book Group supports the right to free expression and the value of copyright. The purpose of copyright is to encourage writers and artists to produce the creative works that enrich our culture.

The scanning, uploading, and distribution of this book without permission is a theft of the author's intellectual property. If you would like permission to use material from the book (other than for review purposes), please contact permissions@hbgusa.com. Thank you for your support of the author's rights.

Grand Central Publishing
Hachette Book Group
1290 Avenue of the Americas, New York, NY 10104
grandcentralpublishing.com
twitter.com/grandcentralpub

Originally published in hardcover and ebook by Little, Brown & Company in June 2016
First oversize mass market edition: October 2017

Grand Central Publishing is a division of Hachette Book Group, Inc. The Grand Central Publishing name and logo is a trademark of Hachette Book Group, Inc.

PRIVATE is a trademark of JBP Business, LLC.

The publisher is not responsible for websites (or their content) that are not owned by the publisher.

The Hachette Speakers Bureau provides a wide range of authors for speaking events. To find out more, go to hachettespeakersbureau.com or call (866) 376-6591.

ISBNs: 978-1-4555-8534-2 (oversize mass market), 978-0-316-29019-7 (ebook)

Printed in the United States of America

OPM

10 9 8 7 6 5 4 3 2 1

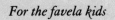

For the favela kids

PART ONE

WORLD CUP FEVER

Chapter 1

Rio de Janeiro
Saturday, July 12, 2014
2:00 p.m.

CHRIST THE REDEEMER appeared and vanished in the last clouds clinging to jungle mountains that rose right up out of the city and the sea. Then the sun broke through for good and shone down on the giant white statue of Jesus that looked over virtually all of Rio from the summit of Corcovado Mountain.

In the prior two months, I'd seen the statue from dozens of vantage points, but never like this, from a police helicopter hovering at the figure's eye level two hundred and fifty feet away, close enough for me to understand the immensity of the statue and its simple, graceful lines.

I am a lapsed Catholic, but I tell you, I got chills up and down my spine.

"That's incredible," I said as the helicopter arced away, flying over the steep, jungle-choked mountainside.

"One of the seven modern wonders of the world, Jack," Tavia said.

"You know the other six offhand, Tavia?" I asked her.

Tavia smiled, shook her head, said, "You?"

"Not a clue."

"You without a clue? I don't believe it."

"That's because I'm unparalleled in the art of faking it."

My name is Jack Morgan. I own Private, an international security and consulting firm with bureaus in major cities all over the world. Octavia "Tavia" Reynaldo, a tall, sturdy woman with jet-black hair, a lovely face, and beguiling eyes, ran Private Rio. And we'd always had this teasing chemistry between us.

The two of us stood in the open side door of the helicopter, harnessed and tethered to the ceiling of the hold. I hung on tight to a steel handle anyway. The pilot struck me as more than competent, but I couldn't help feeling a little anxious as we picked up speed and headed southeast.

I used to be a helicopter pilot in the U.S. Marine Corps; I got shot down in Afghanistan and barely survived. A lot of good men died in that crash, and because of their deaths, I'm not a fan of helicopters despite the fact that they can do all sorts of things that a plane, a car, or a man on foot can't. Let's just say I tolerate them when the need arises, which it had that day.

Tavia and I were aboard the helicopter courtesy of Mateus da Silva, the only other person in the hold. A colonel with the Brazilian military police, da Silva was also head of all security for the FIFA World Cup and the man responsible for bringing Private in as a consultant.

The final game of the tournament—Germany versus Argentina for the soccer championship of the world—was less than a day away. So far there'd been little or no trouble at the World Cup, and we wanted to keep it that way. Which was why da Silva had asked for an aerial tour of the Marvelous City.

After two months in Rio, I agreed with the nickname. I've been lucky enough to travel all over the world, but there's no place like Rio de Janeiro, and certainly no more dramatic an urban setting anywhere. The ocean, the beaches, the jungle, and the peaks appear new at every turn. That day a million hard-partying Argentine fans were said to be pouring over Brazil's southern border, heading north to Rio.

"This will give us a sense of what Rio might look like during the Olympic Games," da Silva said as we peered down at dozens of favelas, shantytown slums that spilled down the steep sides of almost every mountain in sight.

Below the favelas, on the flats, the buildings changed. Here, on the city's south side where the wealthy and superrich of Rio lived, modern high-rise apartment complexes lined the sprawling lagoon and the miles and miles of gorgeous white-sand beaches along the coast.

We flew over the tenuous seam where slums met some of the world's most expensive real estate toward two arch-shaped mountains side by side. The Dois Irmãos—the Two Brothers—are flanked by the Atlantic Ocean to the east, the ultrachic district of Leblon to the north, and a sprawling favela known as Rocinha to the west.

Once one of the most violent places in any city on earth, Rocinha was among the slums Brazilian military police tried to "pacify" in the years leading up to the World Cup. The government trained a hardcore group of elite fighters known as BOPE (from the Portuguese words for "Special Police Operations Battalion") and declared war on the drug lords who had de facto control over the favelas. Da Silva was a commander in BOPE.

The special unit killed or drove out the narco-traffickers in dozens of slums across the city. But they'd succeeded only partially in Rocinha.

The favela's location—spilling down both flanks of a mountain saddle—made access difficult, and the police had never gained full control. Da Silva remained nervous enough about that particular slum to demand a flyover.

We went right over David Beckham's new place in a canyon above Leblon. The British soccer star had caused a stir when he'd bought land in a favela; some of Rio's wealthy were indignant that he would stoop to living in a slum, and advocates for the poor worried it would start a trend and displace people who desperately needed shelter.

The helicopter climbed the north flank of the mountain, allowing us to peer into the warren of pastel shacks built right on top of each other like some bizarre Lego structure.

"You might want to stand back from the door, Jack," Tavia said. "They've been known to shoot at police helicopters like this."

Tavia was very smart, a former Rio homicide detective, and she was usually right about things that happened in her city. But da Silva didn't move from the open doorway, so I stayed right where I was too as we flew over the top of the slum, dropped off the other side, and curved around the south end of the Two Brothers.

We stayed low to avoid the ten or fifteen hang gliders soaring on updrafts near the two mountains. To the east, the coastal highway was clogged with traffic as far as we could see. The Argentines had come in cars and buses. They hung out the windows waving blue and white flags and bottles of liquor. Bikini-clad girls danced on the hoods and roofs of the vehicles and crowded the beach on the other side of the highway.

"They'll be coming all night," Colonel da Silva said.

"Can the city handle it?"

"Rio gets two million visitors on New Year's Eve," Tavia said. "And five million during Carnival. It might not be managed flawlessly, but Rio can handle any crowd."

Da Silva allowed himself a moment of uncertainty, then said, "I suppose, besides traffic jams, as long as the final goes off tomorrow without incident, we're good to—"

"Colonel," the pilot called back. "We've got an emergency on Pão de Açúcar. We've been ordered to get a visual and report."

"What kind of emergency?" the colonel demanded.

As we picked up speed, the pilot told us, and we cringed.

I hung out the door, looking north toward Pão de Açúcar, Sugarloaf Mountain, a thirteen-hundred-foot monolith of dark granite that erupts out of the ocean beyond the north end of Copacabana Beach.

"Can people survive something like that?" Tavia shouted at me.

Even from eight miles away, I could clearly make out the sheer, unforgiving cliffs where they fell away from the peak. I thought about what we'd been told and how bad the injuries might be.

"Miracles happen every day," I said.

Chapter 2

IN A LAB at the Oswaldo Cruz Institute in Rio's Centro District, Dr. Lucas Castro tried to steady his trembling hands as he waited impatiently for a machine to finish preparing a tissue sample for examination.

Please let me be wrong, Dr. Castro thought. *Please.*

There were two others in the lab, young technicians who were paying more attention to the television screen on the wall than to their work. Soccer analysts were discussing the next day's game and still shaking their heads over the thrashing Brazil had taken in the semifinal against Germany.

Seven to one? Castro thought. *After everything done to bring the World Cup to Brazil, after everything done to me, we go down by six goals?*

The doctor forgot about the tissue sample for a moment, felt himself seized by growing anger yet again.

It's a national embarrassment, he thought. *The World Cup never should have happened. But, no, FIFA, those corrupt sons of—*

The timer beeped. Castro pulled himself out of the thoughts that had circled in his brain ever since the crushing loss four days before.

The doctor opened the machine. He scratched his beard, a habit when he was anxious. He retrieved and cooled a small block of sterile medium that now encased a sample of liver tissue he'd helped extract from a very sick eight-year-old girl named Maria. She and her six-year-old brother had been brought to the institute's clinic violently ill in a way Castro had rarely seen before: sweating, shaking, decreased function in almost every major organ.

The doctor took the block to another machine that shaved razor-thin slices off it. He stained these, mounted them on slides, and took them to a microscope. Castro was a virologist as well as an MD. In any other situation, he would have run a time-consuming test to determine whether a virus was involved, but if his suspicions were right, looking at the cells themselves would be a much quicker indicator.

He put the first slide under the lens.

Please let me be wrong about this.

Castro peered into the microscope, adjusted it, and saw his fears confirmed in several devastating seconds. Many of the cells had been attacked, invaded, and hideously transformed.

They looked like bizarre, alien reptiles with translucent coiled-snake bodies and multiple heads. Seeing them, Dr. Castro flashed on a primitive jungle village exploding in flames and felt rattled to his core.

How many heads? he thought in a panic. *How many?*

Castro zoomed in on one of the infected cells and counted five. Then he looked at another and found six.

Six?

Not five? Not four?

He looked and quickly found another six-headed cell, and another.

Oh dear God, this can't be—

A nurse burst into the lab, cried, "The girl's crashing, Doctor!"

Castro spun away from the microscope and bolted after her.

"Who's with her?" he demanded as they raced down a hallway and through a door that led them outside onto a medical campus.

"Dr. Desales," she said, gasping.

Castro blew by her and sprinted down the street to the institute's hospital.

He reached the door of the ICU two minutes later. A man and a woman in their thirties stopped him before he could go in.

"No one will tell us anything, Doctor!" the woman sobbed.

"We're doing our best," Castro told the girl's parents, and he dodged into the ICU, where he yelled at the nurses, "Get us hazmat suits. Quarantine the room. Then quarantine the entire unit!"

Castro grabbed a surgical mask, went to the doorway, saw Dr. Desales working furiously on a comatose eight-year-old girl. "John, get out of there."

"If I do, she dies," Dr. Desales said.

"You don't, you could die."

Various alarms started sounding from the monitors and machines attached to a six-year-old boy in the bed next to the girl. Dr. Castro scanned the numbers, saw the boy was crashing too.

Throwing aside all caution, Castro yanked on sterile gloves and went to work, frantically adding a series of medicines to the IV.

"What the hell is it?" Desales demanded.

"A virus I've seen only once before," Castro said. "We called it Hydra. Goes after the major organs."

"Transmission?"

"Not certain, but we think body fluids."

"Mortality rate?"

"Roughly sixteen percent the last time it appeared," Castro said. "But I think there have been mutations that made it deadlier. C'mon, Jorge, fight."

But the boy continued to fail. The doctors tried everything that had helped in these cases before, but no matter what they did, Jorge and his sister kept slipping further from their control. Their kidneys shut down. Then their livers.

Eleven minutes after Castro entered the ICU, blood began to seep from the little girl's eyes. Then Maria was racked by a series of violent convulsions that culminated in a massive heart attack.

She died.

Fourteen minutes later, in the same terrible way, little Jorge did too.

Chapter 3

FOUR HUNDRED YARDS off the shore of Copacabana, Colonel da Silva and I, harnessed and tethered, hung out the side of the helicopter and peered through binoculars.

Tens of thousands of crazed Argentine fans were partying on the famous beach. But my attention was totally focused on Sugarloaf.

"Do you see them, Jack?" Tavia shouted.

Through the shaky binoculars, I kept getting various glimpses of a thousand feet of black rock, but nothing—

"There," I said, spotting something bright yellow against the cliff several hundred feet below the summit and something red and white below that.

"Jesus," I said. "That's bad."

The pilot flew us beneath the cables of the aerial tram that took tourists to the top of Sugarloaf and hovered a hundred yards from the climbers, a man and a woman dangling by harness, rope, and piton. The man was lower than the woman by twenty or thirty feet.

Neither of them moved their arms or legs, but through the binoculars I could see that the woman's eyes were open. She was crying for help. The man appeared comatose. His rib cage rose and fell erratically.

"I think we're looking at possible spinal damage," I said. "Does Rio have a search-and-rescue team?"

"For something like this?" Tavia replied dubiously.

"No," da Silva answered. "Not for something like this."

"Then we need to land on top," I said.

"And do what?" the colonel demanded.

"Mount a rescue," I said.

"You can do something like that, Jack?" Tavia asked.

"I had a lot of rope training in my early Marine years," I said. "If the right gear's up there, yeah, I think I can."

Da Silva gave me a look of reappraisal and then shouted at the pilot to find a place to land on the mountain's top. We spiraled up, away from the climbers. The pilot coordinated with security officers at the summit to clear the terrace, and in a minute or two, we put down.

An off-duty Rio police sergeant who'd been on the summit when the accident occurred led us around to the tram station, where one of the big gondolas was docked and empty.

Next to the tram, a sandy-haired woman in her twenties sat with her back to the rail, sobbing. A wiry olive-skinned man crouched next to her, staring off into space. Beside them, turned away from us, stood a taller, darker man who was looking over the railing. All three wore climbing gear.

Ignoring the few other people on the dock, we went straight to them and quickly learned what had happened. Alexandra Patrick was an American from Boulder, Colorado. Her older sister, Tamara, was the woman on the rope.

The young man beside Alexandra was Tamara's boyfriend, René Leroux, a French expatriate living in Denver. The three of them had been traveling around Brazil seeing various games in the World Cup tournament. All were experienced climbers.

So was the tall Brazilian, Flavio Gomes, who worked for Victor Barros, the comatose man on the rope. Barros's company had been guiding advanced climbers up the face of Sugarloaf the past eight years. Nothing even close to this had ever happened.

"We set every anchor," Gomes said. "We check them every time. It all looked solid. And then it wasn't."

Gomes, Leroux, and Alexandra had been on a different, easier route than Tamara and Barros. Tamara was a far better climber than her sister or boyfriend and had asked to go up a more difficult way. Gomes's group had gone first and was one hundred and fifty vertical feet above the other two when, apparently, an anchor bolt gave way, and then another. Only Alexandra saw the entire event.

"They fell at least fifty feet," she whimpered. "And then they just kind of smashed into each other, whipsawed, and crashed into the wall. I could hear Tamara screaming for help, saying that she couldn't feel her legs. There was nothing we could do from our position."

Gomes nodded, chagrined. "I'm a solid climber, but I only just started guiding, and I've never been on a rescue like this. It's out of my league."

Leroux hung his head, said, "She's gonna be paralyzed."

I ignored him, went to the rail, and saw an anchored nylon rope going over a pad on the belly of the cliff and disappearing into the void.

"Were they on this line?" I asked.

"No, that line runs parallel to their rope, offset about eight inches," Gomes said. "Another one of our normal safety measures."

Thinking about the position of the injured climbers, thinking about what I was going to have to do to get them off the cliff, I decided against going down the secondary rope.

I looked at da Silva and said, "I need you to make a few things happen very fast, Colonel. Two lives depend on it."

Chapter 4

THIRTY-EIGHT MINUTES later, I was on my belly on the floor of the tramcar. The doors were open. I was looking over the side, straight down more than a thousand feet, and fighting vertigo.

The second I spotted Tamara Patrick on the cliff, I said, "Stop."

Colonel da Silva repeated the order into a radio. The tram halted and swung on the cable about twenty-five feet out from the summit station.

"How far down are they?" da Silva asked.

"I'm calling it three hundred feet," I said, getting up to look at two Brazilian soldiers who'd come from an army base located less than a mile from the bottom tram station. They were almost finished attaching a truck winch to the steel floor of the cable car.

"One hundred meters," I said to the soldiers. "Does it get me there?"

Tavia translated my words into Brazilian Portuguese, and they answered her.

She said, "With the extra rope, they think so."

Gomes was checking the knots and carabiners that connected a climbing rope to the winch's quarter-inch steel cable. I checked the space that separated the winch drum from the floor. Three, maybe four inches of clearance. With that much rope going onto the drum, it would be a tight fit.

We threaded the other, looped end of the climbing rope through a large carabiner we'd attached to a steel hook above the door frame. A closed D ring connected the rope to the harness I wore.

"Radio?" da Silva said.

I reached up and double-clicked the mike clipped to my chest.

The other people in the car—da Silva, Tavia, Gomes, the two soldiers, and the off-duty sergeant—nodded. They got in a line and grabbed hold of the rope with gloved hands.

I went to the edge of the open door, willed myself not to look down. Just before I stepped out, I said, "No slipping, now."

Then my weight came into the harness and my legs were in space, and I was pushing off the bottom of the tram. Free of the car and dropping, I went into a slow twirl that got me dizzy and forced me to close my eyes to the jungle treetops so far below.

Sometimes I think I'm crazy. This was one of those times.

It took them a full minute to lower me the entire length of the climbing rope.

"You're on winch now." Da Silva's voice crackled over the radio.

"Got it," I said, feeling the descent go smoother and faster.

A minute later, I was almost to Tamara Patrick, eight, maybe nine feet above her and four feet out from the wall.

"Stop," I said into the mike, and the winch halted.

"Help me!" Tamara called out weakly.

"That's what I'm here for," I said. "My name is Jack, and we're going to get you out of here."

"I can't feel anything from the waist down," she said, starting to cry.

"But you can feel your arms?"

"A little," she said. "Yes."

"Both hands?"

"The left more than the right," Tamara said, getting herself under control.

"That's good, that's a start," I said, looking down twenty-five feet to the guide hanging there limply.

"Has your guide said anything since the fall?" I asked as I started to kick and pump like a kid on a swing.

"No," Tamara said. "How are you going to get me off here?"

"With a little imagination," I said, swinging closer to the wall and then farther away.

On the third swing I caught that secondary rope coming down from the top. I rigged my harness to it and called into the mike, "Give me eight feet of slack, then bring the litter down."

"Got it," Tavia said.

I waited until a loop of rope hung almost to the injured climber before I started down. When I reached Tamara's side, she rolled her head over to look at me, another good sign.

"I'm scared," she said.

"Me too," I said. "I hate this kind of shit."

She smiled feebly. "And I love this kind of shit."

"Your sister told me that."

"Am I gonna be paralyzed, Jack?"

There was so much pain and fear in her voice and

face that I felt tears well up in my eyes. I looked away and said, "I'm no doctor."

She said nothing. I glanced at her. She was staring up.

I craned my head back and saw the stiff backboard twisting lazily on a second rope dropping from the tramcar.

"Jack?" Tamara said. "Could you hold my hand until it gets here?"

"I'd be honored," I said, reaching out and taking her left hand. It felt cold and clammy, and I realized she was probably almost in shock.

"Did you see René up there?" she asked.

"I'm wearing his harness."

Tamara nodded, her lower lip trembling. "He can't deal with stuff like this."

"Like what?"

"A paralyzed girlfriend," she said, tears dripping down her cheeks.

"What is he? An imbecile of titanic proportions?"

Tamara laughed through her tears. "Sometimes."

I kept up the light chat with her until the backboard reached us. It took quite a bit of finagling on both our parts to get Tamara strapped to the board, and the winch cable rope attached to the four lines supporting it. But we did it.

"Have a nice ride," I said after I'd separated her from the rope that had saved her. "Very few people have ever done anything like this."

"Thank you, Jack," she said.

"You're welcome," I said, giving her hand one last squeeze. "And whatever happens, you're going to be fine in the long run. Okay?"

"You think?"

"Only an imbecile of titanic proportions wouldn't."

She smiled and closed her eyes.

"Take her up," I said into the mike, and I watched her rise for a few moments before starting toward Victor Barros.

By the time I'd climbed down to the guide's side, Tamara had disappeared inside the tram, and the cable car was moving to the summit station.

"We'll be right back, Jack," Tavia called into the radio.

My fingers were on Barros's neck by then. His skin was still warm to the touch, but there was no pulse that I could feel.

"Take your time," I called sadly into the mike. "He's gone."

I hung there on the side of the cliff with the dead guide until the tram came back and lowered the winch rope. Then I clipped it directly to his harness and released him from the rope that had snapped his back and killed him.

Twenty minutes later, they pulled me into the tram. I sat against the wall opposite the corpse, feeling wrung out, and the cable car began to drop toward the mid-station.

"You okay, Jack?" Colonel da Silva asked.

"Honestly? I feel like I could sleep for a week."

Tavia looked at her watch and grimaced. "I'm afraid you can't, boss. We're already running way late."

I glanced at my own watch, closed my eyes, and groaned.

Chapter 5

IN A *BOTECO,* a small, open-air bar not far from the hospital, Dr. Lucas Castro took another belt of *cachaça,* Brazil's potent sugarcane rum. He stared numbly at the television screen, which showed some American guy hanging off a rope running out of one of the tramcars on Sugarloaf Mountain.

Castro turned to Dr. Desales, said bitterly, "A climber dies. A climber's rescued. It's on every channel. But two kids from the favelas dying from a virus? The day before the World Cup final?"

"Not a chance," Desales said, nodding.

Dr. Castro ordered another shot, unable to stop the events of the past five hours from spinning again in his head, getting him angrier and more resentful by the moment. He and Desales had stood there after little Jorge died, drenched in sweat as they watched the flat lines on the monitors, stunned by how fast the boy and his sister had deteriorated and succumbed. The children had been in their care less than three hours.

"We've got to get out of here and decontaminate," he'd said at last.

Shaken, Desales had followed Castro through the

plastic sheeting the nurses had put up while the doctors tried to save the children.

They went to a special room off the ICU, stripped, and put their clothes in a hazardous-waste bin for incineration. Then they examined each other for any possible body-fluid exposure. Satisfied that there had been none, they lathered head to toe in a mild bleach solution that they rinsed off under high-pressure hoses.

When they'd emerged from decontamination they found Manuel Pinto, the hospital administrator, waiting for them.

A puffy-faced fifty-something man in a finely cut linen suit, Pinto asked, "What the hell's going on?"

"We lost two, a young boy and a girl from the favelas," Dr. Castro replied. "It'll take a PCR test to confirm it, but I believe it's a virus that has broken out only once before. Upper Amazon Basin. Three years ago."

"You were there?"

"With a World Health Organization unit," Castro said.

"Mortality rate?"

"Sixteen percent," Desales answered.

"But we've just had a hundred percent incident," Castro said. "We need to quarantine the hospital and the entire favela where those kids lived."

"An entire favela?" Pinto said doubtfully. "I don't have that authority."

"Then find someone who does. I'm going to talk to the parents."

The mother, a sweet young woman named Fernanda Gonzalez, looked pleading and afraid when Dr. Castro walked out of the ICU into the waiting room.

"There's no easy way to say this," Castro said. "We lost both of them."

Fernanda collapsed into the arms of Pietro, her husband, and sobbed.

"How can that be?" Pietro demanded hotly. "I want to see them."

"I'm afraid that's not possible, sir," Castro said. "We believe they died from a highly infectious virus."

"What? Like Ebola?" Pietro asked in disbelief.

"Different, but yes, dangerous like that."

"Where are they?" Fernanda sobbed.

"Their bodies are under quarantine. And we need to do blood tests on both of you and anyone else who came into contact with your children in the past twenty-four hours."

"Oh God," the kids' mother moaned. "Oh God, this is not happening."

Her husband held on to her and sobbed too. Castro stayed with them until they could answer his questions. He learned that they lived in a sprawling slum in northeast Rio that was home to almost two hundred thousand people.

The father had a decent job as a security guard at the monument of Christ the Redeemer on Corcovado Mountain. Fernanda stayed home and took care of the children. They'd both noticed that Maria had been lethargic the evening before. In the middle of the night, she'd started vomiting. An hour later, so had Jorge.

"Where did they get the little cuts on their feet?" Castro asked.

"I don't know," Fernanda said. "They're kids. They're outside all the time."

Barefoot? Castro thought, suppressing a shudder. *In a slum?*

The doctor had grown up in one of Rio's favelas and knew all too well that hygiene in many of them was minimal at best. So whatever the kids stepped on had been infected with Hydra. But who or what had carried the virus there in the first place?

"Dr. Castro?"

He had looked up from the parents to see the hospital administrator standing there, rubbing his hands nervously. Beside him was an imperious little—

The bartender put a full shot glass of *cachaça* on the bar in front of the doctor, taking Castro from his thoughts.

Castro picked up the shot glass and held it up to Desales. "To Igor Lima," he said. "The dumbest cover-your-ass idiot I have ever met."

The doctors clinked glasses.

They took the rum in one gulp, ordered another round, and almost immediately Castro's thoughts began to swirl again to Igor Lima.

Lima worked in the office of the mayor of Rio. He specialized in public-health issues, and when Castro and the hospital administrator had met with him just a few hours before, the man had been mightily annoyed to have been called to work on the Saturday before the World Cup final.

"Viruses and diseases have a way of ignoring such things," Castro had told him.

"What viruses?" Lima had asked. "What diseases?"

After looking at the hospital administrator, who turned his head away, Castro had brought Lima up to speed. The doctor finished with a plea to put the favela where the children had lived under quarantine.

The mayoral aide's chin retreated. His lips did a stiff dance, and then he shook his head. "That's not happening."

"What?" Castro demanded. "Why?"

"Because you're not sure it's a virus that killed those kids."

"I *am* sure. I—"

"You haven't run the PCR tests," Lima said. "You said so yourself."

"Not yet, but—"

"But nothing, Doctor. We'll keep the bodies and the ICU in quarantine pending autopsies and figure out where we are on Monday."

"Monday?" Castro sneered. "You mean after the World Cup final, don't you? That's what's behind this. You don't want to have the mayor and FIFA embarrassed; you want the media broadcasting only good thoughts all over the world tomorrow afternoon. Right? That's the reason you're burying a potential epidemic, isn't it?"

Lima sputtered, "I'm not burying an epidemic."

Castro poked the bureaucrat in the chest with his finger, said, "When a variation of this virus hit a village up in the Amazon a few years back, we had a sixteen percent mortality rate. But this is a mutation of Hydra. The cells have six heads instead of five. It killed both those children. One hundred percent mortality."

"Again, without tests and without autopsies, you can't know that," Lima said. "So for the time being, the quarantine begins and ends with those bodies and that ICU."

Castro started to argue again, but the mayoral aide stepped back, said, "Doctor, I hate to do this, but given your history, I don't think you can be considered rational enough to handle this situation. I think you should be quarantined too."

"What?"

"You're off the case, Dr. Castro," Lima said, and then he turned to the hospital administrator. "Senhor Pinto, you are in charge of making sure that everything in that ICU is sanitized and those bodies autopsied tonight so they can be cremated as soon as possible. And test the doctors."

The administrator shook his head. "Tonight? I...I can't."

"And why not?" Lima demanded.

"I have a ticket to the FIFA party at the Copacabana Palace," Pinto said.

"That's your problem, not mine," Lima said.

"You can't be serious."

"Deadly serious," the mayor's aide replied, and he turned to depart.

Castro's hands balled into fists. He wanted to belt the little man but restrained himself, said, "Anyone else dies, it's on your head, not ours!"

"Go into quarantine, Dr. Castro, and you as well, Dr. Desales," Lima said over his shoulder.

Chapter 6

THE BARTENDER PUT two more shot glasses in front of the doctors.

They'd been drinking since their tests, and the children's parents', had come back negative. Dr. Castro drank his down and ordered another. Dr. Desales finished his and said he was done. He and his wife had dinner plans and he didn't want to be wasted when he got home.

Dr. Castro wasn't done and he had no one to go home to anyway. He suddenly wanted to get good and drunk and do something brazen, or vengeful, or both. He didn't know what yet, but Lima's actions could well have doomed many people. Even though he and Desales were clean, there were bound to be others. There needed to be a response. Right?

He couldn't just turn the other cheek again. Right?

That was right. There had to be a response, a just response, a goddamned wake-up call.

Desales set an envelope on the bar in front of Castro.

"Ticket to the big FIFA bash at the Copacabana Palace," Desales said. "Pinto gave it to me because he couldn't use it, but we have plans with the in-laws and my wife won't break them. You should go."

"Screw that," Castro said, and he picked the envelope up, pivoted, and flicked it into a trash can behind him.

Desales sighed, clapped Castro on the shoulder, and left.

The bartender set another shot down in front of the doctor just as the television screen changed from news back to World Cup coverage. More analysts. More dissection. More ruminating on Brazil's brutal loss.

Seven to one? After everything, seven to one? For Brazil to go out before the finals was bad enough, but to get demolished? Annihilated?

Castro's thoughts turned circular again, brought up old bitterness and grief he'd told himself a thousand times to leave behind. But the doctor couldn't leave bitterness and grief behind. They were such constant companions, they might as well have been friends.

The doctor drank the shot down and ordered one more.

The screen cut to Henri Dijon, a FIFA spokesman, a French guy with a superior attitude and a five-thousand-dollar suit. Dijon was standing at a bank of microphones in front of the Copacabana Palace.

A reporter asked whether FIFA considered Brazil's World Cup a success despite the protests in the months leading up to the tournament. Hundreds of thousands of Brazilians had gone into the streets in cities across the country to decry government corruption and the spending of billions on sports stadi-

ums that might never be used again while the poor of
Brazil got nothing.

"FIFA considers the tournament a smashing success for Brazil, for Rio, and for everyone involved,"
Dijon said, and he kept blathering on in that vein.

For everyone involved? Castro thought, tasting acid
at the back of his throat. *For* everyone *involved?*

Maybe the greedy bastard politicians who'd
skimmed millions could consider it a success. And
the construction companies. And FIFA, the most corrupt sports organization in the world. For those three
groups and some others, the World Cup and the 2016
Summer Olympic Games would be smashing suc-
cesses.

But not for the poor, Castro thought angrily. The
poor, as usual, had gotten shafted. Thrown out of
their homes to make way for the stadiums, doomed to
substandard health care, poor sanitation, and inferior
educations.

Or destroyed, like that favela family today. Or like
Castro two years ago.

He shook his head. He wouldn't go there. He
wouldn't allow those memories to cripple him. Not
tonight.

Instead, he watched the FIFA spokesman prattle
on, ignoring the misery created by the sporting event
and speaking only of the joy. Castro couldn't ignore
the pain or the misery. He couldn't have if he'd tried
because he had suffered as much as anyone and more
than most.

As a result, Dr. Castro hated all of them, everyone
who had anything to do with the World Cup. In his
mind, the suffering was entirely their fault. And now,
probably starting in that favela where Maria and little

Jorge had lived, there would be even more pain because of a stupid soccer game.

There has to be some kind of response, Castro decided as the bartender put down the new shot glass full of rum. *There has to be some kind of balance restored, some kind of penalty, something to...*

A thought came winging out of the blind rage he'd worked himself into. The doctor dismissed it out of hand at first and picked up the shot glass.

Then he thought about it some more, and again.

Dr. Castro put the glass down, understanding that restoring balance would mean crossing a line, after which there was no coming back. Ever.

I don't care, he thought. *This isn't vengeance. It's the right thing to do.*

Castro sat there a moment, swelling with justness, purpose, and resolve. Then he pushed the shot glass aside, paid his tab, and went over to the trash can, feeling stone-cold sober.

Chapter 7

BY SIX THIRTY that evening, Avenida Atlântica was jammed with partying Argentines. The police had shut down the lane closest to the beach to take care of what had become a dangerous situation: the drunken revelers wandering off the famous black-and-white-mosaic sidewalks directly into traffic.

With traffic moving in only one direction, taxis and cars were slow bringing guests to the Copacabana Palace. Though more celebrities stayed at the Hotel Fasano in Ipanema these days, the Palace remained the place to throw a high-society bash.

As he walked along the sidewalk toward the main entrance, Dr. Castro was thinking that the Palace was also FIFA's hotel. It only made sense that the final big party of the tournament would be held here.

Castro was wearing his best suit, navy blue, tropical wool, with a lightly starched white dress shirt and a red tie with soccer balls on it. He saw security men eyeing him as he approached. He lifted his hand to scratch his beard then remembered he'd shaved it off and put his hand in his coat pocket instead.

A couple climbed out of a cab just ahead of him.

Both wore FIFA credentials on lanyards around their necks. The woman carried an invitation.

For a moment, the doctor hesitated.

Did he need FIFA credentials to get inside? Would he be turned away?

Castro forced an easy smile and held up his invitation.

Security waved him up the stairs.

A doorman opened one of the double doors. Castro stepped into a crush of well-dressed partygoers, his left hand still holding the invitation. His right hand protected his front pants pocket and all that it contained.

Slipping to the outside of the knot of people, Dr. Castro saw a table where guests were checking in. He also noticed a second security team: a big, beautiful Brazilian woman to the left of the grand staircase, and a tall, muscular blond-haired guy on the right. Both wore radio earpieces. Both were attentive and scanning the crowd.

It took four or five minutes for the doctor to reach the table. He held up the invitation to a grinning woman wearing FIFA credentials, said, "Manuel Pinto."

She turned a few pages on her list, found Pinto's name, and ran a pink line through it. Then she handed him a small ID badge that he clipped to his breast pocket. He smiled, thanked her, and walked around the table.

Joining others moving toward the staircase, Dr. Castro kept that easy smile going, trying to look as if he were about to meet an old friend. He turned his head slowly toward his left shoulder and then toward his right as he got close to the second security team.

The doctor was using body language; by exposing his neck to the Brazilian woman and then the blond man, he was saying, *I am not a threat. Not a threat to anyone at all.*

It seemed to work, as neither of them paid him much attention. He stole glances at the badges they wore: REYNALDO, PRIVATE. MORGAN, PRIVATE.

Dr. Castro stiffened as he went by them.

Private.

He vaguely knew of the company and its reputation.

What were *they* doing here?

Where the staircase split, the doctor went right, climbing to the mezzanine and wondering whether having Private around made going through with his plan too risky. Maybe he should just have a drink and slip out. But then he flashed on images of bulldozers and rubble and a torn, bloody lab coat and those kids dying today, and the anger came back, along with his purpose and resolve.

Dr. Castro turned left on the mezzanine and moved with the crowd past walls covered with photographs of notable guests of the Palace, almost all of them Hollywood actors, European royalty, music greats, or the superrich and powerful. He found it all of only mild interest, although he did note that novelist Anne Rice's picture was above and in a much more prominent position than Brigitte Bardot's.

The doctor entered a ballroom set up for a banquet and continued along with the throng out onto a terrace that overlooked Avenida Atlântica, the beach, and the ocean. Night had fallen.

Across the street, under spotlights, men were playing beach volleyball. There were drums beating and whistles blowing somewhere, and Argentine and German fans were crushed in around the open-air bars and kiosks along the waterfront.

The crowd on the terrace was much more well-heeled. Dr. Castro guessed dignitaries, FIFA officials, local politicians, and a smattering of tycoons.

Everyone who had benefited, he thought bitterly.

The majority of people he'd come in with were already pressing on toward the bars on either side of the terrace. The doctor figured he'd had enough for one night but thought he'd look out of place without a drink in his hand. He waited patiently and ordered club soda with lime on the rocks.

When Dr. Castro turned away from the bar, he glanced through the crowd and was startled to see Igor Lima six people away and to his left. The mayor's aide was drinking champagne, talking to a blonde six inches taller than him, and looking very self-satisfied. For a long moment the doctor got so enraged he considered making Lima the direct object of his wrath.

But he restrained himself. Too obvious. And Lima might recognize him, and that would do Castro no good in the long run.

It had to be a more fitting choice, the doctor thought. A statement. A...

The party dynamics shifted, some guests leaving the terrace to check on their seating for dinner. The exodus opened up space in the celebration and revealed new faces, including another one that Dr. Castro recognized.

He felt the rightness of that choice begin to vibrate everywhere in and around him. His skin tingled. It made him shiver.

Breathe, he told himself. *Breathe, and then calmly, coldly, finish this.*

Castro shifted his drink to his left hand, reached into his pants pocket, found the long thin cylinder, and grasped the length of the slender barrel. With his thumbnail, he flicked off the cap.

"Please, if you will all come inside, dinner is about to be served," a woman called, prompting the crowd, including his target, to surge toward the banquet hall.

Castro forced that easy smile onto his face and lifted his drink before him, which got people to move out of his way. He angled and slipped and sped up until he was right behind Henri Dijon.

Quick as a whip, he drew his weapon, held it tight to his body, and then...

"Ahh!" Dijon yelled.

The FIFA spokesman spun around, slapping at his butt cheek and looking everywhere. His shoulder collided with a young waitress carrying a tray loaded with cocktails. He knocked her off her feet. The drinks and the tray crashed to the stone terrace, sending booze and shards of glass flying.

During the same three or four seconds, Castro kept moving and pocketed his weapon. Far enough away now, he blended in with the other guests as they all turned to check out the carnage. Dijon looked mortified as he helped the waitress back to her feet, saying, "I'm so, so sorry. I got stung by something, and I..."

The doctor drifted off. He didn't want to seem too interested. Besides, the job was done.

As he moved through the banquet hall, he monitored his reaction. He had crossed the line, and yet he felt no remorse and no guilt. None whatsoever.

That's easier, he thought. *Better.*

Dr. Castro left the banquet room, walking with a slight hitch in his stride so he wouldn't accidentally jab himself with his weapon. He found a men's restroom. He took a stall, put his drink down, felt wobbly, and leaned against the wall with his eyes closed for several long beats.

Then Castro gingerly went into his pocket and drew out the syringe. He studied it, feeling more than satisfied. When the doctor had gone out onto the terrace, there had been five ccs of little Jorge's blood in the cylinder. And now?

Now there were only three.

Chapter 8

I PLAYED DIVISION 1 football. I know what it's like to be an athlete surrounded by a raucous crowd on a big game day, how you feed off it, how the fans feed off your play.

I have also been lucky enough to be in the stands for four World Series games, three NBA Finals, two Super Bowls, a Stanley Cup contest, and the men's hundred-meter track final at the London Olympics.

But I will tell you flat-out that I have never felt anything close to the extraordinary energy inside Maracanã Stadium after ninety minutes of nail-biting regulation play and fifteen minutes of dramatic overtime left Germany and Argentina locked zero to zero in the winner-take-all game for the soccer championship of the world.

Going to their respective benches for water and coaching before the second overtime period began, the players looked like they'd been through a war. The fans in the stadium looked like they'd witnessed a war and were holding on to one another for strength.

I got it. Like them, I'd seen twenty-two men playing beyond their hearts for one hundred and five minutes, striving for supremacy under incomprehensible pressure, while all around the globe, literally billions of fans were living and dying on their every fevered move.

This is different, I thought as I climbed up the stands and scanned the crowd. *This is a whole other dimension of sport.*

Don't get me wrong. I love baseball, football, basketball, and hockey, but you can't tell me those games yield true world champions the way soccer does. More people play soccer than the four of those sports put together, and the World Cup pits all nations against all nations, with almost every country on earth competing during the four years of qualifying that lead to the final tournament.

As the players returned to the field, the emotion in the crowd of seventy-five thousand rabid fans was off-the-charts electric. I had trouble staying on task when the referee blew his whistle and Maracanã Stadium morphed again into a madhouse crackling with hope and pulsing with fear.

When the ball went out-of-bounds and the din died down a little, I triggered my lapel mike, said, "Tavia?"

"Right here," she said from the opposite side of the stadium.

"Tell everyone that this is not over yet, and we stay sharp until the very last person leaves this place."

I heard her speaking Portuguese and then the crowd roared, drowning her out and sucking me right back into the game at the hundred and twelfth minute.

In a full sprint, Germany's André Schürrle drove the ball down the left side of the pitch with Argentine defenders in hot pursuit. Schürrle dribbled toward the corner and just as he was about to be double-teamed, he struck the ball with his left foot.

The rising ball flew beautifully between both Argentine defenders and past a third before dropping to the chest of Germany's Mario Götze, a substitute player sprinting toward goal. The ball bounced off Götze's chest. Before it could hit the ground, he let loose with a nifty feat of kung fu, booting the ball out of the air and into the net.

The place went insane with a roar that hurt my ears. The Germans were deliriously singing "Deutschland über Alles" while the Argentines screamed in disbelief, ripped at their hair, and cried as if a wedding had just turned into a funeral.

I'd never seen anything like it.

More than seven minutes remained in the overtime, but I began to move laterally through the stadium toward a blue stage erected in the stands high above midfield. This was where the trophies would be awarded. I figured that if there was going to be a security issue, it would happen when the politicians and lords of FIFA emerged from their bulletproof hospitality suites and exposed themselves to the players, the fans, and the world.

Only four minutes remained on the clock by the time I got to the area. Already a large company of burly Brazilian policemen in matching blue suits, ties, and white gloves were moving to positions on either side of the aisle of steps the players would climb to reach the stage. Colonel da Silva was coming down the stairs on the opposite side, inspecting the security line.

On the stage itself, on a long table draped in white, the trophies were being assembled and positioned. Behind the table, overseeing the arrangements, was a man I knew slightly, an acquaintance, really. Henri Dijon was French and the primary spokesman for FIFA.

In every encounter I'd had with Dijon, he'd been unflappable, well spoken, and impeccably dressed. He was also a health nut and ordinarily appeared tanned and fit. But in those last minutes of the World Cup final, Dijon looked pale and weak as he patted his sweaty brow. And his clothes seemed, for him, anyway, disheveled.

The crowd roared. I spun around, saw Argentina's superstar Lionel Messi lining up for a free kick about thirty-five yards from the goal with less than two minutes on the clock. If Argentina had a chance, this was it.

Instead of raising the decibel level, all the Argentines had gone silent and apprehensive. Then Messi booted the ball over the top of the goal, and a great wave of groaning broke over the stadium.

When the referee blew the whistle a short while later, ending the game, the Argentines were wretched and the Germans dancing. Down on the field, it was the same, the world champions celebrating and the almost champions grieving and despondent at what might have been.

"Jack, da Silva says the VIPs are ready to move," I heard Tavia say in my earpiece. "Chancellor Merkel will come last with her own security contingent."

"Roger that," I said, turning away from the field.

My intent was to climb high above the stage before any of the VIPs started down. But I'd taken no more than two steps when I saw Henri Dijon come toward me as if he were drunk and forced to walk a high wire.

The man was drenched with sweat and trembling. He lurched and stumbled, and I caught him before he could face-plant on the concrete.

"Henri?" I said.

"Doctor," he said thickly. His eyes were unfocused and bloodshot.

"We'll get you a medic," I said.

"No," Dijon gasped. "Not here. I don't want to ruin the ceremony."

Tavia had seen Dijon falter and came across the stage in time to hear him. She said, "Let's get him to the clinic."

We held him under his arms and supported and lifted him up the twenty or so stairs. Having the wall of guards on either side made it easier for us and less humiliating for the FIFA spokesman.

"Oh God," Dijon moaned. "Something's wrong. Terribly wrong."

Tavia put her hand on his brow after we'd gotten him out of the stands and into the deserted halls of the stadium.

"He's burning up," she said, and we dragged him to the clinic.

The nurse on duty got him on a bed and tried to check his vital signs. But Dijon went into some kind of seizure; his whole system seemed to go haywire, his body arching grotesquely with violent spasms.

"Call for a doctor," the nurse cried as she tried to hold Dijon down. "There has to be one in the stands. I can't handle something like this, and I don't think he'd survive an ambulance ride."

Tavia radioed Colonel da Silva, who relayed the message. A moment later, over the loudspeaker, a man's calm voice asked for any physicians in the stadium to go to the clinic, where there was a medical emergency.

In two minutes, a shaggy-haired blond man with a mustache came running up to the clinic. "I'm a doctor. What have you got?"

The nurse started firing off the patient's vital signs as the doctor grabbed sterile gloves and a mask and went to Dijon's side. The man's spasms had slowed to tremors. The doctor set to work and the nurse drew the curtain.

In the hall outside the tiny clinic, Tavia, shaken, said, "I've never seen anything like that."

"I saw some rough stuff in Afghanistan, but that was right up—"

The doctor tore back the curtain and hustled toward the door with the nurse crying after him, "Are you sure?"

"Sure enough to be getting out of that room," he yelled. "You should too."

"What's happening?" Tavia demanded as he rushed out.

"He's dead," the doctor said, hurrying by us.

"Where are you going?" the nurse cried.

"I'm a plastic surgeon, no expert on infectious diseases, but that looks like Ebola to me," he shouted over his shoulder. "And because I am no expert, I am getting the hell out of here before this entire stadium is put under quarantine!"

The doctor broke into a run and left us there. Gaping at this news, I stared in at the lifeless form of Henri Dijon, who was sprawled on the bed at an unnatural angle, his skin now livid, almost purple, and blood trickling from his lips.

I looked to Tavia and the nurse, who were also in shock.

"Call da Silva," I said. "And tell the nurse to shut that door."

Tavia put in the call while the nurse sealed off the room where Dijon lay.

"Da Silva's on his way," Tavia said. "Says to talk to no one. Jesus, Jack, we could be infected. What do we do?"

Feeling afraid and shaky for the first time, I said, "Strip, burn our clothes, and cover ourselves in Saran Wrap?"

Chapter 9

LUCAS CASTRO WAITED until he was blocks away from Maracanã Stadium before he removed the blond wig and fake mustache and dropped them in a trash can.

They can't ignore that, the doctor thought, looking back at the brilliantly lit stadium where Shakira was singing. *Someone will pay attention now. The deaths of Jorge and his sister won't be in vain. The death of—*

A firework rocket soared over the stadium and exploded in a series of thundering claps and flashes, then dwindled away to silver glints that rained down on the World Cup venue like a brilliant mist. The image was satisfying enough to turn Castro toward home.

Dr. Castro had no doubt that he would hear how the crisis was handled. Once the body was examined, someone would come to him, and he'd be able to blame it on Igor Lima. No histrionics that might raise suspicions. Just a clear account of the truth.

I warned Senhor Lima. But he was more interested in protecting the World Cup than the people of Rio.

Dr. Desales would back him up. No doubt. And when it came to it, Pinto, the hospital administrator, would do the same, if only to save his own ass.

When Dr. Castro reached home, he was pleasantly tired, and he poured himself a glass of wine, proud of himself. He hadn't stood back. He'd fought for something, sacrificed for it, even spent four thousand dollars for a scalped ticket to the game.

The doctor had watched Henri Dijon through binoculars for the entire match, or at least whenever he was visible. After seeing those same two from Private catch the FIFA spokesman and lead him away, he knew it was only a matter of time before a call went out for a doctor, a call that he would answer.

Encountering Morgan and Reynaldo again, he'd had a moment of panic that they would recognize him from the night before. But his disguise and the urgency of the situation had been enough to keep all attention on the dying man.

Dijon had conveniently expired before Castro had time to make even a mock examination. Then it was simply a matter of suggesting Ebola was the culprit and acting the scared, unethical plastic surgeon out to save his own hide.

By now the entire stadium must be under lockdown, the doctor thought as he poured himself a second glass of wine and turned on the television, expecting the late local coverage that Sunday night to be all about the virus outbreak.

But there was nothing. Just stories about the game and how smoothly it had all gone. Not even a protest had marred the event. FIFA and the government were declaring the tournament and the final a classic, one for the ages. Never once was Henri Dijon mentioned. And watching a live stand-up inside Maracanã, he could see that the stadium was empty.

Castro couldn't believe it.

They're burying Dijon's death, he thought with growing bitterness. Even the death of someone like Dijon wasn't enough to shatter the facade. They were burying the story for FIFA's and Rio's image, just like they'd buried the two poor kids.

The doctor sat there for hours staring at the screen, telling himself that at some point, word of Dijon's death and its manner would get out. But by dawn, watching the early newscasts, he wasn't even trying to believe it anymore.

Dijon's death will be attributed to a heart attack or something. The virus will never be mentioned. I'll never be contacted. And more will die until...

No, that's not happening, Castro decided, feeling angrier and more obsessed than ever. *There has to be payback. That is all there is to it.*

He owed those dead kids payback. He owed all the poor of Rio payback as well. And Sophie? He owed her most of all.

Castro went to his refrigerator and pulled out a vial. He held it up to the morning light and swore he could see the ghosts of Sophie, the children, and even Dijon swirling in the rest of the contaminated blood.

Every single ghost was howling at him to go on.

TWENTY-FOUR MONTHS AND TWO WEEKS LATER

PART TWO

A TALE OF TWO CITIES

Chapter 10

Thursday, July 28, 2016

ONE WEEK AND one day before the opening ceremony of the 2016 Summer Olympic Games, Rio was almost ready to show the world how to party.

Construction went on around the clock as workers finished up the Olympic venues spread across the city. Corporate hospitality tents had gone up on the beaches and in the parks. The new subway line to the Olympic Park in Barra da Tijuca had opened the week before, to much fanfare.

In Ipanema and Copacabana, hotels were fully booked for the upcoming sixteen-day event, and the few apartments available were going for twenty-five thousand dollars U.S. a week. The first of several massive cruise liners had already sailed into Rio's harbor to provide overflow sleeping space for the five million people expected to come to the Marvelous City for the games.

Newspapers wrote about nothing but the Olympics. It was the only topic on the radio, the only thing you saw on television. Even in squalid places like Alemão, the so-called German favela of northwest Rio, there was an energy in the air; anticipation, yes, but something more that Rayssa couldn't quite put her finger on.

Standing behind a four-foot masonry wall high up one of the six steep hills of the Alemão slum, Rayssa was pissed that she couldn't name that energy.

What was it? And what was everybody in Rio anticipating anyway? Didn't they know the whole thing was rigged from the get-go? Completely and totally rigged? *No, they don't. Fools. So we have to show them, educate them.*

It's the only way anything will change here.

As these thoughts weaved through her head, Rayssa rested her elbows on top of the wall and looked through a pair of high-dollar Zeiss binoculars. It was late on a Brazilian winter day, the sun already behind the towering mountains to the west, and the shadows lengthened with every moment. But from her position, Rayssa still had a sweeping, panoramic view of the favela, all six hills, all six aerial gondola stations, many of the alleys, many of the broader pathways, a few of the little markets and stores, the ditches that funneled raw sewage downhill, the roof of the police station on the far, far hill, and the new school the government liked to tout.

To anyone who'd not grown up in a favela, this was a hellish existence, devoid of culture or enriching experience. But Rayssa loved the favelas, their vibrancy, their music, their art, the close-knit fabric of life. Favelas didn't just exist. They pulsed, and Rayssa loved each throb and each cry.

She moved the binoculars, paused, and held them on a group of church volunteers standing on what passed for a playground at the school, distributing clothes and food. She studied the line of slum dwellers awaiting their handouts as well as the knot of young, foreign do-gooders doling out the contributions. Two

girls, roughly nineteen, pretty, fair-skinned Cau-
casians, stood out. She watched them for a long time,
seeing how tense and uncomfortable they were. Then
Rayssa panned beyond the girls to two beefy guys
watching over the whole scene.

Rayssa studied them for fifteen or twenty seconds
before lifting her eyes from the binoculars and looking
up at the sky. It was already dusk. Within minutes it
would deepen into the time when jaguars hunted.

A fourteen-year-old boy came padding up to her.
"They're ready."

"Get ready to disappear, Alou," she said.

"Like smoke in the wind. The binoculars good?"

"The best," she said. "Good steal."

Alou grinned. "Lightest fingers in the city."

Rayssa picked up a cell phone, sent a group text:
Set.

She brought up the binoculars again. Lights were
starting to blink on in shacks all around the slum.
She peered toward the police station just over a mile
away, scanned the paths and alleys below it. No men
in SWAT gear. Just the good people of the favela going home after a day of backbreaking work.

Rayssa lowered the binoculars. She looked at the
school with her naked eye now, gauging the deepening gloom. You didn't want to go too early because the
element of chaos and surprise would be reduced. You
didn't want to go too late because the chaos and surprise might be too much and it would all be for—

She snatched up the phone, texted *Now.*

Rayssa had just enough time to grab the binoculars
before two rifle shots barked and echoed over the
slum. Two bullets hit the beefy guys watching over the
church group, one in each man's head, dropping them

in their tracks a split second before a thudding explosion lit up a street two miles away.

Every light in the favela died.

"Go, Alou!" Rayssa whispered, and she heard the boy leap up and run.

Under cover of night, Rayssa stood there a moment, hearing shouting and yelling far below her near the school, none of the words clear or distinguishable from that distance, just panicked voices all melding together and sounding to her like the throaty, hissing-whip roars of one very pissed-off jaguar.

Chapter 11

DARKNESS WAS STARTING to fall over Botafogo Harbor, ending the splendor we'd been watching from the spectacular table that recently promoted General Mateus da Silva had gotten us at Porcão, a restaurant that boasted dramatic views of the harbor and Sugarloaf Mountain.

Porcão offered Brazilian *churrasco,* with guys walking around carrying big skewers of freshly braised meat that they sliced off for you at your table. Tavia and I had eaten and drunk enough that we waved off a chance for more excellent rib eye, and I held my hand over my glass when da Silva attempted to fill it again.

"You don't think there's even a chance of a terrorist act at this Olympics?" I asked incredulously.

The general looked annoyed, poured more wine for Tavia, and said, "It's not something I stay awake thinking about, my friend, and I'll tell you why."

I sat back, tried not to cross my arms, said, "I'm listening."

"Do you think a foreign terrorist could mount some kind of action in Rio without help from the locals?" da Silva asked.

"I'm not following you," Tavia said.

"Black September attacked at the Munich Olympics," da Silva replied. "They were all Palestinians, but they had help, people in Germany who believed in their cause. But in Brazil, you will not find people to help foreign terrorists, just as you will not find homegrown terrorists here."

"And why's that?" I asked.

Acting as if it should have been obvious, the general said, "Brazilians and, especially, Cariocas do not have the right mind-set for terrorism. They're too happy with their lives. Let's say you are some crazy Middle Eastern terrorist and you come to Brazil and you say to your neighbor, 'Hey, Senhor Carioca, let's build a bomb to change the world.' You know what Senhor Carioca is going to say?"

I raised my eyebrows. Tavia smiled as if she knew the answer.

The general continued, "He says, 'No, you go on, Mr. Crazy Terrorist. I am heading to the beach. Cold beers, soccer balls, the ocean, many fine women in bikinis with big round *bundas* for me to look at and many muscular men with six-pack abs for the women to look at. This is all we want in life. This is all any Brazilian wants in life. Not terror, Mr. Crazy Man. Not bombs.'"

I glanced at Tavia, who was highly amused.

"You agree with this argument?" I asked.

"For the most part," she said, chuckling.

"But what about Henri Dijon?" I asked.

General da Silva groaned. "Not again, Jack. That was no attack. No evidence of intentional harm was found."

"Because the autopsy was not exactly thorough."

"You blame the doctors for not wanting to risk their lives if there were no other incidents of infection?"

"Can I speak freely?"

"I've never known you not to."

"You guys wanted the way Dijon died to be hushed up."

Da Silva went stone-faced, said, "We wanted to avoid a panic if it was unnecessary, and history has proven us right. Dijon and those two children were the only ones who contracted that virus. You and Tavia didn't get it, did you? The nurse didn't get it, did she? If the mysterious plastic surgeon had gotten it, we would have heard, but we didn't, did we? In fact, there were absolutely no new cases after Dijon, isn't that so?"

"Correct," I said.

"There you go. End of story."

Tavia said, "But General, you have to admit it's strange that two kids from a favela and one visiting dignitary were the only victims."

"Why strange? Who knows where Dijon had been in the prior few days? And again, it doesn't matter. No new cases in more than two years now."

Tavia's cell rang. She looked at it, said, "The office."

She got up from the table, answered, and walked away.

I said, "I still think you'd be smart to beef up the number of hazmat teams at the venues."

The general thought about that, shrugged, and said, "My budget is stretched thin as it is, thanks in part to Private's exorbitant fees, but I'll see."

I had no time to respond to the not-so-subtle

charge of price gouging because Tavia came back, highly agitated. "Sorry to dine and dash, General, but we have a problem with another client."

Da Silva looked mightily displeased. "I didn't know Private had another client in Brazil during the Olympics."

"During the games, we don't," Tavia said. "These clients are supposed to leave next Wednesday night, before they start."

I blinked, felt hollow in my stomach. "The twins?"

She nodded grimly. "They've gone missing, Jack. And Alvarez and Questa are dead."

Chapter 12

FIVE MINUTES LATER, Tavia and I were in a cab speeding through tunnels and over bridges and down highways toward northwest Rio and the Alemão favela, one of the biggest slums in the city.

"This wasn't how I'd hoped the evening would go," Tavia said wistfully.

"I had other plans too," I said, and squeezed her hand.

"You want me to make the call to Alvarez's and Questa's wives?"

"I'll do it," I said. "But let's get the facts straight first."

She nodded. "I think you did the right thing."

"Not telling da Silva all of it? I don't know. I may live to regret it."

When the general had asked about our clients, I'd told him that the nineteen-year-old Warren twins, Alicia and Natalie, were from Ohio and that their father was an old college friend of mine who'd asked me to look after them while they were in Rio on a church mission. Most of that story was fabricated, and it had to be. Our contract stated that we could not reveal their true identities unless the family gave us permission to do so.

Still, I didn't like misleading General da Silva. He'd been a big supporter of Private's involvement in security for the Olympic Games and for the World Cup before them, and I did not want to alienate him in any way. If I got permission from the parents to tell him, I would. Until then, I wouldn't.

To keep my mind off that dilemma, I said, "Tell me about the favela where they were taken."

"Alemão's one of the biggest and oldest favelas in Rio," she said. "Close to four hundred thousand people live there on six steep hills spread out over, I don't know, eight square miles?"

"Pacified?"

"About as well as Rocinha. There's still a constant battle to keep it clean."

"How bad was it back in the day?"

Tavia raised her eyebrows, pursed her lips, said, "In the 1980s and 1990s, Alemão may have been worse than Rocinha, an outlaw city inside the city. No police would go there. The drug traffickers developed their own justice system and social codes. Rape, burglary, murder, and disloyalty to the gang were forbidden. The punishment was almost always death."

"But the BOPE changed that?"

She nodded. "The German favela was one of the first they tried to pacify. The BOPE made an announcement that they were coming to drive out the narcos. The traffickers were waiting, armed to the teeth. When a police helicopter flew over the slum to call out movement to the BOPE ground forces, someone fired a bazooka and blew the helicopter out of the sky."

"Is that right?" I said, shocked. Despite what Hollywood might lead you to believe, back in L.A., you

just didn't hear about bazookas firing on police choppers.

"The bazooka was the last straw," Tavia said.
"They brought in da Silva as commander the next day,
and he was ruthless. Fifteen or twenty gangsters were
killed in less than eight hours. The others escaped into
the jungle, and even now they keep trying to come—"

I saw what had stopped her. Up ahead, in what
had been blackness, lights were coming back on, flickering and then strengthening and spreading across hill
after hill.

"That's Alemão," Octavia said as the taxi slowed
down and stopped a short distance from several police
cars blocking the road, their blue lights flashing.

We climbed out, paid the driver, and moved toward the officers in the squad cars. Octavia did the
talking, showing her Private badge and gesturing to
me. They didn't seem too impressed until she told
them that the two dead men had worked for us, and
we worked for General da Silva.

In short order we were led to the gondola base and
told to get out at the fourth station up the line. When
the gondola shut and we swung out into space above
the slum, I admit that I was thinking about bazookas.

But then I looked out the window and saw troops
of military police in body armor, all of them carrying
automatic rifles and moving across the twisting paths
of the slum, passing one rickety building on top of five
others on top of ten more. Lit up like that, the favela
looked post-apocalyptic, right out of *Mad Max*.

Two heavily armed officers met us at the fourth station and, with flashlights, led us down to the school.
The slum was an assault on the senses: putrid smells,
unsavory odors, shacks that looked ready to tumble, a

general din punctuated by music blaring, voices yelling, and babies crying. The deeper I went, the more claustrophobic and inescapable the favela seemed.

Lieutenant Bruno Acosta of the Brazilian military police was waiting for us at the school, which had been cordoned off. Acosta was in his mid-thirties, built like a tombstone, and very bright.

The lieutenant knew who we were and the connections we had, so he seemed to hold nothing back. The attack had come in the last light of day. Two different snipers had shot Alvarez and Questa just before the favela's main transformer was blown with an improvised explosive.

"There were a lot of people here when it happened," Acosta said. "The shooting and the bombing caused a near riot. In the darkness, a ground force of four, maybe five masked men swept in on the church group. They had flashlights, found the sisters, took them, and left. There were threats, but no other shots were fired."

"How long until police were on the scene?" I asked.

"Nine minutes," the lieutenant said.

"Enough time to hide them or get them out of here," Tavia said.

"Who are they?" Acosta asked. "Why were they targeted?"

Mindful of the agreement we had with the twins' parents, I said, "The Warren family is very wealthy."

"So a kidnap for ransom?"

"You have another motive?" Tavia asked.

Acosta shook his head. "The parents know?"

"Not yet," I said. "Can we talk to some of the witnesses?"

The lieutenant thought, replied, "It was basically mayhem in here and it was dark. Several of the kids in the church group got trampled and were taken to the hospital. The group leader's still here, though, I think."

We found Carlos Seitz, coordinator of the twenty-person church contingent. Seitz was understandably distraught.

"What am I going to tell their parents?" he said.

"We'll take care of that," Tavia said. "How were they?"

"Up until the shots? They seemed fine."

Seitz described the twins as hardworking, unlike some of the others, who went on missions only because it looked good on their résumés.

"You know, the two-month good deed of their lives," the mission's leader said. "But the Warren girls, you could tell they believed they could really help down here. They were smart, idealistic, and passionate about things."

"Can you give us a way to reach you?" I asked.

"I have a cell," Seitz said. "And I'll write down the address of the hostel where we're staying until we leave next Wednesday."

We each gave Seitz a card and then left him and returned to Acosta. I offered him the use of Private Rio's lab and our forensics team, which were FBI- and Interpol-accredited. Acosta politely but firmly turned me down.

"We're more than capable of handling a crime scene, Mr. Morgan," he said. "You'll have the parents contact me?"

"Of course."

Again with a police escort, we left the area, climbing back toward the ski lift that was our escape from the slum. It wasn't until we were aboard one of the red gondolas that the claustrophobic feeling left me.

"One good thing?" Tavia said.

"What's that?"

"No one seems to know who they really are."

"I'm praying you're right, but then why would they have been targeted?"

I pulled out my cell phone, looked at it and then at the head of Private Rio.

"These aren't going to be easy calls," I said.

"I imagine they won't be," she said. "My offer's still there to talk with Questa's and Alvarez's wives."

"Appreciate it, but I can be a big boy when I have to be."

"Really?" she teased. "I've never once noticed."

"And here I thought you were a world-class investigator."

She tickled me. I winked at her and dialed a U.S. phone number with a 650 area code.

Chapter 13

THE PALO ALTO, California, phone rang three times before going to voice mail. A robotic female voice repeated the phone number, instructed me to leave a message after the beep.

"Andrew, it's Jack Morgan," I said. "Sorry to use your personal line, but please call me. It concerns the girls."

Ten minutes later, after Tavia and I had left the gondola and climbed down the hill to look for a cab, my phone rang.

"Andrew?"

"It's Cherie, Jack," the girls' mother said. "Are they sick or something? I told them that the water could be—"

"Cherie," I said, interrupting. "The girls were taken by armed men earlier this evening. Their bodyguards, my men Alvarez and Questa, were shot and killed."

"What…" Cherie replied in a soft, bewildered voice that trailed off.

I was starting to explain exactly what had happened when she cut me off, screeching at me, "Everyone said you and Private were the best! You told me to my face that you were the best! But the goddamned best would not have let this happen! Not to my babies!"

"No, Cherie, you're right," I said evenly. "I said we were the best, and today that's not true. My men were ambushed by snipers. There was no warning, just two shots out of the blue. When I get off the phone with you, I have to call their wives and families and explain that they're dead and never coming back, which is not the case with your girls. We are going to get them back."

"How?" she demanded curtly.

"I don't know yet, Cherie, but I promise you and Andrew that I will find them and bring them back to you."

"Unless they're already dead."

"You can't think that way."

There was another long pause. I heard her crying softly.

"What is it?" she asked at last. "Ransom?"

"I would assume so, but no one's been contacted yet as far as I know."

"I thought you were going to give them aliases."

"We did," I said. "And no one we've spoken to has mentioned the family name. Everyone still believes they're the Warren girls from Ohio."

"Somebody doesn't," Cherie said. "This can't be a coincidence."

"How do you want me to handle their identity in the future?" I asked.

"Keep our name out of it as long as you can," she said. "I have to tell Andy now. He told me that Rio was the wrong place for them to be, and I...I wouldn't listen."

"I can call him," I said.

"No," she replied. "He needs to hear this from me. And then, no doubt, we'll be on our way to Rio in the jet. Immediately."

My brow furrowed as I said, "Honestly, Cherie, I don't know if that's such a good idea right—"

"Sorry, Jack," she said. "But when it comes down to it, the money aside, our daughters are all Andy and I really have."

She hung up just as a cab pulled over. I climbed in after Tavia and made the calls to Alvarez's and Questa's widows. They were devastated. Questa's wife collapsed and her sister told me she was taking her to the hospital. After hanging up, I leaned my head back against the rest, closed my eyes, and groaned.

Tavia said sympathetically, "You look like you've been through the wringer."

"Twice."

"Lot of stress," she said.

"Muito," I said. A lot.

"I think I know how you could relieve some of that stress," she said quietly.

I couldn't help myself, and I smiled. "I bet you do."

When I opened my eyes, her lovely face and her lips were there. We kissed softly and everything felt a little bit better, and safer, and right.

Chapter 14

LUPITA VALENCIA LOOKED as frail as a newborn bird.

But after Dr. Castro examined the four-year-old girl that evening, he smiled at Lupita's mother and said, "I think she's over the worst of it. She's going to beat it. You'll probably be taking her home sometime tomorrow."

"Bless you, Doctor," the woman said, tears in her eyes. "Bless you for saving her."

"Glad we could help," Castro replied. He patted her on the shoulder and exited the room into a crowded hallway at the Hospital Geral on Santa Luzia Road in Central.

In Brazil, there were two kinds of hospitals: public, for the poor, and private, for the rich. As public hospitals went, Geral was very good, and the doctor was happy to have found work there.

"Who's next?" he asked the triage nurse evaluating the line of patients that wound out the door.

"No one for you, Dr. Castro," the nurse said in a disapproving tone. "You've been here thirty-six hours as it is. Go home. Sleep."

For once, Castro didn't argue. He said, "See you next time. I'm at the university tomorrow."

"Get some sleep," the nurse repeated and shooed him away.

The doctor changed out of his scrubs and left the hospital, mindful of the line of patients that seemed to get longer every day. Castro hailed a cab and almost gave the driver his home address but then changed his mind and gave him another.

Dr. Castro fell asleep and did not wake until the taxi stopped in a light-industrial area on the western outskirts of Rio. The doctor walked beneath sodium lights toward a long, low steel-walled and -roofed building that had a door with multiple locks. Beside the door, a small cheap plaque read:

AV3 PESQUISA—RESEARCH

Castro got out his keys, looked around, and then unlocked the door. He went inside quickly, shut the door behind him, and flipped on a light, revealing an empty room. He locked the outer door and went to a second locked door opposite it. Beyond that was an airy warehouse space dominated by a large white rectangular tent made of laminated cloth. A myriad of ducts and hoses ran into and out of the tent roof.

Without stopping to admire his ingenious design, Dr. Castro went through a flap into an anteroom of sorts. There he donned a full hazmat suit, duct-taped all the seams, and entered a pressurized decontamination shower. Only then did he pass through an air lock into his clean room.

Despite having worked for thirty-six hours, Castro felt renewed energy being back in his secret lab. He loved some parts of his other life—helping patients, teaching students—but it was only here that he felt buzzing and alive.

The doctor crossed the clean room to five glass tanks arranged in a row. Above each was an alphanumeric code and a small camera attached to a plugged-in Samsung digital tablet.

Castro paused at each tank, studying the white rats within. In the first four tanks, the rats were moving around, but there were sores visible on all of them, and several were stumbling as if they had lost their motor skills.

In the fifth tank, the rat was dead. Its sores were more grotesque, and there was dried blood around the eyes, nose, and mouth.

That's interesting, Dr. Castro thought. *When did that happen?*

The doctor went to the tablet and called up a video that featured a running time display at the bottom. Castro sped the video in reverse until he found the moment the rat convulsed and died. According to the time stamp, death had occurred one hour, forty-eight minutes, and sixteen seconds after the doctor had left the lab.

One hour, forty-eight minutes, and sixteen seconds.

The doctor stared at the frozen time stamp for several long moments, thinking that if he weren't so tired he might be doing a victory dance right now.

One hour, forty-eight minutes, and sixteen seconds!

It was the breakthrough. It was what he had been working two long years for, and he was too zonked to celebrate.

Wait. He had to replicate his experiment. He had to know for sure before he did any rejoicing.

Castro noted the code above the dead rat and went to a stainless-steel tank, where he donned insulated gloves to twist open the top. Fog curled out of the liquid nitrogen. He lifted a tray of steel vials and found one with the code that corresponded to the one above the dead rat's tank.

He took the vial and waited fifteen minutes before running water over it, gradually increasing the internal temperature. Done, he retrieved a syringe and removed a tiny amount of blood from the vial. He injected the remaining rats with it and went to a refrigerator.

Before putting the vial inside, he shook it. He watched the blood film and settle, film and settle, thinking that this might just be the mutation of Hydra he'd been imagining in his daydreams, the one that struck quickly, the one that caused total devastation, the one that produced cells with nine heads.

One hour, forty-eight minutes, and sixteen seconds.

Castro glanced at the clock, did the math, and felt enough of a thrill to shiver.

Chapter 15

IN THE HOURS before dawn, I slept fitfully, my mind spinning nightmares about the twins and the men who'd died trying to protect them. I jerked awake, breathing hard and in a cold sweat, around three in the morning.

"Shhh," Tavia said, stroking my cheek in the darkness. "It was just another bad dream."

"I need some good ones once in a while," I said, calming down.

"Then dream of me," Tavia said, and she laid her head on my chest.

Within minutes, her breathing slowed into a deep and gentle rhythm that calmed me even more. I smelled her hair, still damp from the shower, and drifted off into dreams of the moment I'd realized I could fall in love with her.

"Come on, Jack," Tavia had said to me. "You can't really appreciate Rio without seeing her from the sea."

We were at the Botafogo marina, and Tavia was coaxing me into a motor launch she'd chartered after a long day of work after a long flight in from Los Angeles. We'd met formally only that morning.

I'd come to Rio to interview Tavia about opening and heading a Private office in the Marvelous City during the World Cup and Olympic Games. She'd been a dynamo from the get-go, and I knew within an hour of meeting her that I'd give her the job.

But Tavia had put together a crash course of all that was Rio so I'd understand the security challenges of the city before making my decision. We'd been to several possible venue sites prior to boarding the boat, and I was starting to get dizzy from jet lag.

I got in and we pulled away from the docks and motored around Sugarloaf Mountain, through the harbor mouth, and out to sea. We stopped about a mile off Copacabana Beach, where we had a panoramic view of the remarkable landscape and de-sign of the south side of Rio, from Leblon to Sugarloaf and the jungle mountains soaring in and behind the ever-growing city.

"Just breathtaking," I said.

Tavia laughed and threw her arms wide as if try-ing to embrace it all.

"I think God was in the mood to celebrate when Rio de Janeiro was made," Tavia said, and she laughed again. "God made Rio so crazy beautiful that it's impossible not to be happy here. I love it. I'll never leave. If I die, bring me to this spot so my spirit can look at her, love her, and be a part of her that washes ashore."

She'd smiled at me and then gazed all around in wonder, as if she were lost in paradise.

That was the moment when I felt I could get lost in Tavia. That was the moment that stirred and sweet-ened my dreams now and for the next couple of hours until the real Tavia kissed my lips and woke me up for good.

"Time is it?" I grumbled.

"Quarter of five," she said, getting out of bed. "We want to be in Alemão before everyone leaves for work."

I groaned, rubbed my eyes, said, "I'll phone room service for coffee."

"I ordered it last night," Tavia called from the bathroom. "Breakfast in fifteen minutes."

"You're a superwoman," I said, entering to see her climb into the shower. "I saw that about you from the start."

Tavia smiled sleepily. "What took you so long to say so?"

"A complicated life," I said, and I climbed in after her.

I'd sworn never to get involved with an employee again. I had had a relationship with Justine Smith, a psychologist who works in the L.A. office. I still love Justine and believe she still loves me, but we both know it will never work for all sorts of reasons. Anyway, after we broke up, I'd vowed never again to mix business and love.

Because of that vow, a long time passed before I acted on the spark I felt constantly between Tavia and me. We had a special chemistry, as if we were always riffing on each other's thoughts. And since I had to be in Rio for repeated, extended periods, first with the World Cup and then with the upcoming Olympics, we'd spent more and more time together.

It felt inevitable in a way. Tavia was smart, funny, experienced, and tough, and like most Brazilians, she genuinely loved life. Study after study has found the people of Brazil, and especially Rio, are among the happiest on earth.

That was certainly true of Tavia. Despite the difficult things she'd been forced to deal with in her early life, first as an orphan, then as a police officer, Tavia still went through every day thinking life was one miracle after another, which was refreshing, comforting, and, well, enjoyable.

Back in January, I'd flown in for a pre-Olympic security meeting and couldn't believe how desperately happy I was to see her waiting at the gate. We'd gone out to eat and had a bottle of wine. It had been two months since we'd last seen each other. We caught up. We laughed. We talked shop. She looked fantastic.

About halfway through the evening, I realized that I wasn't just smitten with her. She'd turned into a good friend, the kind of person I could and did confide in.

Someone very wise once told me that if you want love in your life, you have to go looking for it. So I broke my vow, and over a bottle of Malbec I'd let it slip that I loved working with her and, well, just being with her.

Tavia had cocked her head. "What are you saying, Jack?"

"I'm saying it's wrong for all sorts of reasons, but I can't tell you how much I've grown to hate being apart from you."

Tavia hesitated for several beats, but her moistening eyes never looked away from mine before she said, "Then don't be apart from me ever again."

Now, standing in her shower, I looked at Tavia washing herself and felt happy and whole, ready to

face any challenge. I could do anything my heart de-
sired with this woman by my side.

Tavia rinsed off, looked at me, and smiled. "That's
quite the grin."

"Is it?"

"Yes. What were you thinking about?"

"True love," I said, and kissed her.

Chapter 16

WE WALKED UP to the Alemão favela, rather than taking the gondola, shortly after dawn. The slum was wide awake and throbbing with life. Dads and moms heading off to work. Moms and dads cleaning clothes in buckets or lounging in their doorways to smoke and watch their children dart with the chickens along the haphazard paths.

After the surreal experience of seeing the slum from the sky at night, I was engulfed by it in the daylight. Yes, there was squalor, but the people seemed to make the most of their lives, and so many were smiling and genuinely happy that I kept having to remind myself that it was a dangerous place, the kind of place that could swallow two missing girls.

Everyone we stopped to speak with asked suspiciously if we were cops. Tavia explained again and again that we had been hired by the parents to look for their girls. We got people to look at photographs of the twins. No one recognized them in that part of the slum, more than a mile west of the school yard where my men had been murdered and the twins taken.

"Police are not liked here," I said after the eighth or ninth person questioned our roles.

Tavia said, "People of the favelas know that police corruption is rampant because the cops are paid so little. It's very dangerous to be a cop in Rio. They die. Often. So the relationship between the police and the favela fluctuates between mutual admiration, suspicion, and outright war. One of the reasons I left to join Private."

"Glad you did," I said.

"Me too," she said, and she smiled in a pleased and playful way.

We kept moving through the slum toward the kidnap site, talking to people, showing pictures. And getting nothing.

There had to be a better way to do this, I thought.

"So they don't trust the cops," I said. "Who do they trust? Who hears things? The priests?"

"Maybe priests, but I don't know how we'd find...wait."

"What?"

"I know someone who might know something. Not a priest. An old acquaintance of mine here in Alemão. Why didn't I think of her before?"

Twenty minutes later we entered a small crowded public medical clinic on the eastern edge of the slum. Tavia went to the window, identified herself, and asked to see Mariana.

The receptionist disappeared but quickly came back to open the door and lead us in. The hallway was crowded with supplies, and we had to squeeze past seriously ill people lying on gurneys.

"Wish I had a surgical mask," I said as we rounded a corner and almost ran into a woman standing there.

"Good thinking," the woman said, handing me one. A kind, grandmotherly type in her sixties, she wore her gray hair in a braid and had an earth-mother style to her clothes.

"Mariana Lopes," Tavia said, throwing her arms around the woman, who hugged her back. "Long time."

Tavia introduced me and said Lopes was something of a saint around the favelas, which caused the woman to blush and wave her off. Later I would learn that in addition to the medical clinic, Lopes ran an orphanage and an after-school program for favela kids, all on a shoestring budget.

"She's around a lot of people," Tavia explained. "She listens to street kids, who often see things adults don't see, or don't want to see."

"If you say so, dear," Lopes said. "How can I help you?"

Tavia explained what had happened the night before, the shooting and the kidnapping of two American church volunteers.

"I'd heard a rumor of gunshots up there," she said. "But nothing concrete. It takes a few days before things like that trickle down to me."

A nurse came up to talk to Lopes, who listened and frowned. She held up a finger, said, "I'm sorry. Crisis of the hour. Listen, Tavia, you know who might know something more recent?"

"Who?" Tavia said.

"The Bear," she said. "Remember him?"

Chapter 17

TAVIA DID REMEMBER the Bear, and she was surprised to hear he was still alive.

"He doesn't live in Alemão anymore, does he?" Tavia asked.

"No, L'Esprit, Spirit," Mariana Lopes said. "But they're not far apart, you know?"

Tavia got directions and we started off again, skirting the German slum to where train tracks separated it from another smaller but no less decrepit favela.

We climbed through the maze up the steep side of the Spirit slum, where teens hung from doorways and men stood at bars the size of closets and televisions blared with the latest soccer highlights. There was music playing everywhere, and it seemed to throb louder as we climbed higher, almost to the top, where the favela met the jungle, bamboo and vine thickets not yet hacked away by someone eager for a newer home.

Drenched with sweat, I looked over my shoulder and was stunned by the view. There was Christ the Redeemer against a crystalline-blue sky, and I could see across the lower basins of Rio all the way to the beaches and the ocean, which looked impossibly aquamarine in the distance.

"Rio's the only city in the world where the poor get the best views," I said.

"True," Tavia said. "But even that is changing."

"People buying up the bottoms of the slums and putting up high-rises?"

"Happens almost every day. So the poor who can't afford the high-rise will just go higher and higher up the mountain, and then down the other—"

Tavia stopped, said, "There's Urso, the Bear."

Urso reminded me of gangster chieftains I'd encountered in L.A. over the years. Big dude. Late twenties. Buff. Heavily tattooed. Cannon-barrel arms. A keg for a chest. Two jackhammers for legs. And bristly jet-black hair that matched the color of his wraparound shades.

At the moment I saw him, however, the Bear's street cred seemed compromised by the fact that he was holding a baby in one arm while handing a woman a wad of cash. She got emotional and bowed her head in thanks.

Urso kissed the baby on the cheek and gave him back to his grateful mother, who bowed again and trotted off past four other gangstas leaning up against a concrete retaining wall just below the edge of the jungle.

As the woman walked away, the Bear smiled, revealing gold caps, two on his upper incisors and two on his lower canines. The grin and the gold caps disappeared when Urso spotted Tavia walking toward him.

"*Oi,* Urso," Tavia said.

He tugged down his glasses to look at her, said in English, "Octavia Reynaldo. Where you been, girl?"

The other gangsters began to leer openly at Tavia, who flipped them the bird, said, "Got a new job. Hadn't you heard?"

"Can't say I did," Urso said. "Who's the surfer boy?"

"My boss," she said. "Jack Morgan, the head of Private. From L.A."

Surfer boy aside, the fact that I was from Los Angeles seemed to impress the Bear because he broke into that gold and stained-enamel smile and reached out a giant tattooed fist to bump mine.

"Where's your crib for real, man?" he asked.

"Pacific Palisades, you know it?"

"Up toward Malibu."

"You've been to L.A.?"

"Lived there four years," Urso said. "South Central–Compton line."

"Rough place."

"No, man, this is rough. South Central's paradise compared to Spirit."

"Why didn't you stay in L.A.?"

The Bear shrugged. "Shit happens. Even in paradise."

"You hear about the shooting and the riot at that food giveaway in Alemão?" Tavia asked.

"I'm not supposed to set foot in Alemão," Urso said. "Ever."

"But you've still got friends inside, right?"

The Bear gestured at the other four watching us. "My friends are all right here. Backs against the jungle, just holding our own. Know what I'm saying?"

"Did you or your friends hear anything about the shooting?"

Urso hesitated and then spoke to the men in Portuguese. The four gangsters shook their heads.

"They don't know nothing. I don't know nothing."

"I can't believe the Bear wouldn't hear about a shooting on his old turf," Tavia said.

Urso acted insulted, said, "If you're not a cop anymore, Reynaldo, why you so interested?"

"The guys who died worked for us," Tavia said. "They had families."

"That right? Now, why would Private bodyguards be in a favela?" he asked her.

"There'd been threats to a church group. My men were volunteers."

"See there?" the Bear said, looking to me. "Dogooders getting killed. Always happens. It's why I try never to do that much good."

He translated, and his buddies broke up laughing and fist-bumped.

I said, "Two American girls went missing after the shooting. Twins."

"That right?" He seemed surprised. "Hadn't heard that."

Tavia showed Urso a picture of Natalie and Alicia. The Bear whistled and held the photo out for his friends to see. They reacted with similar admiration.

Urso said, "We'd remember those two *lindíssimas*. You don't see too many gorgeous *americanas* in Alemão or Spirit."

"Will you ask around for us? There'd be real money in it if you came up with something strong," Tavia said.

"Yeah? How much?"

"You put us onto them, I'll give you fifty thousand *reais*."

Urso snorted. "Make it worth my time. Make it dollars and I'm yours."

Tavia glanced at me, and I nodded.

"All right, L.A.," Urso said with that gold-capped grin, and he bumped my knuckles again. "Bear's on it, and I'll find you those girls, 'cept I need an advance for me and the boys to go to work."

"Give him five," I said to Tavia.

"Ten," Urso said.

"Seven."

The Bear winked and grinned lazily as if he'd just scratched his back against the bark of an old tree.

Chapter 18

AT THREE FIFTEEN that same day, Tavia and I stood on the tarmac of a private jetport at the domestic airport on the Rio harbor front. We had a Mercedes-Benz armored limousine at our backs and four operators armed with H&K submachine guns nearby.

I still felt nervous as the Gulfstream appeared out of the sun.

"What are they like?" Tavia asked. "I mean, in person?"

"The mom, Cherie, can be intense, passionate, idealistic, and, at times, irrational," I said. "Andy's your typical engineering über-mind: brilliant, but socially awkward, probably two or three clicks along the autism spectrum."

The Gulfstream landed, revealing the logo: *WE*. The jet taxied and rolled to a stop in front of us. Tavia signaled her guards. They moved in pairs, two men on each side of the exit ramp as it lowered.

Cherie Wise, a pale redhead in her early forties, came out wearing red capri pants, sandals, a blue Hamilton College sweatshirt, a straw hat, and oversize sunglasses. Andy Wise, a lanky, balding man with round wire-rimmed glasses, followed her. He wore

Wranglers, a green polo shirt with the WE logo on the breast pocket, and running shoes, and he carried an iPad under one arm.

A structural engineer with a Stanford MBA, Andy and his company, Wise Enterprises, had slain giants, making billions in public works and telecommunications projects around the world: Hotels in Dubai. Tunnels in China. Hydroelectric dams in southern Africa. Cellular networks all over the Third World. In Brazil, WE had been involved in the construction of the World Cup stadiums and many of the Olympic venues.

Wise's wife was no slouch either. An English major and former Peace Corps volunteer, she was a tough administrator with an advanced degree from Wharton. She ran WE Help, the Wise family's philanthropic foundation, which gave away tens of millions of dollars every year to various worthy causes.

"Tell me again why I shouldn't fire you, Jack?" Cherie said coldly by way of greeting.

"As ineffective as we were in this case, we're still the best," I replied, having anticipated the challenge. "Without Private's help, you'll be significantly weakened in your effort to find and free your daughters."

Andy Wise stared at me like I was a disappointment, said, "Status of your investigation?"

"We've got every agent in the Rio office assigned to your case," Tavia said, and she introduced herself.

"And I've mobilized a secondary team of my top operators. They'll be leaving Los Angeles within the hour," I said.

"So you are in the organizational stage," Wise said, staring over my shoulder as if there were something behind me only he could see.

"And data-gathering," I said, trying to speak his language. "Tavia's joined forces with a favela insider who has a team tracking your daughters' whereabouts. But, please, I'd feel better if we were in the limo."

Cherie glanced around, said, "We aren't safe here?"

"I think we're perfectly safe here," I said. "But I don't want to take any chances until we know why your daughters were abducted. We'll bring you to your hotel, talk on the way."

The four of us climbed into the limo. Tavia and I sat in the seats facing backward, across from the couple.

When the doors were shut and locked, Wise rolled his head and rocked slightly, said matter-of-factly, "I don't think there's a question about why they were taken, Jack. The hostage and ransom business is booming in South America. Talk to the people at Global Rescue and they'll tell you that."

"Andy, stop," Cherie said. "I'm sure they—"

Wise ignored her. "I've seen the statistics. I know the odds of us ever seeing our daughters safe and—"

"Stop it!" Cherie snapped. "They're not statistics, Andy. They're our daughters, for Christ's sake!"

"Get emotional if you wish," Wise said. "But the numbers don't lie. It's why I didn't want them down here in the first place. I knew the threat. I informed you of the threat. But, no, I was ignored. The statistics were ignored just so you could make the girls look better on some future résumé."

"That had nothing to do with it," Cherie shot back. "I wanted them to see the world for real, not in the abstract. I wanted them to understand people and their plights on a gut, emotional level, not as some goddamned number or statistic."

"And look where it's gotten us," Wise said.

Tavia's cell phone rang. She answered, listened, said, "We'll be right there."

She hung up, turned around in her seat, and knocked on the divider, which lowered. "Change of plans," she said. "We're going to Private Rio."

"Why?" Cherie asked. "I need a shower, a change of—"

"We've been contacted by the kidnappers, Mrs. Wise," Tavia said. "They've sent a video of the girls."

Chapter 19

"MOM? DAD?" NATALIE Wise sobbed. "You've got to help us."

"Please?" Alicia whimpered. "We want to come home."

"Oh God," Cherie Wise said, and she buried her face in her husband's chest.

We were in the lab at Private Rio, watching the video on a big screen. The billionaire rubbed his wife's back mechanically and looked at his daughters with little affect, as if he considered the images nothing more than a gathering of blips and algorithms.

But I was studying everything the camera revealed. The girls were bound with leather straps to ladder-back chairs. The chairs were set about a foot from each other in front of a black curtain parted to show a painting of children on their knees praying.

Natalie and Alicia were frightened, filthy, and showing signs of abuse. Natalie, a redhead like her mother, had a severely swollen left cheek. Alicia, sandy blond and the smaller of the two, had a split lip and eyes that looked like she hadn't slept in days.

Two masked figures in black appeared, a male and a female. The man's mask had feathers and green sequins; the woman's was more primitive, a rudely carved face with a diamond-shaped mouth and painted cat's eyes.

In stilted, accented English, the man said, "We know who is these girls. Tell the Wises we want fifty million dollars or daughters to be executed. You have forty-eight hours to comply. Instructions to follow."

The screen went blank.

"Pay them," Cherie Wise said, unable to control the tears. "Tell them right now, we'll pay."

"Wait," her husband said. "I want to hear—"

"Your options?" Cherie demanded, mouth open, incredulous, tears dripping down her cheeks. "There is no option, Andy. We pay. We get our daughters back, and we go on."

He blinked, said, "Should the police know we've been contacted? That a ransom has been demanded?"

Tavia said, "You have to make that call."

"Why wouldn't we tell the police?" Cherie asked. "I want a manhunt."

"No, you don't," I said. "A manhunt makes them want to run. And if they run, at some point they'll consider your daughters excess baggage, and they might decide it's easier to kill them than let them go. We want to keep this small, contained, controllable."

Cherie bowed her head, then said, "But no police?"

Tavia said, "The way the kidnapping went down says to me that it was done by people who'd had training. Military or police."

"I've read about police kidnappings in Mexico," Wise said. "Here too?"

Tavia nodded. "Seven, eight years ago, a prominent Brazilian businessman was kidnapped and held for ransom. The police took over the operation. They tracked the ransom money, found the kidnappers, and killed them. Then they kept the ransom money, claimed the kidnappers had taken off, and orchestrated a second payment. The businessman was later found dead at the bottom of a well."

"I hate it here," Cherie said, wiping the tears off her cheeks.

Wise studied his wife's anguish, looked over at me, and said, "Find and rescue my girls before that ransom's due, Jack, and I'll pay you twenty percent of it—ten million dollars cash."

Chapter 20

THE LAB SCREEN flickered, split, and then the aging–Grateful Deadhead face of Dr. Seymour "Sci" Kloppenberg was on the left and the kidnappers' video on the right.

"You there, Jack?" Sci asked, staring out at us from inside Private's jet.

"Right here, Sci," I said. "Have you seen the video?"

"Yes, hold on a second, we're having problems with the Wi-Fi in the jet and I want to have Mo-bot in on this as well," he said before the camera went haywire and then went dark.

"Who was that man?" Cherie Wise asked. "He looked like a Berkeley refugee."

"Sci used to teach at Berkeley, actually, but now he works for me."

I explained that Kloppenberg was the polymath criminologist and computer forensics analyst who ran Private's lab in Los Angeles and oversaw all of the company's labs around the world. Sci was also the driving force behind making Private's criminology labs so state-of-the-art that they met FBI, Scotland Yard, and Interpol standards.

"Kloppenberg's quirky, but he's the only person I know who's an honest-to-God genius," I said, which provoked odd looks from both of the Wises. They obviously considered themselves somewhere high in that lofty realm.

"Who is Mo-bot?"

"Maureen Roth. She works for Sci as a technical jack-of-all-trades. She's also one of the most well-read people I know."

The screen flickered and returned, divided into thirds, the video of the girls in the middle, Sci on the left, and Mo-bot's motherly face smiling on the right.

"We've got you," I said. "Can you see us?"

"Yes, we've got it working now," Mo-bot said.

"Apologies," Sci said. "But we've both had a run at the kidnappers' video in the last hour and come up with a few things for you."

Kloppenberg said the video had been sent to Private Rio from an Internet café in Kuala Lumpur through a server in Pakistan.

"Got enemies in either of those places, Mr. Wise?" Mo-bot asked.

Wise thought and then said, "Not that I'm aware of."

"Done work in those countries? Pakistan? Malaysia?"

"Both," he said.

Sci said, "I find it telling that the video was sent to Private Rio and not to the Wises."

"Good point," Tavia said. "The kidnappers must have known the girls had Private Rio bodyguards. So they sent the video here first."

"But how did the kidnappers know the guards were with Private?" Mo-bot asked. "They were in street clothes, correct?"

"Correct," Tavia said.

Wise said, "Then someone in Private Rio talked, or my girls did."

"The girls?" his wife said. "That's absurd. They knew the risks. Why would they do such a thing?"

Wise cast an even gaze at her, said, "Natalie could have fallen in love again. Or Alicia could have been trying to impress someone. You know how naive, trusting, and impressionable they can be. So quick to become someone's best friend forever or rally to some politically correct cause without doing the research necessary to justify their support. They're just like…"

"Me?" Cherie demanded. "Why don't you just say it?"

Her husband blinked, took off his glasses, said, "At times, yes."

"Andy, I honestly don't know why you stay with me."

Wise frowned, clearly puzzled, said, "How do you make that logical jump?"

Sci cut them off, said, "We blew up some stills from the video, Jack."

The images appeared one after another: the Wise twins in the chairs, the painting of the children kneeling in prayer, and the masks their captors wore.

Mo-bot said, "See how the painting has no frame? And there's the suggestion of other figures to either side of the children. It's part of a mural."

"Why cover the rest of it?" Cherie asked.

"The mural might be recognizable," Tavia said.

"Then why show it at all?" Wise asked. "Why not just cover up the whole thing?"

"They're trying to play on your emotions," I said. "Two kneeling, praying children behind your girls. What about the masks?"

Tavia said, "The feather-and-sequin mask is samba. You could find one like it in many places in Rio. But the primitive one I've never seen before."

"Looks animist to me," Sci said.

"Are there animists in Rio?" Cherie asked.

"Macumba," Tavia said, nodding. "It came with the slaves the Portuguese brought from Africa to work on the rubber plantations. Macumba's more widely practiced up on the northeast coast in Bahia, but it's here in Rio too, especially in the favelas."

"Make a note to figure out where this second mask came from," I said. "Anything else from the video?"

"Sounds," Mo-bot said. "Three different background noises."

She typed. Dogs barked, one with a gruff tone, another a yapper. Then we heard a train whistle blow close by, followed by a gentle tinkling melody that changed to clanging and then died.

"What was that sound?" Cherie asked.

"High-tone chimes," Mo-bot said. "Moving on a gust of wind."

Chapter 21

THE WIND, DR. Castro thought. *What will it be?*

Castro sat in a small cramped office at the medical school of the Federal University of Rio, hunched over a laptop computer, studying real-time meteorological data displayed on the screen. He paid scant attention to the temperature and barometric-pressure readings from various stations around Rio, focusing instead on wind direction and speed.

The doctor jotted notes on a chart. Then he reviewed those notes before coming up with a hypothesis. Now he just had to conduct an experiment to see if his hypothesis was right.

Pensive, the doctor exited his browser and shut his computer down. He put the laptop in a knapsack and then picked up a mason's leather and canvas bag from the floor beneath his desk.

Outside, it was a mild, midwinter day in Rio, temperatures in the low seventies and an ocean breeze that was northeasterly, coming down off the equator. As Dr. Castro walked, he wondered whether the breeze would stay prevailing and steady with a building warm trend or change out of the south, as the latest forecasts indicated.

"Dr. Castro? Professor?"

The doctor had hoped to get off campus quickly, but he turned. A smiling young man ran up, trying to catch his breath.

"I'm sorry, Professor," he said. "But I have a question from last week's lecture on retrovirus reverse transcription."

Castro had important things to attend to, but he was devoted to his students, especially this one: Ricardo Fauvea. Ricardo reminded Castro of his younger self. Like the doctor, Ricardo had grown up desperately poor in one of Rio's favelas and had defied the odds. Despite a public-school education, he had scored well enough on an entrance exam to earn a spot in one of Brazil's excellent tuition-free universities. He'd done it again getting into the medical school, just as Castro had.

"Walk with me," the doctor said.

"What's in the bag?" Ricardo asked.

Dr. Castro flushed, slightly embarrassed. "A new hobby."

Ricardo looked at him quizzically. "What sort of hobby?"

"Come along, I'll show you," he said, and hailed a taxi. "How are you anyway?"

Castro's young protégé recounted the latest events in his life on the short cab ride to the village of Urca, on the bay in the shadow of Sugarloaf Mountain. They got out of the cab and walked the rocky shoreline to a secluded, crescent-shaped beach.

"So that's me up to date," Ricardo said. "How about you, Doctor?"

"I'm fine," Castro said, walking out onto the sand and happy to see the little beach was empty.

"What did you want to know about reverse transcription?"

"Right," Ricardo said. "I wanted to know why RT doesn't produce exact copies of viruses all the time."

"Because retroviruses are unpredictable. I suppose that's why I enjoy my new hobby so much."

The doctor opened the mason's bag, revealing the components of an Estes model rocket. "This toy is ingenious and predictable. I know for certain that if I put everything together correctly, it will fly spectacularly."

Castro loaded the nine-inch rocket with an engine and attached it to a starter and battery. "Now, some viruses are like this toy: stable, predictable. Those kinds of viruses reproduce predictably."

Setting the rocket on its launchpad, he said, "But retroviruses are notoriously unstable and mutate constantly. Those unpredictable ones are the ones you have to fear, because by the time you've figured out a cure, the one you're trying to kill has already mutated into something else."

Ricardo nodded his understanding, but not convincingly. "Give me an example?"

Castro thought of his private lab work but said, "The virus that causes the common cold. It's constantly changing. That's why so many have tried and failed to cure it. Ready?" He held out the ignition key and switch. "You do the honors."

Ricardo smiled, took the device, said, "It's not dangerous?"

"No," the doctor said. "Just fun."

His student twisted the key and flipped the switch. An intense flame shot out the bottom of the little rocket. It gathered thrust, soared into the sky, and blew a white contrail for five, maybe six hundred feet before a parachute popped open and the rocket dangled there, floating on the sea breeze.

Still northeast, Dr. Castro thought, and then he noticed the parachute stutter and float on a slightly different tangent as it fell slowly into the harbor and then sank.

"You lost it," Ricardo said.

"Still fun," Castro said, grinning. "You didn't like that?"

"No, I did," his student said. "I liked it taking off the best."

"I kind of like the whole experience," Castro said, laughing. "I honestly do."

"Why, do you think?"

"I don't know," the doctor said. "I read about these when I was a boy, but of course we could never afford such luxuries. I suppose the rockets make me feel like the kid I was never allowed to be."

Chapter 22

WHILE THE WISES checked into the Copacabana Marriott under assumed names, Tavia and I went to the hostel where the other members of the church group were staying. We took the newly restored tram from Centro across the Carioca Aqueduct and up Santa Teresa Hill. Santa Teresa, more than any other area of Rio, feels European and old, and trendy restaurants and bars thrive there.

We got off near Monte Alegre and found our way to the hostel on Laurinda Road. Carlos Seitz, the church-group leader, was waiting, along with eight other members of the mission. They were all concerned and frightened for Natalie and Alicia. They were also nervous about returning to the favelas after the attack. One girl said she wanted to go home but her parents wouldn't let her.

All of them described the twins as inseparable and very hard workers, gentle and caring, though reserved. Not one of them felt close to either Natalie or Alicia despite the fact that the group had been together for three weeks.

"Do you do all of your work in Alemão?" I asked.

Seitz shook his head and told us they'd worked

at three charity sites around Rio. Most recently they'd been with Shirt Off My Back, an NGO that delivered clothes and food to the desperately poor. Before that, they'd worked on a sanitation project in Campo Grande. When they'd first arrived, they volunteered at an orphanage in Bangu.

"Mariana Lopes's orphanage?" Tavia asked.

"That's right," Seitz said.

"That's odd," I said. "She never mentioned that she'd met the girls."

"We never named them," Tavia reminded me.

Seitz gave us the addresses of the charities, and we left with promises to keep him updated on the twins.

Outside, we caught a taxi that returned us to Alemão favela. Night had fallen by the time we reached the tram station. We moved with the sparse crowd toward the red gondolas. The doors opened automatically.

We got inside, meaning to return to the scene of the attack, to see it again at night and perhaps find someone who'd seen something and neglected to tell the police. Two men in their twenties climbed into the gondola, sat opposite us, pulled out cell phones, and studied them.

The doors closed. We cleared the station and were soon high above the lights of the slum. Tavia and I turned to each other and spoke in soft English about how best to pursue the few leads we had.

Click. Click.

Two minutes out of the base station, I heard it. *Click. Click.*

Out of the corner of my eye I saw stiletto switchblades. The men never said a word, just lunged at us, blades leading.

Chapter 23

I HAMMERED MY right fist back and sideways, just inside the path of the oncoming knife aimed for my ribs and lungs. My blow struck the bundle of nerves, tendons, and ligaments that pass through the underside of the human wrist. The strike not only deflected the blade but sent a shock through my attacker's fingers and thumb, loosening his grip.

Beside me, Tavia had seen the attacker coming her way and had kicked him in the kneecap with her shoe. He'd staggered back screaming at the same time I twisted my upper body and hammered again at my assailant's wrist, then tried to punch him in the face with my left.

He was quick and dodged the punch, leaning backward so it passed just out of range. I drove myself to my feet, wanting to strip him of his knife.

But he got underneath me and popped his shoulder up under my solar plexus, slammed me against the closed doors. I hammer-smashed my fist against the scapula and rotator cuff of the arm with the knife. On the second blow, over the noise of Tavia fighting the other guy, I heard the stiletto clatter to the floor of the gondola.

I tried to knee him in the face. He blocked it, got hold of my belt, and spun me around and into Tavia, who crashed into the corner. My guy squatted, tried to punch me in the groin. I shifted my hips, took the blow on the thigh. He snatched up the knife before I could get at it.

He slashed at my right side, high along the ribs, but I got hold of his elbows and pinned them against the glass. He had the knife in his right hand, gripping it like an ice pick. He seemed high on something, manic, and I feared I wasn't going to be able to hold him for long.

The tip of his knife blade crept closer and closer to my left eye. Staring at it, I saw a little sign behind and above the knife; I didn't get the exact words, but I caught the drift. I drove my head toward his, trying to smash the bridge of his nose. He twisted and took the blow to the side of his face. It rocked him.

I let go of his left elbow, reached up, and tugged the lever below the emergency-release sign. The doors flung open behind him. He had a moment of understanding what I'd done, of terror, and he tried desperately to regain his balance before he pitched backward, flailing and screaming, into the night air and then was gone.

Behind me, I heard an "Uhh," and I spun around. Tavia heaved for breath as she stepped back from the second guy, her hair disheveled, her forearm cut in two places, and the stiletto sticking out of the low center of his chest. He gasped like a fish out of water, quickly at first, then slower, and then not at all.

She glanced at me, said, "What do we do with him?"

The next station was still two hundred meters away. We looked ahead, saw a wide stripe of pitch-darkness on one particularly steep hillside, and, after checking his pockets and finding nothing, we pushed him out the door too.

Tavia had a spray of his blood on her blouse and there was blood on her hand from the cuts to her forearm. We used her jacket to mop up the blood on the floor and seats. I gave her my jacket. We left the gondola, walking casually until we cleared the station and found a side road and then as quickly as we dared.

We went to the clinic where we'd talked to Mariana Lopes the day before. She wasn't there, but her nurse cleaned, stitched, and bandaged Tavia's wounds, never once asking how she'd gotten them.

"You all right?" I asked after we'd left.

"Not a chance," Tavia said.

"Is that the first time you've had to kill someone?"

"No, but it still takes you over."

"Like his ghost is still with you."

She nodded, and shuddered. I wrapped her in my arms, kissed her temples, said, "You did what you had to. We both did."

"I couldn't get my gun drawn," she said.

"Happened too fast."

"They didn't try to rob us."

"Just went for the kill."

Tavia turned stony. "So they were gangsters. On assignment."

We returned to Spirit favela and that same spot against the retaining wall high in the slum, up against the jungle. Urso was there, eating and drinking with four or five of his homeboys.

Tavia marched up to him with the bandages on her arm exposed and a .380 in her hand.

"We had an agreement, Bear," she said, aiming at his head. "Does your word mean nothing?"

Urso's hands flew up. "Hey, fuck, Reynaldo! What you talking about? The Bear's word is gold."

"We got attacked on the Alemão gondola. Street trash with knives. They targeted us."

"That's nothing to me," Urso said. "I can't keep freelancers from moving into Alemão. That's the BOPE's job."

Tavia was still mad and skeptical. "You saying those weren't your boys?"

"Hello?" said the Bear. "We got a deal, right?"

"So why aren't you out looking?" I asked.

"Been looking all day, L.A.," he said. "You're getting your money's worth."

"So what have you heard about those girls?"

"People saw them dragged into a gray van down the hill from all the shooting. No license plate, so that doesn't tell us anything, but we're working out from the point where they were put in the van."

"Narrow your search area," Tavia said, and she told him that the girls were being held within hearing distance of train whistles and close to barking dogs and wind chimes.

"Trains?" the Bear said. Then he nodded. "Okay. That helps. But chimes? Shit, man, everyone's auntie got chimes. Different size, shape, tone. And there are dogs everywhere."

"We can send you a digital file of the exact sounds," I said.

Urso brightened. "That works. After we eat, me and the boys will go down by the tracks, listen for chimes and dogs barking. We good?"

Tavia studied him critically again for several beats before saying, "Okay, Bear, we're good."

Chapter 24

DRESSED TO KILL in heels, a tight black leather skirt, and a black silk blouse that showed off her ample figure, Luna Santos was in her mid-thirties with lush black hair and a gorgeous olive complexion. Her heart pounded with anticipation as she exited a taxi by the aqueduct, two stories and eight hundred feet of stark white arches in the heart of Lapa, an edgy entertainment district in Centro.

On one side of the aqueduct, fans were already lined up to get into a sprawling outdoor music club. The square on the other side of the arches was jammed with revelers. Seven days to go until the Olympics, and already the city was packed with people ready to bust loose and celebrate. Luna was more than ready to party with them.

She bought a *caipirinha,* a potent *cachaça* rum drink and sort of Brazil's national cocktail.

Luna walked on, sipping the minty, sweet booze, feeling the alcohol fire through her, aware of but not acknowledging the men who openly admired her as she passed. The fact that Lapa could be a little dangerous after dark only added to the general thrill.

I want fear tonight, she thought. *I want drama and passion and sweat.*

Her brain began to imagine the forbidden pleasures the night might bring, and she felt herself tremble with excitement and—

Luna's cell phone rang. She stopped on the crowded sidewalk, dug her phone out of her evening purse, checked the number, and felt the anticipation drain out of her.

Cupping her hand around the mouthpiece, Luna answered. "Antonio?"

"I'm sorry, baby," her husband said. "I have to work late."

"I figured," she said. "Sleeping at the office again?"

Her husband, defensive, said, "Just a few more days, Luna, and I'll be—"

"Gone for the next sixteen."

Exasperated, Antonio said, "You understand what I'm doing is important?"

"Sorry, but I've got to go. My movie's about to start."

Luna hung up and then turned the phone off.

Tonight is not about Antonio and his career, she thought. *Tonight has zero to do with the Olympics. It's about me. It's about the needs of Luna Santos.*

That decided, she set off again toward the entrance to Rio Scenarium, a famous samba club, trying to imagine what her new lover had planned for the evening. He'd said that after drinks and dancing he would take her someplace *gostosa,* someplace hot.

Luna hoped it was a first-class love motel. Rio was peppered with facilities that catered to couples in need of a discreet meeting place. Some of these were spectacular, just like the finest suites in the finest hotels in Copacabana and Ipanema, except you paid by the hour.

The year before, with her old lover, Luna had been in one that had its own pool, sauna, and all sorts of accoutrements that made her... well... very satisfied.

The bouncer at the samba club leered at Luna as he opened the door for her. She didn't give him a hint of encouragement. She would never cheat on Antonio with such a man.

Luna had a high standard for lovers. They had to be educated, well spoken, and within ten years of her age. They had to be physically fit and more than capable in bed, and a sense of mischief and daring helped immensely.

Her new lover met all these requirements and more. He was frankly gifted in affairs of the flesh. Luna shivered as she entered the club. Pounding samba music played. Lights flashed over a packed dance floor. The ceiling soared two stories up. The second floor was more like a balcony where partyers drank and commented on the skills of the writhing bodies below.

Luna sniffed at the sweet smell of sweat and raging pheromones in the club and got even hornier. She scanned the eclectic interior, paying scant attention to the suits of medieval armor on one wall, clock collections on another, and mirrors and paintings on a third. She wasn't seeing her man.

Luna got a double *caipirinha* this time, sipped at it, loving the way the mint, ice, sugar, and rum slid down her throat and made her feel like someone else indeed. She moved closer to the dance floor. In the strobe light, the mob of dancers looked like one sensual creature and—

Luna felt strong hands on her hips, felt a man press himself just hard enough against her *bunda* that she knew he was as aroused as she was. Purring with pleasure, Luna threw her arm up, back, and around his neck, delighting at the way he nuzzled her.

She gasped softly at his slow, grinding embrace and then pivoted to press her breasts and hips against him.

"Doctor," she said, pouting. "I was beginning to think you weren't coming to see me tonight."

Dr. Castro let his eyes go dreamy, kissed her passionately, and said, "How could a man ever stay away from a woman like you, my little orchid?"

Chapter 25

AS THE MUSIC beat faster and the dancing became more and more frenzied, Luna throbbed in his arms. Doctor was a master of samba, of offering and denying, of sweating and sliding against her until she was drunk with wanting him and then changing to cold and removed, which drove her passion to flames.

Doctor was a mystery and that made him all the more alluring to Luna. She had no idea what his name was; she called him Doctor, and he called her Orchid. They'd met two weeks before at another dance club and there'd been this immediate physical connection that didn't require details like backgrounds and names.

The music wound down into a slow bossa nova that made her want to press into him all the more. But Doctor held her at bay, a brush of hips here, a moment chest to chest, but no delicious melding of bodies.

Luna said, "Sometimes I see you staring off, Doctor. Are you thinking of your other lover?"

"There is no other lover," he assured her.

"Wife?"

"I had one. She passed."

"So sad for you, but a pleasure for me. Where are you taking me?"

"That's a surprise," he said. "Shall we get our drinks and go?"

Luna just wanted to go, but he'd ordered them glasses of wine. He got plastic cups, poured the wine into them, and they left the club arm in arm to join the rest of the mob drinking and partying in the streets.

"To pleasure," Doctor said, touching his cup to hers.

"To no strings," Luna said saucily, and she downed the wine.

In his car, she rubbed her hands all over his chest, said, "I can't wait to be alone with you."

Castro kissed her, said, "It won't take long for my little orchid to bloom."

He drove. Luna felt pleasantly hammered, not thinking a bit about her husband, only about Doctor and how unbelievable he'd made her feel their first time together. She prayed she was going to feel even better tonight.

"Where are we going?" she asked once she realized they'd gotten onto the highway. "There are excellent sex motels around Lapa."

"But nothing like this one," Doctor said, and he rubbed her thigh.

Luna purred, realized she was drunker than she'd thought. Not sick drunk, but stripped of any and all inhibitions.

Free to do what I want.

She squirmed her hips in protest when his hand left her leg.

"You torturing me?"

"There's a fine line between pain and ecstasy."

Ecstasy. When was the last time Antonio spoke of such things? *Maybe I should leave Antonio before*

I do something stupid like get pregnant. Maybe I should...just...

Her vision blurred and distorted. She was aware they were driving through an industrial area she didn't recognize.

"Where you taking me, Doc?" she slurred.

Luna's eyes drifted shut. She felt as if she were spinning slowly off a cliff, like a bird hovering on updrafts.

Far behind her, from back on that cliff as she twirled and glided toward nothingness, she heard Doctor reply, "My lab, Luna."

Chapter 26

SCI AND MO-BOT arrived in Rio around eleven that night, and Tavia and I took them to see Andrew and Cherie Wise in their suite at the Marriott. We brought the couple up to speed on what we'd learned in the past five hours and gave them an overview of our strategy to find their daughters.

Maureen Roth typed on her iPad, linking it via Bluetooth to the flat-screen on the wall. A satellite image of Rio appeared, the mountains, the canyons, the beaches, and the sea. Mo-bot typed a few more commands, and six flickering pins appeared, three red, three yellow, superimposed on the image.

"These three in red are the charities where the girls worked in the past three weeks," Maureen said. "The yellows are the hostels where they stayed. And now, I'll filter out all areas more than two miles from a train or Metrô track, and…"

Large pieces of the image vanished, and it was like we were looking at Rio as an incomplete jigsaw puzzle. But it was clear from the pins that the hostels and all three charities were within our search area. So were the Spirit and Alemão favelas.

I said, "We've got people working the tracks near

the abduction site first and then expanding out. In the morning, we'll be at those charities and hostels."

"How can this help?" Cherie asked. "I mean, look at the density. Millions of people live in those parts of the city."

"True," Tavia said. "But at some point, Mrs. Wise, your daughters appeared on someone's radar. Likely at the hostels or the charities. If we can figure out where and how they were targeted, we can figure out who has them."

Wise said, "A search is your only strategy, Jack?"

"It's the one that seems most promising at the moment."

"You've got less than forty-two hours," he said. "I've arranged to withdraw thirty million dollars' worth of Brazilian *reais* on Sunday."

"They said fifty million," Cherie said.

"I can't get fifty," he said. "And they'll never know the difference. It will be a big stack of money all strapped down, and that will be enough. Why? Because they won't stop to count it and we'll put newspaper cut like cash deep in the pile. They'll give us the girls and take the money at the same time or no deal."

His wife looked dubious, but she nodded.

"That is going to be a big stack," Sci said.

Wise nodded, said, "The bills are roughly the size of U.S. currency. Given that every dollar weighs a gram, and using a fifty as the likely denomination, we're talking about eleven hundred pounds."

Sci said, "They'd be smarter to ask for it in gold. At this morning's spot price, that drops the weight to nine hundred and thirty pounds."

Wise stared at him, said, "Well done."

Cherie looked disgusted, shook her head, and said,

"It's always about mental gymnastics with you, Andy. Can't you just once look at life emotionally?"

"Emotion won't get Alicia and Natalie back," he snapped. "Strategy, a plan, and meticulous execution of that plan will get them back."

"And what if it doesn't?" she said, starting to cry as she gestured at the screen. "What if they take the money and kill the girls, and we never see them again?"

"That's not happening."

She wiped her bloodshot eyes, looked at the four of us from Private, said, "You see it, don't you? With everything we've got, my girls are all I have."

Chapter 27

YOU'RE ENOUGH TO get what we need, Rayssa thought as she shone a powerful flashlight beam in the frightened eyes of her captives.

The Wise twins were bound at the wrists and ankles and sitting on filthy mattresses, backs up against the concrete wall.

"Do we have to wear the gags and blindfolds again?" Alicia Wise said in a pleading whine. "We won't scream."

"You know we won't," Natalie said. "Who would hear us anyway?"

Rayssa thought a moment, said, "Fine. No gags. No blindfolds. But start screaming for help or try to escape and they go back on."

"What about our parents?" Natalie asked.

"I'm sure they've seen the video by now."

"Mom must be freaking out," Alicia said.

"They'll pay," Natalie said, as if trying to convince herself.

"Sure, they'll pay," Alicia said. "Why wouldn't they? They've got, like—"

"Billions," Rayssa said. Then she shut the door and locked it.

Rayssa turned and used the flashlight to make her way down a long, low-ceilinged corridor. It smelled of tobacco and led to a steep staircase. She climbed to a heavy wooden door and thumbed off the flashlight.

Turning the dead bolt, she opened the door and stepped out into a high-ceilinged space, dark but for narrow slats of light coming in between boards nailed over the windows. Except for broken glass crunching under her feet and the wreckage of wooden tables and stools, the place was empty.

Rayssa let her eyes adjust, then crossed the space to another flight of stairs. She paused at the bottom, listening.

The wind was up. She heard chimes and the not-so-distant rattle of a train.

And then something more?

Something or somebody outside?

Dogs began to bark, but this was different from their normal yapping. The dogs were agitated, alarmed.

Rayssa reached to the small of her back beneath her sweater, retrieved a blunt-nosed .38. She slid her shoes off and crept up the stairs.

She returned to the long-abandoned office where she'd been sleeping but didn't turn on the light. Rayssa went to the window, looked out between the slats, and peered down. Except for a weak cone of light cast by a spot on the warehouse next door, there was only gloom, and the chimes, and the wind, and the far-off blare of a train horn.

Rayssa stayed there, waiting, scanning the shadows for many minutes, before her suspicions were confirmed. She spotted a buff guy moving along the rear of that cone of light. Then he stepped into it. She saw his tattoos and, when the chimes rang again and he looked up, his face.

Rayssa gripped the revolver tighter and fought the urge to panic.

What the hell was the Bear doing here?

Chapter 28

LUNA SANTOS AWOKE slowly, groggily, aware that she was under sheets and naked. Well, that was good, right? Must have been a heck of a—

Luna heard movement, blinked her eyes, saw only fuzziness. Her head started to clang. A stark white room came into focus, spinning slowly. She was lying in a hospital bed. There was an IV bag on a stand next to her, with a line running below the sheets.

Confused, Luna tried to raise her arm to look at the IV, but her wrists were lashed to the bed rails. She tried to move her legs and found her ankles tied to the rails too. And there was something between her legs.

Like a thin hose or something!

Luna rolled her head, the pain splitting, said, "Help me. Where am I?"

But her tongue was so thick and her mouth so dry, the words came out weak and garbled. Despite the pounding in her skull, she forced herself to lift her head, looked around, and saw someone standing there in one of those hazmat suits like they had for Ebola, white smock, hood, visor, gauntlet gloves, and all.

The figure came to Luna's side, looked down at her, spoke through a small speaker clipped to the smock, his voice as strange as an astronaut's coming from outer space.

"There you are," Dr. Castro said.

"Where am I, Doctor?" she said.

"In my lab."

"What happened to me?" she asked, bewildered. "Am I sick?"

"Just side effects. They'll clear up soon."

Side effects? Luna thought. *Of what?*

But before she could ask, Castro said, "Just relax. You were chosen, you know. For so many good reasons, I chose you. And now here you are, Luna, where I always dreamed you'd be."

"What?" she said, vaguely aware that he'd used her real name and not Orchid. "I don't…chosen for what?"

The doctor held up a gloved index finger as if to hush her and walked off.

Luna rolled her pounding head, watched him cross the lab to four glass cages beneath digital readouts. She saw a white rat moving around in one of the containers and no movement in the others.

Doctor reached into two of the tanks and lifted out two dead rats.

He turned to show them to her. "This is the way virology works. You have to experiment on several or sometimes ten or two hundred or even thousands before you get the key."

Luna blinked at the dead rats. "What virus killed them?"

Doctor seemed pleased at her interest, said, "I call her Hydra-9."

The fogginess cleared, and she understood somehow that she was in danger, grave danger. Luna wanted to move, to get up, but the lashes held her tight.

A virus. Chosen.

She fought against a growing panic. "Why am I tied up like this? And what's the hose thing between my legs?"

Putting the dead rats into a lift-top freezer, Castro said, "The restraints are so you don't hurt yourself. The hose is a catheter."

Catheter? She felt humiliated, said, "Untie me."

The doctor tilted his head, said, "I can't do that."

"Untie me!" she shouted. "I know when I can and can't fulfill my needs."

"This isn't about your needs. *I* chose *you*, remember, Luna?"

A dread came around her like mist and caustic fog. She struggled against the lashes and screamed, "Help! Help!"

"No one can hear you," Castro said, twirling his gloved index finger, "the outer building has been soundproofed."

He crossed to a refrigerator, opened it, and retrieved an eight-inch stainless-steel canister fitted with a hose and nozzle. Attached perpendicularly to the base of the nozzle was a four-inch-long green canister and a pressure gauge.

"What is that?" she asked, trying to squirm away as he came toward her with it.

"A modified airbrush system," he said, and he gestured at the larger canister. "This contains a propellant."

He pointed to the smaller one, said, "And this one contains rat blood infected with Hydra-9. I modified the airbrush so the propellant drives the blood through a series of screens inside the nozzle. Exiting under pressure, the blood will become an aerosol. Think of it like a virus cloud or fog."

Luna stared at him, horrified, screamed, "You can't do this!"

"I have to do this," he said, fiddling with the control.

"Please, this isn't right!"

"Lots of things aren't right, Luna. Ask Antonio."

"You know my husband?" she choked out.

"We've never met, but I'm acquainted with his work."

The doctor grabbed Luna by her hair. She screamed, tried to fight, but he got the nozzle in front of her face and mashed some kind of trigger.

There was a whooshing sound. A short, sharp burst of fine pink haze blew out of the nozzle, coated her nose, lips, and eyes like sea spray.

"No!" Luna screeched and writhed. "No!"

Chapter 29

ONE HOUR AND thirty-seven minutes postinfection, Luna was deteriorating rapidly. Sweating. Feverish. Borderline delirious. Dr. Castro had taken blood samples every fifteen minutes since the start of the experiment. Hydra-9 was definitely in her system, and wreaking havoc.

With each blood sample, Castro could see evidence of the virus spreading like a flame through Luna's major organs, leaving in its wake those nine-headed husks; the Hydra-9 infection was like a horde of insects breeding and feeding. The virus invaded cells and spun cocoons inside them that cracked to yield multiple offspring of the virus that in turn invaded more cells. And so on.

It was an exponential assault that caused a cascading effect within the host's system as one after another of the major organs burned out and shut down. The kidneys always seemed to be the first to go.

Luna's temperature had hovered around one hundred and two but now began to climb. One hundred and three point one. One hundred and three point six. One hundred and four point zero.

Luna's eyes were glazed. She looked over at the

rat still moving in the tank and laughed madly. "You're going to save me. That's why you chose me, right?"

"That would be counterproductive, Luna," Castro replied. "I really don't know yet what Hydra-9 does to a human in the full course of an unchecked infection."

"You're insane," she hissed weakly.

"Actually, I'm the sanest man I know."

Her fever began to spike higher. One hundred and four point five. One hundred and four point seven. Luna trembled and twitched, closed her eyes.

"Why're you doing this?" she said, gasping.

"Science."

"You said ask Antonio."

Castro paused, nodded. "Your husband played a significant part in the motivation behind the science. He and others stole precious things from me."

"Stole? Antonio? Never."

"Definitely."

"What'd he steal?"

"My dignity," Castro said. "And my wife."

Luna's glassy, bloodshot eyes snapped open. Sweating and shaking, she gaped at Castro as if he were a fading light on a dark highway. She moved her lips, tried to form words but couldn't. Then she arched up into a convulsion and writhed, her eyes bugging out and unseeing. As suddenly as it had started, the neurological frying ended. Luna collapsed as if deflated and died with blood seeping from her eyes and nose.

Castro felt a pang of remorse but no regret. Luna's death was just. It was fair. A way of restoring balance. And it served a nobler purpose. He looked to the clock and felt the remorse ebb away. Elapsed time from misting to last heartbeat: one hour, fifty-two minutes, and twenty seconds.

"Perfect," he said.

Chapter 30

Saturday, July 30, 2016
4:20 a.m.

TAVIA DOWNSHIFTED HER BMW and weaved in and out of traffic in the tunnel that linked Copacabana to Botafogo. The fog I'd been in at Tavia's apartment after we got the call was long gone.

She roared out of the tunnel and through the night toward the favelas while yelling into her cell phone's mike, "Urso thinks he's found the girls. Activate the response team. I'll text the coordinates once we reach the location."

She hung up, still speeding and weaving, said, "Do we notify the Wises?"

"Not until we have something to tell them," I said.

"The Bear said he is positive he has the place; it's got the chimes, proximity to the train, dogs, plus one of his guys says the whole building has recently been boarded up, no activity during the day."

"I'd rather tell the Wises once we've got the girls," I said. "Otherwise they'll be second-guessing us at every turn."

"Your call," she said and took an exit off the highway that brought us northwest of Alemão and into an area of run-down, tin-roofed structures (auto-body shops, upholsterers, tool-and-die makers), ware-houses, and abandoned factories.

We pulled over and parked.

"We're not far," she said. "We'll go the rest of the way on foot."

I got out. Tavia went around to the trunk, popped it, and took out two sets of body armor, two pairs of night-vision goggles, a 12-gauge Mossberg tactical shotgun, and a Beretta .380 with a short, fat sound suppressor.

She handed me the Beretta, wrapped the shotgun in a blanket. "People might get unhappy if they saw this. Easier to hide it until we need it."

Tavia led us quickly through a maze of buildings. As I followed, I heard a train whistle blowing not far away. We rounded a corner. Urso stepped from the shadows.

"Anything change?" Tavia asked, catching her breath.

"Nada," the Bear said. "My boys have the place locked down; you wanna hit it now?"

Tavia looked at me, said, "Full response team is fifteen minutes away."

"Where are they?" I asked him.

Urso pointed to a two-story stone structure down the block. "Used to be a cigar factory when I was a kid."

Dogs began barking nearby.

"Pit bulls," he said. "They're in the lumberyard beyond the cigar place."

"You see any activity in the factory?"

"Heard movement inside, first floor and upstairs, about two hours ago."

I checked my watch. Four forty-five. It wouldn't

be light for more than an hour, and the Marines had taught me to infiltrate before dawn.

"You and I go in now," I said to Tavia. "Urso, put your men by the escape routes in case we flush something."

"I went all around it," the Bear said, showing us a crowbar. "Already found the best places to go in and out."

Tavia unrolled the blanket, revealing the shotgun. She racked a shell into the chamber, and we set off. Urso led us behind the cigar factory to a boarded-up window above an alleyway. Down the alley, a single spotlight shone from a warehouse next door.

The Bear fitted the crowbar under the boards and slowly, quietly pried them free, leaving a black gaping hole where a windowpane used to be.

Chapter 31

I DREW THE Beretta and lowered the night-vision goggles. My world turned a murky green. I peeked inside a hallway strewn with trash and debris. Seeing it was clear otherwise, I slipped over and in.

The air reeked of cured tobacco more than dust.

Tavia lowered her goggles too and came inside. We moved as one then, me bent over, navigating us around the obstacles on the floor as silently as possible, and her behind, putting her feet where I did, shotgun shouldered, scanning ahead for movement.

We reached a door. I pushed it open and winced at the creaking noise the rusted hinges made. I pulled back, tense, squinting, waiting for a volley of gunfire. It didn't come.

I paused for a count of thirty, pushed the door wide open, and pulled back a second time. Count of thirty. Nothing.

In a crouch I slid around the door into what seemed a cavernous space where the smell of tobacco was everywhere. Broken tables and chairs. Cabinets hanging off the wall. But there was no movement, not even in the dimmest corners.

"Room clear," Tavia whispered over my shoulder.

I gestured at the stairs at the far end of the room. She understood and nodded. Urso said the chimes were hanging off a windowsill up there.

We crept up the stairs, listening but hearing nothing. We reached the landing and Tavia got to her knees on the stairs, aiming over the top riser at the door. I went up to it, touched the handle, and prayed it wasn't booby-trapped.

I pressed down, heard the click, threw the door open, and ducked back into the corner. Nothing.

Tavia eased up, her cheek welded to the shotgun stock. The Beretta leading, I edged around into what used to be an office, saw a filthy mattress, a broken bookcase, and an open window. Outside, chimes tinkled.

"Those are definitely the same chimes," Tavia whispered in my ear.

I nodded, sweeping my attention around the room again and seeing something odd sticking out of the bottom of the bookcase.

I crossed to it, crouched, and saw it was a feather. I pulled on it and out came the samba mask from the video.

Chapter 32

WE WERE IN the right place, which was both a relief and a ratcheting-up of our anxiety levels. The Wise twins were here in the cigar factory. But so were the kidnappers.

"Whatever happens, we do not shoot the girls," I muttered to Tavia.

"Clear fields of fire," she said.

We left the mask on the floor and crept down the stairs as quietly as we'd climbed them. Twice as we crossed the old rolling room, our weight provoked creaking noises in the floorboards, and we froze for more than a minute each time.

The girls and the kidnappers had to be in the basement. Every noise we made was a potential warning. Every noise could get them killed.

We went to the only other door off the old factory floor. Outside in the lumberyard, the pit bulls went nuts, barking and snapping. After a moment's hesitation, I motioned for Tavia to cover the door while I reached around the jamb for the handle. It twisted as if oiled. I let the door sag ajar, waited, and then pushed it open with two fingers.

Something shot out of the darkness. For some reason, I thought, *Pit bull,* and I almost took a shot before I saw it was an enormous black cat. It darted between us and across the factory floor.

After several deep breaths, I looked around the corner, saw a steep, rickety wooden staircase down into a cellar. My gut said it could be a trap, but I pointed it out to Tavia and we went anyway, trying to place our weight where the riser had the most support. We still ended up making several more soft squeaking noises.

But we reached the bottom of the stairs without incident. It was cooler and drier in the cellar than it was above. There was so little light down there that the goggles only barely revealed a blurry green hallway with doors on both sides.

"Take your goggles off," I murmured. "Go to flashlight."

"You sure?"

"I'd rather risk being shot at than make a mistake because of the goggles."

She understood, pulled her goggles off, and went to her vest for a Mini Maglite. I did too, setting my goggles down on the floor and sliding the thin, powerful flashlight under the barrel of the Beretta before flipping the switch on.

The beam cut the gloom all the way to the back of the hallway. We went down it, trying the doors, finding them unlocked, and peering inside each. These rooms were evidently where the tobacco had been stored, but they were empty now.

The hallway reached a T. A heavy wooden door stood at each end of the stubby arms. The right-hand door was padlocked. The left was ajar. A breeze from the other side caused it to move slightly.

I heard a voice. Female. Scared. Crying behind the padlocked door. I immediately cupped the end of the flashlight, and Tavia did the same, both of us letting just enough light through our fingers to see our way toward the voice.

Tavia and I snuck forward. Another woman spoke, louder, threatening in tone, but too muffled to make out. Tavia pressed into the wall two feet shy of the door, shotgun up.

I stepped right up to the door, started to check my watch.

Beyond the door, there was a loud, flat crack of wood on flesh. The first woman began to scream and sob.

I shot the lock.

Chapter 33

THE BULLET SNAPPED the hasp.

I ripped the lock free, pressed the latch, and shouldered my way into a dirty concrete-floored room with a painting on the rear wall. The mural depicted scenes from a town during a tobacco harvest. Dead center of the painting, on their knees in front of a church, were the two praying children we'd seen in the background of the ransom video.

The Wise twins were gone. There was no one in the room. All we found were two mattresses, a filthy yellow cotton scarf, a thin hemp bracelet, several empty water bottles, some greasy waxed paper, and, on a stool, a tablet computer playing a two-minute video loop.

In the video, Natalie was slumped in a chair, unconscious, the yellow scarf around her neck. The camera swung, revealing Alicia on her knees, praying like the children in the mural, showing the hemp bracelet on her wrist. She was begging her parents to pay the ransom and not try another rescue.

Then the woman in the primitive mask appeared. She hit Alicia with a blackjack, knocked her senseless and bleeding to the floor. Then she spoke evenly to the camera.

"You will be contacted tomorrow regarding payment, Senhor Wise," she said. "No cops. No Private. The money for your daughters, a quick exchange. Unless you try to fuck with us. In that case, all you'll get back is their worthless bodies."

Tavia bagged the tablet, Natalie's scarf, and Alicia's bracelet and went back for the samba mask. I checked the other door, the one that had been ajar and moving slightly in a breeze. The hallway continued on. At the far end it met another staircase that went up to another door.

I opened it. The pit bulls came at me like blitzing linebackers.

I yanked the door shut just in time, heard them thud, howl, and scratch violently against it. I knew now: the kidnappers had taken the girls out through the lumberyard.

It was almost daybreak when we slipped back out the window.

Urso eased out of the shadows. "They in there?"

"They were until they spotted you," I said.

"That's bullshit," Urso said. "No one sees the Bear unless he wants to be seen."

"Then they saw one of your friends," I said. "They escaped through an underground passage to a shed in that lumberyard. You see anybody coming out of it? A gray van?"

The Bear looked uncertain, said, "I dunno. We were watching this place."

"Did you go in there before us?" Tavia asked. "Look around?"

"No way, Reynaldo," Urso said hotly. "I heard the

chimes, figured the train distance, left to call my boys into position. End of story until you showed up."

"How long were you gone when you went to get your friends?" I asked.

He shrugged. "Ten minutes? I walked around the corner to make the call where I wouldn't be heard."

"Whatever it was, something spooked them," Tavia said.

Urso said, "I still get paid, though. I found them."

Tavia hesitated, but I said, "He did his job. Pay him."

I'd no sooner said that when my cell phone rang. It was General da Silva.

"General?" I said, stifling a yawn. "You're up early."

"I'm always up early," the Olympic security chief said.

"That's why you've always got things so well in hand."

"Not this morning," he said. "We've had a murder in the ranks, Jack. I want you and Octavia at the crime scene as soon as possible."

Chapter 34

TRAFFIC WAS BUILDING. It took us almost an hour to drive from the cigar factory to Barra da Tijuca, a newer district of Rio south of Leblon. Shopping malls. Strip malls. Tract houses with red-tile roofs. It looked like large swaths of Orange County, California, had been slapped down in coastal Brazil.

We followed General da Silva's directions to a residential street on a hillside that had a view of the beach and the ocean. Da Silva was waiting for us by a police barrier along with Lieutenant Bruno Acosta. There was a fire truck up the street, and firemen reeling in hoses. The air was tainted with a sickly smoke.

"Media hasn't gotten word of it," Tavia said.

"Yet," da Silva said, not happy.

"We meet again," Lieutenant Acosta said to me. "You find those missing girls?"

"No."

"Ransom note?"

"Not yet," Tavia said a little too quickly. "At least, we haven't heard about one."

"Let's focus on what's going on right here, okay?" the general said.

Acosta studied Tavia and me a beat and then motioned us through the barrier and down the road. The smell became more ungodly the closer we got to the driveway of a single-family home set behind lush hedges.

We came around the corner of the hedge and saw a tropical garden in front of a beautiful Mediterranean-style two-story home. The only thing that marred the idyllic setting was an incinerated car with the silhouette of a charred corpse in the driver's seat; puddles of water surrounded the vehicle.

"The water's unfortunate," Tavia said. "Probably compromised evidence of whoever—"

"Get out of my way!" someone yelled behind us. I looked over my shoulder, saw a fit man in his late thirties wearing a business suit and no tie running up the street toward us. "What the hell is going on?"

"Senhor Santos. Antonio," da Silva said, trying to stop him. "You don't want to see this."

"See what?" Antonio Santos cried, and he dodged around him, went to the end of the driveway, and halted.

His jaw sagged open and his eyes got hazy with disbelief. Then the corner of his lower lip began to quiver, and he sank slowly to his knees.

"Luna!" he howled. "Oh God. Oh…"

He retched and then fell over and curled up into a fetal position. We waited until the spasms that racked his body eased and then helped him to his feet.

"Can we talk to you inside?" da Silva asked.

Antonio Santos nodded numbly. Then he stole another glance at the horror, said, "Did they…was she…burned alive?"

The medical examiner, a big-bellied man named Cardoso who'd been studying the body, joined us, and the general looked to him. Cardoso shook his head. "Gunshot wound to the back of the skull. She probably died instantly and long before the fire."

Santos stifled a sob, turned away from the car and the ME, and walked unsteadily to the front door. He fumbled for his keys, dropped them. He let Tavia pick them up and open the door.

It was as beautiful inside as it was outside, and spotless, nothing out of place. Santos did not seem to know where to go. Da Silva motioned him to a seat in the living area, where he began to corroborate much of what we already knew.

The victim's husband worked for the Rio Olympic organizing committee and was a liaison to the governments of Rio and Brazil. Santos was charged with cutting through red tape and seeing that projects were completed on time. He'd done much the same job in the years leading up to the World Cup in 2014.

Santos said he'd been working insane hours the past month or two and had hardly seen his wife. He'd had a late dinner with Luna two nights before but had not been home in a week and had been sleeping on a couch in his office.

"Your wife have enemies?" Tavia asked.

"Luna? No. She loved everyone and everyone loved her."

"*You* have enemies?" I asked.

"You mean people who hate me enough to kill Luna? No. No, I don't think so."

"Where were you last night?" da Silva asked.

"I worked until two a.m. and then fell asleep on my office couch."

"Can witnesses put you there?"

"I'm sure the security records will show I didn't leave the building."

"When was your last contact with your wife?" I asked.

"Last night," he said. "Around nine. I called to tell her I couldn't make it home again. She said she was going to a movie."

"What movie?"

"I don't know."

"How'd she seem? Happy? Sad?"

"She wasn't happy...she was pissed at me..." Santos broke down. "Maybe if I'd come home she'd still be alive!"

Chapter 35

WHEN SANTOS GOT control of himself again, Tavia gave him water, said, "Luna wasn't happy."

"She hasn't been happy with me in a long time," Santos said. "She always said I was married to my job more than I was to her. But the World Cup and the Olympics. The biggest things to happen in Brazil in my lifetime. I was desperate to be a part of it. I was determined to make both events succeed, and now...I've lost her for..."

Tavia said, "Did she have a lover?"

Santos cocked his head and shrugged. "Everyone in Rio has lovers. She had appetites and I...I wasn't around. So, yes, I assume so."

"Any idea of who the lover might be?" I asked.

He shook his head bitterly. "I've never gone looking for anything like that."

"And you, Antonio?" the general asked. "Extramarital relationships?"

Santos hesitated, but then said, "Last year for a few months, with an American journalist."

"She the angry type?" Tavia asked.

"No," Santos said. "She's the faraway type."

"Luna usually have a phone with her?" I asked.

"Always, like it was Velcroed to her hand."

"We haven't found it yet," Lieutenant Acosta said. "Do you know her account passwords for her telephone and whatever text-messaging system she used?"

"I don't know them, but she kept a file in her office."

"Show us," Tavia said.

Santos got up and trudged to the door of his wife's home office, from which she'd run a successful business renting short-term, high-end apartments in Rio. There were pictures of various outrageous flats on Ipanema Beach, all decorated in an over-the-top style, with a Post-it note on each photo declaring the asking price during the Olympic Games. Eight, nine, ten thousand *reais* a night.

I gestured at several of them. "Who are her clients? Russians? Arabs?"

"And Chinese," Santos said. "They're the only ones who can afford to pay these kinds of prices. The few she got from New York and London wanted places that were less...I don't know."

"Gaudy?" Tavia said.

Santos shrugged, went to a cabinet, and retrieved a file. With da Silva's and Santos's permission, Tavia got onto a laptop and into the victim's telephone and texting accounts.

Luna Santos had more than twenty text messages waiting for her. Tavia didn't bother opening any, but she quickly determined that Santos's late wife texted roughly ninety times a day. In the past year she'd texted more than thirty-seven thousand times.

"I'll send the passwords to our analysts and they'll start digging through these," Tavia said to Santos. "With your consent, of course."

"Whatever you think will help."

Tavia sent an e-mail with the necessary information to Private Rio's lab, and then she opened up Luna Santos's cell-phone account. She wormed her way into the Cloud copy of calls to and from Luna's number.

"Any way you can tell the position of the phones?" Lieutenant Acosta asked.

"I think so," Tavia said, and she gave the computer and the website another order.

The screen blinked and then showed a map of Rio with a yellow pin at the address of the Rio Olympic organizing committee in Barra and another pin in Lapa.

Santos came over, and his face fell.

"You know that address?" Lieutenant Acosta asked. "Where your wife was when you called?"

Santos nodded morosely. "That's down the street from her favorite club. It's where she likes to go samba."

"And perhaps to meet her lover?" da Silva asked. "And maybe her killer?"

Luna's husband nodded again, hung his head, and cried.

Chapter 36

DR. CASTRO HAD watched much of it through binoculars from well up the jungle hillside above Luna and Antonio Santos's house. At a quarter to five that morning he saw Luna's car go up in flames and with it all evidence that he'd put her there.

The car had burned furiously thanks to the two gallons of gas and denatured alcohol he'd dumped inside it. The flames had swept through the car by the time the doctor had crossed the street and started climbing. He was high above the house when the gas tank ruptured and blew a fireball into the sky.

Ten minutes later, the firemen came, and then the police. An hour after that, the head of Olympic security himself, General da Silva, showed up. Castro recognized him from television. Twenty minutes later, those same two Private operators he'd seen at the Copacabana Palace the night before the World Cup final crossed the police lines.

Jack Morgan. Octavia Reynaldo. He'd looked them up.

For several moments, Castro got anxious. Private's investigators were among the best trained in the world. And those two down there were the best of the best.

The doctor wondered if he'd gone too far by targeting Luna. She'd offered him both an excellent, healthy subject for his experiment and a way to take some personal revenge, but should he have just gone for somebody anonymous? A street person? Someone unlikely to be missed?

Then Antonio Santos had shown up, running down the street, stopping in heartbreak in the driveway, and collapsing in an agony of grief. It had been worth the risk, Castro decided instantly. It had been worth the wait.

Antonio knew the guts-ripped-out-of-you feeling now. Let him wallow in it.

The doctor fed on that idea long after da Silva, Morgan, and Reynaldo had gone into the house and forensic techs had arrived on the scene. He stayed up there in the jungle, ignoring the building heat, ignoring the bugs that whined and bit at his flesh.

An hour passed. The techs removed the body and put a tarp over the burned-out car. Autopsy next, the doctor thought. But maybe not. The Rio system was backed up as it was. With a bullet through the back of the head and a burned corpse, why bother?

Four news trucks were parked down the street now. There were cameras aimed at his handiwork. Dr. Castro was feeling pleased when the front door of the house opened and da Silva, the other cop, the two from Private, and Antonio Santos exited.

Through the binoculars, he studied the slumped shoulders and the expression of shock and bewilderment on the new widower's face. That posture and state of being were bitterly familiar to Castro.

Grief. Loss. Disbelief.

Seeing Santos suffer like this made the doctor smile.

He hoped that the tearing to pieces of Antonio Santos's heart would continue for many, many years to come.

Chapter 37

THE JAMMED STREETS around Lapa throbbed with music and happiness. There were thousands of men and women, young and old, all of them dressed for mystery, provocation, and celebration. Some sang lustily. Some danced lustily. Others hooted and clapped encouragement. Caught up in the good time of a pre-Olympic warm-up party Rio-style, all of them had smiles on their faces in addition to their masks.

All of them, that is, except the Wises, who moved deliberately and without masks ahead of Tavia and me through the joyous throng. The crowd was in constant flux, masses of people shoulder to shoulder, hip to hip, which made the job of staying close to the Wises but unobserved that much more difficult.

Andy Wise had gotten a text message around nine that evening telling him to be in Lapa in two hours. He was to walk specific streets until someone made contact and gave him the ransom instructions.

I didn't like the situation. Neither did Tavia. Cherie Wise had insisted on accompanying her husband and walked with her arm crooked through his, her purse over her right shoulder. The Wises were a tall couple and stood out, so we weren't worried about losing sight of them. But we had no idea who the masked, anonymous people swirling around them were.

They reached an intersection, and Andy paused.

"Go left," Tavia said into her lapel microphone. I heard her over my radio earpiece.

They were a good thirty yards ahead of us and entering one of the most choked spots in the entertainment district, a scene of controlled mayhem and unbridled fun, people drinking and singing and howling at the pitch-dark sky. The Wises disappeared around the corner.

"Pick up the pace," I said into my lapel mike, and I turned my shoulders angular and narrow, tried to squeeze my way forward to cut the gap between us.

Fifteen feet from the corner, we heard a chant go up. Boys, ten or eleven of them, masked street urchins, were shouting and waving sticks in the faces of the partyers, who all surged back.

If you have ever been in a mob being turned, you know it can be a claustrophobic, tense, and frightening experience. The crowd pressed against us, pushed us hard to our left. Tables and chairs of sidewalk cafés began to tumble, and people started shouting in anger and alarm.

I fought against the wave of humanity, got around the corner, and saw the Wises being swept ahead of us down a wider street. We were still thirty yards apart, but the mob pressure was easing. Several of the boys with the sticks squirmed through the crowd like greased pigs and got past me.

"What the hell is going on, Tavia?" I said. "Who are those kids?"

"Pickpockets," she said an instant before one of the

boys dropped his stick, accelerated, and ran by Cherie Wise, bumping her and then darting to his right.

Cherie spun around, holding her purse strap in outrage. "My purse! He cut it off me!"

Her husband twisted and went after the boy, who was trying to get the heck out of Dodge. But I had a better angle on him and took off, Tavia right behind me.

The kid ran with uncanny moves, ducking, twisting, spinning off one surprised reveler after another while I bulled my way after him. He led me on a chase through a maze of streets I couldn't name if you'd shown them to me on a map, zigzagging and using people like a skier uses slalom gates.

He was slight and dark, built like one of those Ethiopian distance runners, but his moves were quick, fluid, and precise. It wasn't like the kid was born to run, more like he was born to flee, and it took every bit of my wind and strength to stay near enough to track him in the thinning crowd.

He kept looking back over his shoulder at intersections, hoping he'd shaken me, but I stayed on him, soaked with sweat. He darted to his right and up onto a brightly tiled red stair that led to another and another, a staircase that climbed steeply up the side of the hill to Santa Teresa.

I sprinted after him, knowing where I was. The Selarón Steps was an iconic place in Rio, an urban staircase with walls and doors flanking it and virtually every square inch of it tiled, up one side and down the other. Some tiles were simple, others ornate, but all of them were unique and yet part of the whole; the thousands of shiny snapshots and miniature paintings covered the entire staircase in a collage. Lanterns lit the steps, and tourists walked and lovers embraced along them as the kid holding Cherie Wise's purse bounced up the stairs and through the crowds like the battery bunny gone mad.

I pounded after him and found his weakness. On the flats he was swift, but climbing slowed him, and I started to gain ground. When I was two flights behind him, nearing the top, the kid glanced back, saw me coming, looked startled, and threw the purse at me.

It was a great throw. I mean, he hit me square in the chest with the purse, and it pulled me up short and briefly stunned me.

He cursed me in Portuguese and sprang away, bounding up the remaining steps and onto the Santa Teresa road, where I lost sight of him. I didn't care. I bent over, desperate for air but happy he hadn't gotten away with the purse.

I found Tavia coming up the lower part of the Selarón Steps, showed her the purse, and told her what had happened. Fifteen minutes later, I handed it to a grateful Cherie Wise.

"Oh, thank you, Jack," she said, taking the purse and hugging it. "It's a favorite of mine. The girls had it made for me a couple of years…"

She looked worn out suddenly, said, "I really need to sleep. I'm getting dizzy."

"Make sure he didn't take anything out while he had it, and we'll go back to the hotel," Wise said, and then he looked at me. "No one tried to contact us."

"I know," I said, glancing back at Lapa and wondering if we should have them troll through again.

Cherie opened the purse, took one look, and let out a soft gasp.

"What?" Tavia asked.

She held the purse out and showed us. Inside, on top of her things, there was an unlabeled CD-ROM in a dirty plastic case.

"That's not mine," she said.

"I would hope not," her husband said. "That technology's a dinosaur."

Chapter 38

Sunday, July 31, 2016
8:30 a.m.

WE ALL GOT a good six or seven hours of sleep after finding the CD, so the Wises, Tavia, and I were looking rested and ready to go when we filed into the lab at Private Rio the next morning.

Seymour Kloppenberg and Maureen Roth, however, had been up all night and looked it.

"You get into the CD?" I asked.

"It was encrypted, but yes," Sci said, and he pushed his glasses back up the bridge of his nose. He turned to his computer keyboard and typed.

The large screen above the workbench opened and revealed instructions in a primitive, blurry font, all capital letters.

LOAD MONEY IN WHITE UNMARKED
FORD PANEL VAN NO REAR
WINDOWS.
ANDREW WISE DRIVER, WEARS
BLUE WORKMAN'S COVERALL, NO
HAT, NO GLASSES.
NO FATHER? THE GIRLS DIE.
NO OTHER PASSENGERS IN VAN OR
THE GIRLS DIE.

NO POLICE OR THE GIRLS DIE.
NO PRIVATE OR THE GIRLS DIE.
NO TRACKING DEVICES OR THE
GIRLS DIE.
EXCHANGE TO TAKE PLACE IN
OPEN, PUBLIC, LIT AREA OF OUR
CHOOSING.
YOU HAVE UNTIL MIDNIGHT
MONDAY, AUGUST 1, TO PREPARE.

"We can get a van like that in Rio, right?" Cherie asked.

"I'm sure," Tavia said. "How soon can you get the thirty million?"

"It's waiting at the national bank," Wise said.

"They want fifty million," Cherie said.

"I'm not giving them fifty."

Cherie's face went cherry red. "They'll kill the girls."

"No, they won't," her husband said. "I told you. They'll see a whopping stack of cash in the back of that van and it won't matter whether it's thirty million or fifty."

"But—"

"Jack?" Wise said impatiently. "What's the likelihood of kidnappers stopping to count when we deliver that amount of money?"

"In a public, lit place?" I said. "Small. They're going to want to see money and lots of it, but they won't be counting exact figures until they're long gone."

"See?" Wise said to his wife. "And the girls will be just as free and safe as if we'd spent fifty million for their return. In business, we call that a bargain."

"In life, we call that endangering the lives of your own flesh and blood to cut costs," Cherie shot back.

Wise ignored her, said to me, "Get one of those vans and put in the most sophisticated and least detectable tracking devices you can find. I want them buried in the money. Can you make that happen?"

I looked to Mo-bot, our expert on these kinds of things. She nodded.

"Wait! What?" Cherie exploded. "Are you kidding me? The note explicitly says tracking them will mean Alicia and Natalie die."

"Not if we have the girls in our possession before turning on the trackers by remote control," her husband said. "That way we win it all. We get our darlings back. We get the money back. And we see the kidnappers thrown in jail."

Chapter 39

EVEN IN THIS day and age of billionaires, it is an awesome thing to see thirty million dollars' worth of currency banded, stacked, and strapped to a pallet. More than a thousand pounds of cash. If it dropped on you, you'd be squished. Kind of takes your breath away, really.

But Wise seemed unimpressed as a forklift loader moved the pallet and the small mesa of money into the back of the van. He shut the rear door, locked it, and then shook the hand of a bank official who wished to remain anonymous.

We jumped down off the loading dock into a wide alley in back of a depository of the Central Bank of Brazil. The overhead door began to descend behind us.

Only an incredibly well-connected multibillionaire had the kind of juice to make a transfer like that happen on short notice in a foreign country. I started reappraising Wise as we walked around the van. Behind the Asperger's facade, he had one of the quickest minds I'd ever encountered. And he had this almost unnatural cool when he had to make his most difficult decisions. I don't think he felt even a flicker of emotion when he'd decided to put thirty million dollars' worth of *reais* into the van instead of fifty.

Wise was confident in the extreme, but I wondered whether he might be riding for a fall.

"Sure you want to be the driver?" I asked one last time.

"It's required of me," he said. "So I'll do it. Now what?"

"You get in the van, I get in that car over there with Tavia and your wife, and we wait for further instructions."

"But we don't even know how the instructions are supposed to come."

"We've got it covered," I said.

We did. The concierge at the Marriott had been told to call us immediately if anything was delivered there. Sci and Mo-bot were monitoring all of the Wises' e-mail accounts and cell phones, and Tavia and I were paired with their phones as well. Anything that came to them, we would see.

I was growing confident that we'd covered all the bases and were prepared for anything. No matter what happened, we'd know where the money and the van went.

Mo-bot superglued tracking beacons that looked like machine-bolt heads in the spaces above the wheel wells and slid other, waferlike versions of the trackers deep in the stack of money. The devices were called slow-pulse transmitters.

Rather than emitting a constant, and therefore more detectable, transmission, the devices could be calibrated to send out a location at specific intervals. Mo-bot had them set on a thirty-two-second and then a forty-second cycle, and she would shut them down during the actual transfer.

Now all we needed was a meeting point.

Wise climbed into the driver's seat. I returned to a black BMW X5 parked down the alley and got into the passenger seat. Tavia was driving. Cherie Wise sat in the back.

"Is my husband's beeper thing working?" she asked.

"Sci?" I said.

"Sending a clear, strong signal," he said.

"Told you we had it covered," I said. "I've even got them tracking this car."

Cherie checked her watch, said, "How long until they make contact?"

"Depends how much they want the money," I said.

"Don't be surprised if they make us stew awhile," Tavia said. "Get us tired, a little disoriented, you know?"

Tavia was right. We sat and dozed in the alley until three a.m. with no contact made. Cherie was starting to make noises about returning to the Marriott where she could wait in bed when her cell phone buzzed an alert. A text coming in.

She looked at it and burst into tears. "It's from Alicia. Or it's coming from her phone, anyway."

"We have a trap on Alicia Wise's cell?" I asked.

"Pulling it up right now," Mo-bot said.

"What's it say?" Tavia asked, twisting around in her seat.

"An address. I think it's in Leblon."

"Give it to me," I said, pulling the car alongside the van. I read out the address to Wise.

"Okay," he said, putting the van in gear. "Let's go bring our girls home."

Chapter 40

AT FIRST, DELIVERY of the ransom payment went down the way I'd thought it would. The kidnappers routed Andy Wise to one address and then another in Centro, and since it was largely vacant at that early hour, Tavia and I and the two other cars manned with Private agents had to stay blocks away, watching the digital trackers' updates on iPads and staying connected in real time over the radio and cellular links.

We never bothered to close the distance and instead paralleled Wise in the white van with four or five blocks between us, shutting down the trackers as he neared each address. After he got to the third, there was no new text message for almost five minutes.

Then my cell buzzed. The pairing between my phone and Wise's was working. I had a text on my screen from Natalie Wise's phone to her father's.

This can be simple. You follow directions, you get your daughters back. In a few minutes we'll give you a location where you are to park the van. You will see your daughters from afar, and you are going to walk away from the van. Someone will pick it up. If you do everything right, the girls will go to you, and our business is done. Simple. Agreed?

Agreed, Wise responded a moment later.

Go to the northeast corner of Rua Frei Caneca and de Março. Park where you can see to the north. Wait.

"Northeast corner of Frei Caneca and de Março," Tavia muttered as she got us turned around. "That's gotta be—"

She floored the accelerator of the X5, said into her microphone, "Andy, you're going to be parking next to the Sambadrome. It's where they have the big samba contests during Carnival."

"Never been there, but I know what it is," Wise said. "Describe what I'll be seeing, please."

Tavia thought, said, "Think the grandstands at the Macy's Thanksgiving Day Parade, and then think twenty times the size of those grandstands and lining both sides of Fifth Avenue for roughly half a mile. You'll be looking up a wide, empty concrete street. Park where you can see the entire length of the parade route, but expose yourself and the van as little as possible. Does that make sense?"

"I guess I'll know it when I see it," Wise replied.

Cherie unclipped her seat belt, shifted so she was behind and between me and Tavia. She stared through the windshield and slowly, gently, moved her hands against each other as if she were washing them.

"This is going to work," Cherie said in a wavering voice. "I'll have them back in my arms soon."

"That's the plan," I said.

"I want us taken to the jet immediately afterward," she said. "The hell with the Olympics. We're just not staying. The girls will understand, I'm sure. And Andy, well…there are some things in life not worth fighting about."

Tavia and I exchanged glances but didn't join the

conversation our client was having with herself. After a while in our business, you learned that people did and said strange things when there were lives on the line.

On the screen of the iPad, the van's icon reappeared.

"You're close, Andy," I said into the microphone.

"Just ahead," Wise replied.

"We're shutting down the trackers in three hundred feet," Mo-bot said over the radio. "Camera will come on at the parking spot. You'll have to adjust its position so we see what you do."

She'd given Wise a high-end digital camera small enough to be hidden in the palm of his hand.

The icon disappeared from the screen.

"Parking," Wise said.

Tavia pulled over six hundred yards east on Valadares Avenue. Cherie leaned over the seat when the iPad screen came to life. We were getting Wise's view via the camera. He'd parked the van diagonally, facing into the Sambadrome. He had us looking through the windshield across a security chain at the road and the flanking grandstands that on a big night during Carnival would be filled with tens of thousands of people. Now the place was so empty it looked forlorn. It was a forgotten venue except for a few nights a year. A secluded spot in the middle of the city. Perfect for trading hostages for money.

The iPad screen flashed with bright lights. Headlights.

Wise said, "There's a white van coming into the other end."

"Hold the camera steady and I'll zoom in," Mo-bot said.

A moment later we saw the van turning sideways about one hundred yards inside the north end of the Sambadrome.

"They had to have cut the security cable at that end," Tavia said.

Wise got a message from Alicia's phone. *Leave the van. Walk south on de Março.*

Wise texted back, *Not until I see girls leave van.*

For a few tense moments there was no reply. Then the side door of the other white van slid open. The girls, bound at the wrists and blindfolded, were pushed out by two figures wearing masks and blue workman's coveralls. They held pistol-grip shotguns to the girls' heads.

Then they tore off the blindfolds and Cherie Wise gasped with joy. "It's them. Oh, thank God, it's them."

Wise got a text from Alicia's phone. *Get out of the van and go,* it said. *Or see them die.*

"Get out, Andy!" Cherie screamed.

He texted back, *Not until I see them walking away.*

After a long moment's hesitation, the gunmen nudged them to move. Uncertainly, the girls began walking east, away from their captors and toward the grandstands.

The camera moved, refocused from its position on the dashboard. Due to the curved windshield, we got a skewed image of the girls starting to climb the grandstands and the audio of Wise leaving the van and shutting the door.

"Walking away south," Wise said.

"Car two, secure the girls, evaluate, and transport to our doctor," Tavia said. "Car one, you've got Mr. Wise."

"Where are we going?" Cherie asked.

"After the money," I said.

Tavia put the car in gear and floored it. We'd no sooner gotten up to speed than a masked man in a blue workman's jumpsuit appeared on the iPad screen, caught by the camera on the money van's dashboard. He had bolt cutters and snipped the security chain into the south end of the Sambadrome.

Someone climbed into the passenger side. We heard the driver's-side door slam. The van took off, screeching into the road between the grandstands, heading north fast toward the other white van, which was turning around.

That's all we saw before one of the people in the van swore and grabbed the camera. The screen went jerky and twisty: The ceiling of the van. The chest of a blue workman's suit. The window opening as the van accelerated, and then the camera was hurled into the stands, spinning in the air and catching fleeting images of the fleeing Wise girls climbing higher and higher.

Chapter 41

TAVIA HAD THE X5 going ninety westbound on Valadares Avenue. She dropped gears crossing de Março, and we shot past Andrew Wise, who was giving us the thumbs-up.

"Don't lose my money," I heard him say in my earpiece.

Tavia dropped the BMW into third, feathered the brakes, and sent us into a drifting power slide through the south entrance of the Sambadrome. She got the car straightened in time for us to see that the money van was almost at the other end of the parade ground. She floored it.

The grandstands became a blur, but we were catching up. We hit ninety again. The money van swerved out onto Salvador Avenue, heading east toward Central. Tavia braked and downshifted again.

"There are the girls!" Cherie yelled. "Stop!"

Tavia glanced at me.

"Do it," I said.

She hit the brakes. We skidded to a stop. Wise's wife jumped out, and Tavia and I squealed off.

A black Toyota turned into the Sambadrome, sped to our left.

"That's car one," Tavia said. "Hold on."

She sent us into another smooth drift that kept the loss of speed and momentum to a minimum, then straightened the car out and accelerated once more. The money van was nowhere ahead of us. I looked at the iPad, saw the icon.

"Go left on Trinta Avenue," I said. "They're heading north."

"I've got them now," Tavia said. "No way a van's outrunning this engine."

Three hundred yards. Two hundred. One fifty. I spotted the van now. It couldn't evade us. And the trackers were performing—

The icon on the iPad disappeared.

"Shit," Mo-bot said in my earpiece. "Either the tracking devices all died at once or they're jamming our signals."

"Doesn't matter," I said. "We've got the van right in front of—"

A second white Ford panel van shot out from the road on our right, and at the same time a third white Ford panel van roared in from our left. Both vans swung into the gap between us and the money van. That van crossed an overpass and took the exit onto a cloverleaf ramp.

We spiraled into a corkscrew left turn that shot us out onto Presidente Vargas Avenue, a wide four-lane thoroughfare that led straight east to the harbor front. The two vans directly in front of us began to slow and weave, keeping us from staying with the money van, which gained speed and distance.

"We've got the girls and the mom, Octavia," a female voice said over the radio. "En route to hospital. Little beat up, but okay."

"And we've got Wise," a male voice said.

Stuck behind the other two vans, Tavia spotted a police turnaround and crossed left through it and into the westbound lane. A pair of headlights came at us. Tavia flicked her headlights and floored it. The car swerved out of our way.

We got past one of the blocking vans in the other lane just before we reached the next police turnaround in the median. With a snap of her wrist, Tavia shot us through and back into the eastbound lane between the two vans.

"One down, one to go," Tavia said.

We were crossing Camerino Road, heading straight for the harbor. The second van was right in front of us, swerving, trying to keep Tavia from getting around. I caught glimpses of the money van's taillights two hundred yards ahead.

Tavia got up on the bumper of the second blocking van. She deked left and then tried to get around on the right. The rear door of the van flew open. In the back, one of the guys in the blue workman's jumpsuit was on his knees aiming an assault rifle at us.

He opened fire.

Tavia slammed on the brakes and swerved, but bullets strafed the hood and windshield of the X5. The glass shattered into a thousand little pieces. We couldn't see a thing. Tavia had to slow and try to steer looking out her window.

But it was too late. The vans had taken a left on a road heading north, and we missed it, forcing us to backtrack. By the time we got turned around, they were nowhere to be seen. We went north and were past Pier Mauá when I spotted a white panel van, probably the one holding all that cash, sitting on the rear deck of a tugboat that was picking up speed out on Guanabara Bay.

"Reynaldo!" a male voice called over the radio. "We are under fire. Repeat, we are—"

The transmission died.

"That was Samuels," Tavia said. "He and Branco had Wise!"

"Andy?" I said into the microphone. I got no answer. "Mo-bot, do you have Wise's beacon?"

"Right here," she said. "Tracker shows current location a half a mile south of the Sambadrome."

"On our way," Tavia said.

When we reached the spot where the tracking signal was coming from—an empty city lot—we found Samuels and Branco alive but unconscious, both with head wounds from blunt-force trauma. The back door of the car was open. Wise was gone. I walked with a flashlight and felt my stomach fall twenty stories when I spotted fresh blood spatter in the dirt and then the blue workman's coverall.

When I picked it up with a stick, I saw that it too was spattered with blood and was in two pieces, like it had been sliced off the billionaire with a utility knife or a razor blade.

Chapter 42

BY THE TIME we got to the private hospital in Leblon, I was thinking that we'd been played by very sophisticated criminals who now held hostage one of the richest men in the world. His abduction could not have happened as a secondary crime of opportunity. This was planned. Get Wise to walk away, expecting to be picked up, and then, when he was far from the Sambadrome, with everyone thinking the play was over, attack.

It had all happened on my watch. I had failed miserably. I felt like the world's biggest fuckup.

Wise's wife certainly thought so. She'd said it to me at least twenty times since we'd brought Samuels and Branco to the same hospital where the twins were being treated. I was actually surprised she hadn't fired us.

"Will Andy be held for ransom as well?" she asked in the hallway outside the girls' room.

"I would think so," I said.

"I can't imagine they'll be happy about being shorted twenty million dollars for the girls," Cherie said. "His own damn fault. The cheap idiot."

She was trying to act tough, but you could see the stress she was under.

"Stay focused on the girls for right now," Tavia said. "They've been through a lot. They're going to need you to be strong for them."

Cherie sniffed, said, "Don't worry about me. I can be Jackie O. when it's called for."

Two doctors came out of the room. They said that Alicia had blunt-force trauma injuries to the right side of her head from being hit by the blackjack. She had considerable swelling, and it had taken them fourteen stitches to close the scalp wound. There were clear indications that she'd suffered a concussion, but the CT scan showed no skull fracture or head bleed. She was occasionally confused, but most of the time she was oriented to self, place, and events.

Natalie's right cheekbone was broken. So was her right orbital bone. So were two small bones in her left hand. She was on narcotics for pain, and the broken hand had already been set and splinted. The doctor recommended that one of Rio's world-famous plastic surgeons be brought in later in the day to work on her face.

"Can I go back in to see them?" Cherie asked.

"Please. They've been asking for you."

Tavia and I went in with Cherie. In a beautifully decorated, homey room, the girls were dozing side by side in hospital beds, surrounded by various monitors. Bandages were wrapped around Alicia's head. The right side of Natalie's face was grotesquely bruised and swollen.

Natalie's good eye opened. "Mom?"

"Right here, baby doll," Cherie said and kissed her delicately on her forehead. "Right here."

"Mom, what happened to us?" Alicia said.

Her mother turned and kissed her other daughter. "You don't remember? You were kidnapped."

Alicia licked her lips, and her eyes widened. "That's right."

"I've told her, like, a hundred times, Mom," Natalie said.

"Where's Dad?" Alicia asked.

Cherie seemed paralyzed by the question for a moment, then said, "He'll be here soon."

Natalie seemed to pick up on something through her painkiller haze. "Mom? What's wrong?"

Cherie looked lost, tears dripping down her cheeks.

Tavia said, "We think he's been taken hostage by the same people who kidnapped you."

Alicia looked more confused than ever. "What?"

"It's true," I said. "So we need your help. Whatever you can tell us about the people who took you—what they said, a name, a noise, anything—might help us in rescuing your father."

Natalie said, "They knocked us down and blindfolded us after the shooting. They dragged us in the darkness. We ended up in the back of a truck and then we were carried into a place that smelled like tobacco."

Alicia nodded. "I remember that. And there was this woman named Rayssa who gave us food."

"You see her face?" Tavia asked.

Natalie said, "She always wore a mask when our blindfolds were off."

"No other names you heard?"

The girls shook their heads.

"No other voices?"

"We heard other voices," Alicia said. "Two different men."

"When they moved us," Natalie said. "Both times."

"They knew who you were, correct?" Tavia asked.

"They knew all about us," Natalie said.

"Did they say how?"

Before she could answer, the door to the hospital suite opened and in stormed a very tired, very angry federal military police lieutenant.

Bruno Acosta pointed at Tavia and then at me, said, "You two are under arrest."

Chapter 43

"ON WHAT CHARGES?" Tavia demanded.

"Obstruction of a federal police investigation, obstruction of justice, failure to report a multitude of crimes," Lieutenant Acosta barked. "Not to mention repeatedly lying to a federal investigator."

"We haven't lied to you," I said.

"No?" Acosta thundered. "What about the real identity of these girls? What about withholding information about ransom demands? What about keeping us totally in the dark!"

"That was our doing," Cherie said. "My husband and I. We would not let Mr. Morgan, Ms. Reynaldo, or anyone at Private divulge to police what was happening. If anyone is at fault for keeping you in the dark, I am, and I'm sorry. We want you to be part of the investigation now."

I glanced at Cherie and had to admit she could indeed play Jackie O. when she wanted to. The way she'd spoken to Acosta, frank, open, yet deferential, coupled with her dazzling looks had charmed the lieutenant and instantly defused the situation.

Still, he glared at me.

"You are a foreign national, Mr. Morgan, and yet you ignore our laws like they are worthless, below you somehow," the lieutenant said. "I'm asking that you be thrown out of Brazil."

Tavia said, "Lieutenant, may I remind you that Mr. Morgan works directly for General da Silva at the highest security levels for the sake of the Olympics. The only person who can have him fired and deported is the general."

Acosta looked ready to ignite again until I said, "So let's figure out a way to work together. Put the past behind us and start over."

I held out my hand. The lieutenant hesitated. He really didn't want to, but he finally took my hand and shook it firmly. "We are partners now, yes?" Acosta asked.

"Equal sharing of information, backup when and if you need it."

Acosta thought it over briefly and then said, "I can live with that."

We brought him up to speed fast. The lieutenant was attentive and smart in his questioning and not happy when we described the ransom drop, the release of the girls, the kidnapping of Andy Wise, and the gunfire in Central. He said the hail of bullets had been heard all over the downtown area. Foreign journalists staying at one of the new hotels were asking questions.

"This kind of Wild West thing is not what Rio needs right before the Olympic Games," Acosta said.

Tavia threw up her hands, said, "They shot at us, Bruno. We never pulled a trigger. The back of the van flew open and this guy was there with an assault gun."

"And no one saw a face?" the lieutenant asked. "A license plate?"

"No license plates and they all wore masks," Tavia said.

"They even anticipated tracking devices and jammed them," I said. "These guys are planners and bold executors."

"And now they have the big fish," Acosta said. "There will be a ransom demand, a large one."

"We were thinking the same thing."

I looked to Cherie, said, "Do you have Andy's power of attorney?"

She nodded. "On most things."

"Access to large amounts of cash?"

Wise's wife thought about that, said, "I would have to get it cosigned by a trustee, but yes. How much?"

I said, "I think it's going to be a whole lot more than before. I'd tell your trustees you may need access to as much as a hundred million dollars in the next twenty-four hours."

Cherie looked to Lieutenant Acosta, said, "I know this might be a sore subject, but can we try to keep this quiet? Out of the press?"

The officer hesitated.

I said, "The last thing Brazil or Rio needs is the story getting out that one of the Olympic Games' biggest benefactors was kidnapped days before the opening ceremony."

Acosta looked frustrated, but he nodded. "We'll do our best, Mrs. Wise."

My cell phone rang. General da Silva.

"General?"

"There will be an autopsy of Luna Santos's body at eight a.m. sharp at the Hospital Geral," he said. "I expect you, Tavia, and Lieutenant Acosta to meet me there."

I glanced at my watch and was surprised to see it was nearly seven. I really needed some sleep, but I said, "We'll see you soon."

Chapter 44

THE COLONIAL FRONT of the Hospital Geral featured a series of archways facing Santa Luzia Road. The arches gave way to an airy colonnade where patients were already lined up waiting for their names to be called.

Ending an overnight shift, Dr. Lucas Castro yawned as he walked through the courtyard beyond the colonnade. He decided he would stop and get an açaí smoothie, double-dosed with guarana and other herbs to keep up his stamina. He was going to need it in the coming—

The doctor stopped short. There in the colonnade he spotted three and then four people he absolutely did not want to see. Ever. Especially here, where he worked. *My God, how did they… What did they…*

Castro pivoted and slowly and deliberately walked away, back toward the building and the clinic. He glanced over his shoulder and saw Jack Morgan, Octavia Reynaldo, General da Silva, Lieutenant Acosta, Antonio Santos, and a tall, wild-haired guy wearing a tie-dyed shirt. They were walking into the courtyard, talking, not looking his way at all.

The doctor felt ill nonetheless.

They had to be looking for him. What else would they be here for? Castro hurried into the building where he worked, took a left, and ducked into a men's room. He stood inside the door, watching through a crack.

If they turn this way, it's over, Castro thought, breathing hard. *I go out through the window, get to the house, get what I need, and then head for the...*

All six of them went right. He watched them go down the hall away from him and his office. Relieved, he told himself to wait until they disappeared before hurrying on his way.

But now he was intrigued. If they weren't in search of him, what were they doing in the Hospital Geral? Where were they going?

Against his better judgment, Dr. Castro exited the restroom and strolled down the hall after them, keeping a few nurses and patients between them and him. They took a left and then a right, then boarded an elevator. They were going down, he saw. He ran to the stairs.

He opened the stairwell door in the basement, saw them already out of the elevator and moving away from him. There were fewer people down on the lower level of the hospital. For a second, Castro hesitated. Then he saw where they were going.

Pathology.

The doctor put it all together in an instant. Luna Santos's body had to be in pathology, awaiting autopsy. He felt a pang of dread but took a breath and calmed himself. He'd made sure the burn was intense. They weren't going to get much off her except carbonized flesh and singed bone.

Castro stood there several more moments, wishing

there was a way he could go to the autopsy and listen to the idiots trying to figure out how and why Luna Santos had died. He supposed he could wander through and...

He shook off this foolishness. These people weren't at the Hospital Geral for him, and they weren't going to get anything from Luna's husk. It was time to go, time to attend to far more important business.

As he began to climb back up the stairs, Dr. Castro figured he had less than three days left to live, and he didn't want to waste a single, precious moment.

Chapter 45

DR. EMILIO CARDOSO adjusted his belly beneath his scrubs, checked the drawstring that held the bottoms up, and then pressed a scalpel to the charred remains of Luna Santos just above her right ear. He cut through scorched flesh to the brittle bone and sliced over the top of her head to her opposite ear. Pieces of skin and muscle fell away like dead coals and ash.

The general, Acosta, and I watched from the other side of a window in an observation room; an intercom allowed us to communicate with Cardoso. The victim's husband had asked to be at the autopsy, but the second they'd pulled back the sheets on her body he'd almost fainted. Tavia had taken him to get something to drink.

"She was subjected to tremendous heat," said Sci, who was assisting the medical examiner at the request of General da Silva.

Cardoso wasn't happy about Kloppenberg being in his autopsy room, but he nodded. "The skull will be brittle."

"We'll tease what's left off the bone," Sci said.

Using forceps and scalpels, he and the medical examiner were able to peel back what was left of her scalp to reveal a small hole in the left posterior portion of her skull and a larger exit hole above the right eye socket.

"She was shot from five, maybe six feet away," Cardoso said.

Sci nodded. "Shooter had to be aiming diagonally at her, and almost level."

Cardoso said, "Thirty-eight caliber. There's our cause of death."

"So why burn her?" I asked.

The pathologist and my forensics chief looked over at me, puzzled. So were General da Silva and Lieutenant Acosta.

"I don't understand, Jack," Sci said.

"She's shot through the back of the head, so why burn her in Santos's front yard? I mean, the killer wanted the body to be there for a reason. And he burned the body for a reason as well."

"I don't know," Dr. Cardoso said. "My job is to examine, not speculate."

"But I'm free to speculate," I said. "Luna's body was not hidden. It was brought to her home, put there to shock and traumatize Antonio, which says to me her murder was probably personal and designed to exact some kind of revenge."

"And burning her body?" the lieutenant said. "Same thing?"

"Could be," I said. "But setting a fire after a murder? That's what killers do when they're trying to destroy evidence."

"Evidence in the car she was in?" General da Silva asked.

"Or on her body," I said. "And it wasn't to prevent us from knowing she was shot to death before she was burned, unless the killer actually thought Luna was going to be cremated by the blaze."

Dr. Cardoso did not seem interested, but Sci got what I was driving at and said, "We're looking for something on or in her body."

I nodded. "Unless the fire took it."

Kloppenberg and Cardoso went back to their work. They cut open Luna's chest and found her organs cooked by the flames. The medical examiner focused on the weight and size of her heart, liver, and lungs.

Sci started dissecting them on another table. For the next fifteen minutes, fatigue-induced negativity crept in and had me starting to believe we wouldn't find anything of value.

Then Kloppenberg, who was working on the heart, stiffened. He stepped over to the liver and made a cut and looked at it under a magnifying glass. Then he turned to me and nodded.

"Dr. Cardoso," Sci said. "Could you take a look at this?"

The medical examiner set his instruments down and crossed the room.

Sci gestured into the heart. "Notice anything missing?"

Cardoso frowned, looked down through the magnifying glass for a few beats before he got it. "There's no congealed or coagulated blood."

"There's no blood in any of the organs," Sci said, looking back at me. "I think she was drained before she was shot and burned, Jack."

Chapter 46

DRESSED IN HIS hazmat suit, Dr. Castro reached into the refrigerator in his lab and retrieved one of the pints of Hydra-9-contaminated blood he'd taken from Luna Santos's body. Castro set the plastic pouch of blood in a pot of water warmed to ninety-eight degrees.

Leaving the blood pack there, he returned to the refrigerator and retrieved five more pints of blood stolen from the blood bank at Hospital Geral. He warmed these too and then used a hypodermic needle to extract a sixth of the volume of contaminated blood and inject it into the clean samples.

He left the newly infected blood at body temperature for twenty minutes, giving the virus time to start to reproduce, and then returned them to the refrigerator to chill and slow the cycle. Before he closed the refrigerator, the doctor stood there, counting. Four pints of Luna's blood, and five new pints. Nine pints. A little more than a gallon.

Was it enough? Could there ever be enough? What was the ideal?

Three gallons, Castro decided. But what would

that weigh? A gallon was roughly eight pounds, so twenty-four pounds. That was too much. Max load according to the specs was fifteen pounds.

So work backward. The delivery system weighs 1.8 pounds, leaving me 13.9 pounds, or just under two gallons. He shut the refrigerator door, knowing he needed another seven pints of blood to do the job.

The doctor left the lab, entered the decontamination shower, and hosed himself off completely with bleach and saline. He rinsed and repeated the process. It was unthinkable for him to get sick, not now, when he was so close to his goal.

Dr. Castro stripped and stepped into a second shower. He shivered as he dried off with paper towels and put them in a biohazard-waste bin. Dressed, he exited and sealed the air lock.

He moved to the door that led to the office and opened it. The doctor flipped on the light, considered the crate on the desk, and felt a thrill go through him. The wood-reinforced cardboard box had been waiting for him when he arrived. He'd wanted to open it right away, but he'd had the blood to deal with first.

Now, however, Castro's remarkable mind turned to focus on the contents of the crate. He'd have to be as precise and gentle opening it as he'd been handling the propagation of Hydra-9. A fortune lay inside; every bit of his savings had been poured into that crate, and he wasn't going to—

Knock.

The doctor felt dizzy and frightened when he pivoted to look at the outside door. Other than deliverymen, no one had come to his door in the eighteen months he'd rented the space, and he had no more orders outstanding.

Knock. Knock.

These were louder than the first, more insistent. A cop? Castro fought against panic. Should he answer? Or just wait for whoever it was to walk away?

He stood frozen, straining to hear the sound of gravel under shoes leaving. Instead, there came a third series of knocks.

A male voice called, "Dr. Castro?"

The doctor almost melted down. It was over. It was all—

"Dr. Castro? Please, it's me, Ricardo. My scooter is broken and my cell is dead and I need to use a phone."

Ricardo Fauvea? My student? He knows this place? How? Why?

In the two seconds that followed, Castro lost what seemed like a pint of sweat. It gushed out of every pore and soaked him in a glistening sheen. His hand trembled as he turned the lock.

He opened the door and saw young Ricardo standing there looking sheepish. "Thank you, Dr. Castro. My scooter broke down, and I need to call someone to get me."

Castro almost handed him his cell phone but then thought better of it.

"Where is your scooter?" he asked.

His student put a hand to his brow, said, "It's around the corner there, about two blocks down."

"What were you doing in the area?" the doctor asked, studying Ricardo's every twitch and tic.

Ricardo looked at the ground, seeming disappointed with himself, and said, "I was following you, Dr. Castro."

That took Castro aback. "Following me? From where?"

"The Hospital Geral," he said, still not looking at the doctor.

"Why would you do such a thing?" Castro demanded in an even voice.

"I don't know."

"What do you mean, you don't know?" the doctor said, firmer. "I have never known you to do anything without a reason, Ricardo. There has to be a reason."

The medical student seemed mortified, but he looked Dr. Castro in the eye and said in a stammer, "I...I admire you, Dr. Castro. I want to be like you. And, I don't know, it just seemed...interesting, that's all, to learn how you live and where you, you know, go."

The doctor believed him but didn't know what to say.

"I'm flattered, but it's a little creepy, Ricardo," he said finally.

"I know," Ricardo said with desperation in his voice. "And I completely apologize. I was wrong to invade your privacy."

"It was wrong," Castro said. "It is wrong."

The young man held up his palms. "I'm sorry, Dr. Castro. I was stupid. I guess I don't know many people here in Rio, not many that I'd consider friends, anyway, and it was just something to do. Nothing more than that."

The doctor gazed at him for several moments. "Who were you going to call to help you with your scooter?"

"Uh, my cousin, probably. Diego."

"Does Diego know you're here?"

"No one knows I'm here," Ricardo said. "I just followed you kind of spur of the moment, that's all.

What is this place? Is this your company or do you just work here? Like, moonlighting?"

After a pause, Castro tilted his head, smiled softly, and said, "No, this company is all mine. Since you're here, would you like the grand tour?"

That pleased Ricardo a great deal. His head bobbed. He broke into a grin.

"Yes, Dr. Castro," he said, his eyes bright and shiny. "I'd like that very much."

Chapter 47

DR. CASTRO STOOD aside, smiled wider at Ricardo, and said, "Come in, then."

The young medical student bowed his head as he passed the doctor and then looked around the small office at the chair, the desk, and the crate with some disappointment. Who knew what his imagination had conjured up about this place?

"From the U.S.?" Ricardo said, tapping the crate. "What's in there?"

Castro double-bolted the outer door and said, "A new toy."

"More rocket stuff?"

"Something like that," the doctor said. He moved by Ricardo and opened the inner door. "This is where the work is done. My personal infectious-diseases lab."

Ricardo walked eagerly into the airy warehouse space and gaped at the big tent with its air ducts, hoses, and electrical lines.

"Air locks?" the medical student asked.

"And a state-of-the-art decontamination system. I designed it myself."

Ricardo looked at him in wonder. "So you're set up to handle the truly dangerous viruses?"

"You have no idea."

Ricardo shook his head. "Must have cost a fortune to build."

"Cost me everything I had," Dr. Castro admitted. "Would you like to go inside? See what I'm up to?"

His student acted like he'd been handed the keys to heaven, and he followed Castro into the air locks. The doctor helped Ricardo into a dry hazmat suit; he took the wet one he'd already used that morning.

He didn't bother duct-taping his wrists and ankles or Ricardo's. With Hydra-9 sealed and on ice, there really wasn't any need. Castro turned on Ricardo's radio and microphone.

"Hear me?" he asked.

"Loud and clear," the medical student said.

Dr. Castro unzipped the final portal and crouched to step through and get inside. Ricardo followed, gazing all around like a sailor in a titty bar. The doctor told him to explore while he took care of a minor task.

His student didn't need to be told twice. He walked past the hospital bed to the glass cages, peered into the ones that held live rats, while Castro busied himself at one of the cabinets.

"Are they infected with a virus now?" Ricardo asked. "The rats?"

The doctor continued what he was doing, said, "Yes, but those rats are very resilient, very resistant to the strain. They've survived it."

"So you're developing a vaccine?"

Castro turned, nodded, walked toward him. "You're a smart young man, Ricardo. That's exactly what I'm doing."

"For who?"

"For mankind."

"Well, yeah, of course," his student said. "But, like, who's funding this? You must have a big research grant. Is it from the government? Or a drug company?"

The doctor realized that he'd underestimated Ricardo.

"I'm funding the research personally," Castro said, stepping up beside him.

Through the hazmat suit's glass visor, he could see his student's confusion.

"But this all had to cost over ten million *reais*," Ricardo said.

"Twenty-two million *reais*," the doctor said. "More than two million dollars U.S. Every penny of the settlement I got from the government after my wife was killed in a...well."

Ricardo looked down. "Oh, I'm sorry, Doctor. I...I didn't know."

Dr. Castro considered him a moment before saying, "Ricardo, I'm sorry to say that there are many things you will never know about me."

He plunged a hypodermic needle through his student's hazmat suit, felt it pierce the young man's abdomen before he mashed the plunger. Ricardo made a sound like pillow plumping and doubled over, staring down through the shield at Castro's hand and the barrel of the syringe.

"What?" he said, gasping, already feeling the effects of the drug.

Castro yanked the needle free, grabbed Ricardo under the armpits.

The young man tried to straighten up, looked at the doctor with eyes that were widening. "Why?"

"Because you have seen too much, Ricardo," Dr. Castro said. "And I need seven pints of your blood."

"Seven?" his student whispered drunkenly as his muscles started to go slack. "That's too much, Doctor. I'll…"

"I know, Ricardo. I'm really sorry it had to be you."

Chapter 48

THE BEAR ADJUSTED his knapsack, pulled on the helmet, and made the sign of the cross before climbing onto the motorcycle behind the driver. Urso hated taking motorcycle taxis, especially the ones in Vidigal favela, south of Leblon. The Vidigal drivers were insane.

The motorcycle engine revved. The driver let out the clutch and gunned it. They shot straight up the hill. Fifteen seconds into the ride they almost collided with tourists coming down out of the slum. That was the new thing: wealthy foreigners coming to Rio and staying in hostels in the favelas.

Why would anyone willingly vacation in a slum? the Bear wondered. Would they do the same thing in South Central or Compton?

The narrow tarred road turned supersteep and switchbacked. Shack shops that sold everything from cigarettes to plumbing supplies crowded the street, which meant people and motorcycles crowded the street, which meant people and motorcycles often smashed into each other on the street.

By the time they reached the top of the favela, Urso was soaked with nervous sweat. He handed the driver his fare and the helmet and hesitated at a path that led past the highest shack, which was right up against the jungle and in the shadow cast by the more eastern of the Dois Irmãos Mountains.

The Bear climbed past the shack and continued on into the jungle. Even in August, the dead of winter in Brazil, since there was no sea breeze penetrating the canopy of trees, the late-day heat was oppressive.

But the heat felt good to Urso. He followed the path through roots and along rock ledges. He could feel the towering cliff of the mountain's east flank above him, and through holes in the jungle canopy he caught sight of the sheer gray rock face.

He passed a few other travelers coming down the mountain, always seeing them before they saw him, which gave Urso the chance to study them, evaluate their threat. Rio's jungles were spectacular places, but given their remoteness right in the middle of a city, they could be utterly lawless.

The Bear was not a regular on this path. Not by any means. But he knew enough about these woods to understand that any smart gangster would hide in a ravine just beyond where the path buttonhooked along the flank of the hill. If the men were in the jungle, they'd be waiting above the pinch point.

By the agitated expressions of two young women who passed him a few minutes later, Urso knew for sure gangsters were up there collecting tolls, or worse. He reached around under his loose shirt and removed an old but well-cared-for .45-caliber Remington Model 1911 pistol. It was a heavy thing, but effective.

The Bear reached into his pants pocket and got out a crude, homemade suppressor, which he screwed onto the threaded muzzle. Even though the police rarely came into the jungle, he didn't want to attract unnecessary attention.

Urso slid the suppressed gun into the front of his pants and let his loose shirt drape over it. He walked on confidently into the pinch point, eyes straight ahead but picking up movement on the slope above. He exited the narrow chute and found a kid, maybe seventeen or eighteen, standing there in the path. Two others, one above, and one below, revealed themselves.

"What are you doing here, man?" the one on the trail asked.

"Taking a walk," Urso said. "Seeing old friends up in Rocinha."

"What's in the knapsack?" asked the one above and to his right.

"Groceries," Urso said. "We're having dinner."

"Let's see," said the one below and to his left.

None of them displayed weapons, but the Bear knew they had them.

"Can't we just make this a cash-and-go thing?" he asked. "I'd hate to see unwanted and unnecessary bloodshed."

A long moment of silence unfolded, during which Urso's decision was made for him. Catching a flicker of the uphill man's hands, he dropped to one knee, drew the gun, and shot the man high in the chest. Then the Bear twisted and put one through the downhill man's throat. He had the kid in the trail in his sights before the boy could even tug his old revolver out.

"No, Senhor," the kid said. "Please. I was just following orders."

Urso considered leniency, but in this case it just wouldn't do. He shot the kid in the face.

It was so steep there by the ravine that it took the Bear less than two minutes to drag the dead bodies over and push them off the side. He watched them tumble, fall, and disappear into the jungle below.

There'd be a stench at some point, and birds circling and rodents gnawing, and maybe they'd find bones. But as Urso picked up his spent bullet casings, he knew there'd be nothing to connect him to the deaths.

Chapter 49

AN HOUR LATER, the Bear emerged from the jungle in the Rocinha favela. He nodded to the gangsters watching this end of the trail. They would think of him when their friends did not reappear, but by then it wouldn't matter.

He wandered with purpose through the Rocinha slum, still a ridiculously dangerous place, as the sun began to set. He spotted the ruins of a mansion that a drug lord had built and that the BOPE had firebombed. He passed through the saddle on the west flank of the Two Brothers and dropped downhill toward the tony enclave of Leblon.

The new top 1 percent of the 1 percent—Russians, Chinese, Europeans, and the odd American—lived down there in flats that cost sixteen million dollars U.S. and more. With the great wealth of Rio below him, the Bear cut back to the eastern edge of the slum and started once more into the jungle. Monkeys scattered. Parrots going to roost scolded him.

Two hundred yards in, a thousand vertical feet below the cliffy north end of the mountains, Urso heard the hum of a generator before spotting a gathering of shacks hidden in the trees at the top of a small clearing, less than an acre. On the roof of the largest building was a satellite dish. That was not an uncommon sight in Rio, except this dish was joined by two others, and all three pointed in different directions.

The Bear saw the shadows of men to either side of the largest shack but went confidently to the door and knocked twice. The door soon opened.

The woman who called herself Rayssa stood there.

"Any trouble?" she asked.

"A little," Urso admitted before handing over the knapsack. "But nothing to be worried about."

Rayssa looked doubtful but took the pack and stood aside. The Bear entered the shack, saw fourteen-year-old Alou sitting in front of a desk made from a door turned flat. On top of the desk were three large iMac screens and a keyboard. Alou finished typing something in and hit Return. The two screens on the outside began to play the evening news. The center one showed the websites of the local papers. After watching several minutes of coverage focused on the upcoming Olympic Games, now just days away, Rayssa said, "The police, the Wises, and Private have kept it out of the news."

Urso gestured with his chin at the knapsack, said, "Let's change that."

Rayssa nodded. She said to Alou, "Be ready in fifteen minutes."

"The security's strong, right?" the Bear asked.

Alou looked insulted, said, "It goes out in bursts, with corrupted and misleading metadata."

"What the hell does that mean?"

Rayssa said, "Don't worry about it. He's tested it. It works. Not even Private was able to track us."

Urso chewed at the inside of his lip, said, "Where's Wise?"

"Next door," Alou said.

They went out the back of the shack and crossed a narrow gap to a smaller, tin-roofed structure. One of the Bear's men stood at the door. He wordlessly moved aside and let them in.

Andrew Wise was dressed in another blue workman's coverall, now with a black hood over his head. Straps held his chest, arms, and legs to a sturdy chair. The American billionaire heard them come in, turned his head their way, and tried to say something through his gag.

Rayssa ignored him. She went to a tripod mounted about three feet in front of Wise. She removed a recently stolen Canon HD camera from the knapsack, checked the SIM card, then attached the camera to the tripod and aimed it at her hostage.

Rayssa handed a black hood to the Bear and put on the primitive mask she'd used during the ransom demands for the Wise sisters.

"Okay, then," Rayssa said, walking toward the billionaire. "It's time to get down to it. The real reason you were brought here, Mr. Wise."

Chapter 50

I HEARD THREE sharp knocks on my door at the Marriott. Despite the disaster of the previous evening, I'd been in desperate need of sleep, and around ten that morning I had gone there rather than to Tavia's flat.

The knocking came again. I groaned, forced my eyes open, and looked at the clock. Six thirty p.m. I'd slept eight solid hours, the longest stretch I'd gotten in a month.

"Jack?" Cherie Wise called through the door. "Are you there?"

"Two seconds, Cherie," I yelled back.

After throwing on sweatpants and a hoodie, I went to the door, looked through the peephole, and saw Cherie standing there, trembling, still wearing her clothes from the night before. I yanked the door open. "Cherie?"

"What am I going to do?" she asked, and burst into tears.

"Come inside," I said, taking her by the elbow. "What's happened?"

"Nothing," she blubbered. "That's the point.

They've had him more than twelve hours and nothing!"

"Andy's a big coup, and they know it," I said, leading her to a seat. "They're going to be extra careful
before they contact us. And after the gunfire, they
have to know there are federal police involved too.
You've got to take a lot of deep breaths. Live in the
moment until we know more."

Wiping at her tears, Cherie said, "I'm sorry, Jack,
I've just never been through anything remotely like
this."

"You have nothing to be sorry about," I said.
"Anybody in your boots has the right to cry."

"Not very Jackie O. of me."

"I'll bet Jackie O. had more than her share of moments like this, times when she hadn't slept and felt
like she was all alone in the world."

Cherie sighed, blew out her breath, and slumped
in the chair.

"I suppose you're right," she said. "It's just left me
feeling so burned, so cheated. One minute I get the
girls back and the next Andy's gone."

Cherie paused, tensing again, acting as if she were
far away and contemplating the unthinkable.

"We'd been having trouble in our marriage, Jack,"
she said. "I won't bore you with the sordid details, but
the truth is…I've been up all night because I want
Andy back. I really do. I want to tell him that all is for-
given. I want to hear him say it to me."

The billionaire's wife looked tortured and forlorn
as she drew her feet up, hugged her knees, and whispered again, "I want to hear him say it to me."

Cherie seemed to grow in dimensions I had not
imagined just a few moments before.

I said, "The fact that the girls were released in return for the ransom is a very good sign. I think if we cooperate, you'll see him—"

My cell rang. It was Tavia.

"We were just contacted," she said.

Chapter 51

FORTY MINUTES LATER, Cherie, Tavia, Acosta, and I were at the lab at Private Rio, watching impatiently as Sci and Mo-bot tried to analyze the metadata attached to the latest video. We'd wanted to watch it immediately, but they insisted on looking at it from the outside first for technical reasons I frankly didn't understand.

Finally, shaking his curly head, Kloppenberg said, "I can't quite figure out how they've done it, but the code's corrupted, like it's got a virus that worms through the code upon our receipt. Don't know how they did it. Mo-bot?"

"It's got me baffled too," she said.

"Play it, then," Lieutenant Acosta said.

Everyone looked at me.

"Put some kind of quarantine around it so it can't attack our files, and then open it," I said, and I glanced over at Cherie, who'd taken a seat and was holding her hands together tightly in desperate prayer.

Tavia went to sit at her side. She looked to me, and we shared a worried moment before the big screen in the lab came alive with the image of Andrew Wise.

He was gagged and strapped to a stout chair, still wearing the blue jumpsuit.

The camera zoomed in and showed Wise's face was bruised. Dried blood matted his hair. Drips and streaks of it showed on the chest of the coverall. He seemed alert, aware of his surroundings, but hurt and in considerable pain.

"Jesus." Cherie moaned, and she buried her face in her hands. "Why are they doing this?"

"They released the girls," Tavia said. "You'll have him back soon."

But then the camera retreated, revealing a white sheet behind the billionaire. On the sheet and above Wise's head, there was crudely painted red lettering that read:

Favela Justice!

"What the hell is this?" Lieutenant Acosta said.

That same woman from the earlier video messages, Rayssa, wearing the primitive mask, appeared to Wise's left. Walking with confidence all around the billionaire, she looked to the camera.

"For those of you who don't know, this cancer of a man is Andrew Wise, the founder and chairman of Wise Enterprises, or WE," Rayssa said in thickly accented English. "Senhor Wise is on trial here for his actions as they relate to the rape and persecution of Brazil's poor through his company's profiteering in the construction of the World Cup and Olympic Games venues.

"Favela Justice has all the damning evidence," she went on. "Evidence you will see in the coming days. We'll let you decide Senhor Wise's guilt or innocence.

If you judge him innocent, we let him go. You judge him guilty, and Favela Justice demands the payback of one billion dollars in gold, which will go to the poor of Brazil."

"One billion?" Sci said.

Mo-bot whistled, said, "Got to be the highest ransom demand in history."

I glanced at Cherie and saw her lose all color.

Rayssa paused at Wise's left side and addressed the camera. "All news organizations gathered in Rio: You have been sent an excerpt from the trial of Andrew Wise. Every afternoon at three thirty eastern daylight saving time, you should expect another one. Tomorrow's excerpt: the evidence revealed."

The screen went blank.

"A billion dollars. Three thirty p.m. eastern," I muttered, seeing where this was going. "Fuck."

I left the room, pulling out my cell phone. "Fuck."

"What?" asked Tavia, following me into the hall.

"I went through a nightmare at the last Olympics in London, and here comes another one," I said, trying to wrap my head around what had just happened in there.

Was all of this solely about the billionaire? Or were they using the billionaire to attack the Olympics? Was Favela Justice connected to Luna's death? Were the games being threatened once again?

When General da Silva answered my call, I said, "I've got news, and you're not going to like it one bit."

I laid it out for him: The story of the ransom and the kidnap. The video and the potential ramifications.

The general said *shit* in Portuguese.

"Exactly."

"Get me that video," he said. "Then we'll talk."

"Straightaway," I said, and I returned to the lab, where Sci, Mo-bot, Lieutenant Acosta, and Cherie Wise were watching the video again.

"Andy's hurt, but not out of it. He knows what's going on around him," Cherie said when she saw me. Then she started to cry. "Can we convince the media not to broadcast this?"

I shook my head and said, "I won't lie to you, Cherie. The Olympics don't start until Friday. That leaves three days with a gaping news hole. There's a reason they're delivering their messages at three thirty p.m. eastern. That's a half an hour before the big news organizations' early deadlines. A billion-dollar demand? The global media will eat this up."

Chapter 52

THAT EVENING, THE video of Andrew Wise played on a flat-screen as Dr. Lucas Castro worked on his invention in the shop outside the clean room. The billionaire's kidnapping and ransom demand dominated every channel.

A billion dollars in gold for the poor? Castro thought. *That's a solid penalty. That'll sting the pockets. I think I like this Favela Justice, whoever they are.*

He stood back, looking at his intricate device. In a titanium frame hung a hammock of black-mesh fabric that held two large canisters fitted to a central green hose; that hose was attached to nine smaller black hoses sticking out of the bottom of the mesh. They hung down several feet, like tentacles with airbrushes attached to their ends.

"Perfect," Castro said proudly.

Now he had to make sure it worked.

Castro removed one canister from the central hose and attached it to a small air compressor with a remote control.

This was a test, after all, and Dr. Castro wished to exceed the pressure his device called for. It wouldn't do to blow a gasket and fail at the moment of truth.

No way that was happening. Not when he had so little time left on earth.

He used the bleed valve to draw off the air in the fitting and closed it when red-dyed water seeped out. Castro flipped on the compressor, stood back, and pulled out his iPhone. He called up an app that connected him to the compressor control. The doctor hit the Go button.

A second later, clouds of red mist shot out of the nine airbrushes, which whipsawed, throwing the aerosol this way and that. It spattered the bench and floor like a measles rash. It raised a red fog that drifted to the doctor, tingled on his face, and gathered until drips of it rolled down his cheeks like bloody tears.

Dr. Castro was grinning wildly, elated.

He'd patterned his delivery system after Hydra-9 itself. Together, the nine-armed device and the virus that produced nine-headed cells were a single organism about to strike Rio with great and terrible wrath.

Chapter 53

Tuesday, August 2, 2016
8:30 p.m.
Seventy and a Half Hours Before the Olympic Games Open

TAVIA DROVE US up a steep hill in the Bangu District of Rio.

"How are you holding up?" I asked.

"I get waves of energy," she said. "And when there's no wave to be had, I drink espresso."

"So you're pragmatic?"

"A pragmatic romantic."

"It suits you. You wear it well."

"You're sweet," Tavia said; she blew an air kiss my way and pulled up in front of a blue gate set in a high stone wall.

There had been little we could do after seeing the video from Favela Justice but leave it to Sci and Mo-bot to wrestle with the corrupted metadata and take Cherie Wise back to the hospital to see her girls. She said being with them was the only way she'd be able to sleep.

Tavia and Lieutenant Acosta and I had decided to work different angles. Acosta was going to plumb the federal police intelligence files for any mention of Favela Justice. We returned to the idea that the Wise girls, who'd been in Brazil under assumed identities, must have been spotted by someone who knew them by sight. Unless the girls had told someone who they were.

When we'd asked the twins, who were both doing much better, about it again, they had once more strongly denied that they'd revealed their identities. We wanted to talk to them some more, but both of them were tired and Cherie told us to come back in the morning. They were all going to sleep the night away.

We left them, realizing that if an individual had taken a particular interest in the girls, somebody at one of the three charities they'd volunteered for might know about it. We couldn't try the sanitation project or the NGO because they were closed.

But the third charity, the orphanage, was a different story.

We heard a television playing and children laughing when Tavia pulled the cord on the bell at the front gate. A man came to the entrance and looked at us suspiciously until we showed him our identification and asked to see Mariana Lopes.

"She's not here," he said.

"We called the clinic, and they said she was here," Tavia said.

"It's late," the guard said. "She's tired. Come back tomorrow."

"It won't wait," Tavia said. "Could you tell her Octavia Reynaldo and Jack Morgan are here and that it is very important?"

He had a scowl on his face and spit out something in Portuguese as he walked away.

"I didn't catch that."

"He said, 'They never leave that poor woman alone.'"

Five minutes later the gate opened. We walked into a walled area surrounding a large, rambling, three-story building painted in a riot of pastel colors. In front of it was a playground with all kinds of toys strewn about.

Mariana Lopes shut the gate behind us and smiled, though we could see she'd been under strain and hadn't slept.

"We're sorry to bother you, Mariana," Tavia said.

"You said it was important, so it's not a bother. Do you want tea? There's some in the kitchen."

"Tea would be fine," Tavia said.

Lopes led us through a maze of hallways, past bunk rooms and common areas and lavatories and a laundry, to a cramped but well-equipped industrial kitchen that was spotless.

"You did all this yourself?" I asked. "The clinic and the orphanage?"

"I had help," she said. "Lots of it."

"But you were the guiding light," Tavia said. "It was all your idea."

"I picked from a lot of good ideas," Lopes said.

"How many kids?" I asked as we sat down at a table.

"At any one time the census is somewhere between sixty-five and seventy-five. Is that why you're here? If you wanted a tour, I could have arranged it for—"

"Do you remember these girls?" Tavia asked, showing Lopes a photo of the Wise sisters on her cell phone.

The orphanage director put on her reading glasses, looked closer. "Of course," she said. "The Warrens. Why? Are *they* the girls who were kidnapped?"

"And returned for ransom," I said.

"Oh my God," Lopes said, her hand at her mouth. "I never put it together."

"We never told you who the girls were," Tavia said. "Tell us about them?"

Lopes shrugged. "We have many volunteers like the Warrens who come through here, usually four, five at a time, so they tend to blur a bit, but I remember those two well. They had a rough go of it at first, but they turned out to be wonderful girls. If I could get those kinds of volunteers all the time, the children would be the better for it. Oh, this is awful. Are they all right?"

"They're going to be fine," Tavia said. "But you said they had a rough go of it. In what way?"

"Well, they came here straight off the plane. First stop. I think they might have believed they'd go to Copacabana or something, but that didn't happen."

Chapter 54

A SECURITY GUARD came into the kitchen. Mariana Lopes went over and spoke to him for a few moments, then returned to us, pushing back a wayward strand of hair as she sat down.

"You were saying that when the twins came here, they thought they were going to Copacabana?" Tavia said.

"I'm saying they were shocked by the poverty," Lopes said. "You could tell it really bothered them. They were well aware that there were poor people in the world, but this was clearly the first time they'd seen it in person. They kept getting tears in their eyes, and on the second or third day, I overheard one of them, I can't remember which, telling the other that she didn't know if she could take it, seeing kids suffering when they'd been given so much."

"But they got through the shock?" Tavia said.

Lopes nodded. "I walked over and told them that this was the point of volunteering. They were giving back because of all that they'd been given. That seemed to change their attitude. And they'd both studied Portuguese before they came, so they could talk with the kids. They befriended many of the children and staff in their time here. I wish my daughter, Amelia, were here to tell you. She had more interaction with them."

"Where is she?"

"She's been down in Porto Alegre the last two weeks, doing fieldwork for her PhD."

"But she was here when the Warren girls were?" I asked.

"For part of their time with us. Give her a call. She'll remember them."

"Do you have her number?" I asked.

"I do," she said, pulling out her phone. "It's best to try her in the evenings. She's been putting in long…" The orphanage director stopped, looked up at us. "If the girls have been ransomed and returned, why are you here?"

We exchanged glances, knowing it was all going to come out soon, if it hadn't already.

"Because the girls' real last name isn't Warren," Tavia said. "It's Wise, as in WE, Wise Enterprises."

Now Lopes seemed completely confused. "Okay?"

"You don't know the company? WE? Big construction projects?"

She squinted. "I guess."

"The girls' father, Andrew Wise, the founder of WE, was grabbed during the ransom exchange. A group called Favela Justice has claimed responsibility and they plan to put him on trial and tape it."

Lopes pondered that. "You mean like vigilantes?"

"Kind of," I said. "They've accused him of gouging the government during the construction of World Cup and Olympic projects and impoverishing the slum dwellers."

That annoyed her. "Slum dwellers? Mr. Morgan,

they prefer the term *favela people*. This group...what did you call it?"

"Favela Justice," Tavia said.

"Well, I don't know who they are, but I'm inclined to believe their charges."

"Why?"

"Government contractors overcharging and paying off politicians in Brazil? It's been a constant story since, I don't know, the beginning of Brazil."

I glanced at Tavia, who shrugged, said, "That's true."

Lopes fought a yawn.

"We should go, then," Tavia said. "And you should sleep, Mariana. We appreciate the help."

"Have I been of any?" she asked, getting up wearily.

"Some," I said.

"Well, as I said, call Amelia," Lopes said. "She knows more about the girls than I do."

Chapter 55

THE ELEVEN O'CLOCK news in Brazil and the cable news shows were dominated by Favela Justice and the plight of Andrew Wise. Several broadcasts featured aerial images of various World Cup and Olympic venues that Wise Enterprises had helped build, including the athletes' village in Barra da Tijuca.

"The charges are price gouging and financial oppression by a man who benefited greatly from the construction boom," one newscaster brayed. "What's next in this strange story? Stay tuned as it unfolds."

"Enough," Tavia said, and she shut off the television.

I handed her a glass of excellent Argentine Malbec. "Here you go. Decompression, stage one."

Her cell phone rang. She sighed, looked at it. "Amelia Lopes, finally."

Like her adoptive mother, Amelia spoke excellent English, and Tavia put her on speaker.

"Yes, of course I remember the Warren girls," Amelia said. "Very sharp and very—how do you say?—sympathetic."

When we told her the girls' real surname, she figured it out fast. "They are the daughters of this guy who's all over the television news right now?"

"The same," Tavia said.

"They told me they came from a privileged background, but I had no idea they were…"

I asked, "Was there anyone at the orphanage who was particularly close to them, someone they possibly confided in?"

"You mean someone they might have told about their real identities?"

"Yes."

"Well, I thought I was close to them, or as close as you can get to people you've known for a week, but they never mentioned having a different last name," Amelia said. "I think I'd remember that."

"I'm sure you would," I said. "Your mother says you're doing fieldwork."

"Almost got it wrapped up. Another two or three weeks and I'll be ready to start writing."

"And what are you studying?"

She paused, yawned, said, "I'm sorry, it's been a long day. I'm pursuing a doctorate in socioeconomics, focusing on one town in southern Brazil for my dissertation. How are the girls?"

"They're both going to be fine," Tavia said.

"Would you tell them hello from me if you see them?" Amelia asked.

"We certainly will," I said. "And we appreciate the call back."

"Sorry I couldn't be of more help."

"If you think of anything, you'll give us a call?" Tavia asked.

"I can do that," Lopes's daughter said. "Thank you."

The line went dead. We returned to our Malbec, and my hand found Tavia's. Her hands were beautiful. Her fingers were long, slender, and expressive. She used her hands when she talked, like they were speaking another language.

My thumb rubbed her palm. "You calm me down, you know. Even when things get crazy, having you near calms me down."

"So you're saying I'm a sedative?"

"No," I said, and laughed. "More like a glass or two of, I don't know, spectacular Malbec?"

"I can live with that," she said with a slight, sly smile as her index finger trailed up my forearm. "Do you want to finish our wine and go to the second stage of decompression before we sleep?"

"Decompression, stage two," I said, leaning in to kiss her. "Best idea I've heard all day."

Chapter 56

CHERIE WISE WALKED to the window in the sitting area of her suite at the Marriott and looked out through a narrow gap in the curtains.

"I feel like food," she said.

"You can order room service," I said.

"No," she said. "I feel like I am the food, and the mob out there is salivating at the idea of eating me and my family."

I could see how she'd feel that way. Matt Lauer, the *Today* show host already in Rio for the games, started off early that morning with a live stand-up in front of the hotel; he gave a brief synopsis of Wise's life intercut with sections of the Favela Justice video and references to the billion-dollars-in-gold penalty.

At last count there had been fifteen cameras on Avenida Atlântica aimed at the Marriott and twice that number of journalists on the sidewalk and white-sand beach.

The front desk had received calls requesting interviews with Cherie from dozens of reporters, including Lauer, who was the most persistent. Either he or his producer left a message every hour on the hour.

Tavia and I had spent the morning interviewing

the man who'd overseen the Wise girls at the sanitation project in Campo Grande and the woman who
ran the Brazil branch of Shirt Off My Back, the NGO
they'd been working for at the time they were kidnapped.

The sanitation guy had called the Wise girls
"distracted," which seemed to mean he didn't think
they worked hard enough. That ran counter to
Amelia's and Mariana's descriptions of the twins.
But then again, latrine duty is nothing to get excited
about.

The woman in charge of the NGO said she'd
never met Natalie or Alicia. Left with no idea how
or where the girls had been identified and targeted,
Tavia and I split up. I went to be with Cherie while
Tavia fetched the girls, who'd been given the okay to
leave the hospital.

At three fifteen, there was a knock on the door.
I opened it, and Natalie entered. She looked high on
painkillers and pressed an ice pack to her bruised face
as she walked by me in search of her mother. Following her, Alicia looked miserable. She was paler, and
her eyes were sunken.

"Why release them from the hospital?" I muttered
to Tavia as she came in behind Alicia. "They look like
hell."

"The doctors figured it would be fine as long as
they were monitored by a nurse," Tavia said. "There's
one on the way."

We joined the Wises back in the suite's sitting area;
the girls sat on the sofa flanking their mother, who
had her arms around both of them.

"My head still hurts," Alicia said. "Why can't I
have something like Natalie's getting? She's sitting

there with that goofy smile and I've got, like, the worst headache ever."

Tavia said, "The doctors don't like to use narcotics with concussions."

"When the nurse gets here, we'll see what we can do," Cherie promised.

My cell rang. It was Sci.

"We got a Zip file just now from Favela Justice," he said.

"Forward it to Tavia's e-mail and then get to work on it," I said.

"Coming right at you."

I hung up, looked at Cherie, said, "It's here."

Wise's wife blanched, said, "Girls, there's something you're going to see that you won't like, but Jack and I think it's important for you to watch in case you recognize anything or anybody."

"What kind of thing?" Natalie asked.

"You'll see," Tavia said, getting out her computer and calling up her Gmail account. "By the way, we talked to a friend of yours last night."

"A friend?" Alicia asked. "Who?"

"Amelia Lopes," I said.

Natalie blinked dumbly, and her chin retreated. Alicia stared at us in a kind of dazed disbelief.

"You talked with Amelia last night?" Natalie said. "How is she?"

"Fine; working hard on her research," Tavia replied as she typed on her keyboard. "She says she hopes you're okay."

"Where is she?" Alicia asked, looking confused.

"Some town near Porto Alegre," I said.

"Oh," Alicia said. "I couldn't remember what it was near before."

"She's, like, the smartest person ever, Mom," Natalie said.

"I think your dad holds that title," Cherie said.

"Sure, but, like, she has insight, you—"

"Sorry, here we go," Tavia said, and hit Return.

The screen blinked to life.

Chapter 57

A BRILLIANT RED logo—FAVELA JUSTICE—came spinning out of a void before leveling out on the screen.

Then it faded, revealing Andy Wise staring out at us. Still gagged and strapped to that heavy wooden chair, the billionaire looked worn from his experience.

Rayssa, the woman in the primitive mask, appeared, said, "We'll let the evidence speak for itself."

She vanished into a series of smash-cut video clips and images crafted like a news segment on Vice.com, a hip, visual story with Rayssa explaining what we were seeing in a voice-over. Documents fluttered onto a wooden table, dozens of them, and then hundreds, piling up on the table, falling off the sides, and drifting in the air.

One appeared in close-up for less than five seconds as Rayssa said, "These are copies of WE invoices for rebar, which is used to reinforce concrete. Mr. Wise's company bought rebar in volume, right off the boat from Poland, for three hundred dollars per metric ton."

Another document flashed by with the WE logo, too quick to read, and then dozens more, one after the other, rapid-fire, as Rayssa said, "But as internal accounting documents show, Mr. Wise's company was charging the Brazilian government and Olympic authority three thousand dollars per metric ton."

Over images of the Olympic village and the World Cup stadiums, she said, "Favela Justice gets that Mr. Wise is in business to make a profit, but a nine hundred percent profit? That's gouging any way you look at it."

The video went on showing images of cement mixers while Rayssa alleged that WE billed raw cement at nearly six times the amount other private construction firms did. Then the scene shifted to images of favelas and favela people all over Rio.

"The Brazilian government took on hundreds of billions in debt to finance the stadiums," Rayssa said. "This was money that could have gone to better schools, better sanitary conditions in the favelas, hope for the vast majority of Brazilians who want a better life. Instead, like the Roman emperors who built the Colosseum, the government bought entertainment for the impoverished, and men like Wise pocketed the lion's share of what could have been our future."

The screen returned to that image of the billionaire in captivity.

"To enrich himself, Wise made us all poorer," Rayssa said. "Took the money right out of our hands and made it look legal, and the poorest will suffer for it. Unless you vote to find him guilty. Then he owes the poor one billion in gold."

The screen went blank.

There was a long silence in the room before Alicia

looked at her mom and said in a trembling voice, "Is that all true? About Dad."

"We have no idea whether those documents are real or fabricated," Cherie said. "I don't think these savages obey any rules of law."

"You think favela people are savages, Mom?" Natalie said.

"I didn't say that, I—"

"Yes, you did," Alicia said. "But what if it is true, Mom? What if Dad did do all these things?"

"Your father has never knowingly broken a law in his life," Cherie said.

"Knowingly," Natalie said. "What does that mean?"

"It means he runs a gigantic company with operations all over the world and thousands of employees," her mother snapped. "He can't possibly know what every one of them does."

"That's true," Alicia said. "But what about the price gouging? What if that's true? What if he did it legally, but unethically?"

Cherie looked from one girl to the other in disbelief. "Are you two suffering from Stockholm syndrome or something? Siding with the people who kidnapped you and your dad?"

"No," Natalie said in slurred protest. "Just asking if it's true."

"I can't answer that," Cherie said curtly. "But I'd expect you to support your father. Can you do that? Or should I send you both home to clear out your things?"

"Mom," Alicia moaned. "We're not saying—"

"Your father would move heaven and earth for you, and you don't feel enough for him to take his side?"

"Mom, that's not what we were saying at all," Natalie said.

"That's sure the way it sounded," her mother said coldly. She got up from the couch, went into her bedroom, and closed the door behind her.

Chapter 58

THE REACTION WAS worse than we'd expected. The world press grabbed and chewed on the six-minute video from Favela Justice, freeze-framing on the documents, which looked genuine enough. They were either excellent forgeries or the real thing.

Spontaneous protests broke out in favelas around Rio. In Alemão, police were shot at with semiautomatic weapons. Two cars were burned. From high up inside Vidigal favela, unseen gunmen fired several hundred rounds. The sounds of them echoed all the way to Copacabana.

Sirens went off all over the city as police who'd gathered for the Olympics now set out for the rioting slums. There had been footage on every channel the evening before, and that morning on the *Today* broadcast, Matt Lauer had brought up the possibility that the Rio Olympics might be canceled due to violence and unrest.

"This has been the rap against Rio as an Olympic host from the start," Lauer said. "The International Olympic Committee was worried that the government would be unable to control the favelas, which would put the games in danger. Though Brazil has cracked down hard on crime in the slums over the past ten years, last night's riots clearly show that there is widespread anger over the money spent on the Olympics and, before it, the World Cup. The potential for danger throughout the—"

The anchor stopped, listening to something being said in his earpiece. "We're getting reports that the United States is threatening to pull its athletes unless their safety can be assured.

"I repeat, in a stunning development, the U.S. Olympic Committee has—"

General da Silva punched off the remote in a large conference room at the Olympic authority offices. Tavia and I were there along with the three top echelons of the security team that had been assembled in Rio for the games.

"This will not happen!" da Silva roared. "Not a chance. These Olympics are going to go down flawlessly from here on out. Are we clear?"

"Yes, sir," many of them shouted back.

"I've spoken with the president and she has assured me that I will have whatever I need, right up to martial law in the favelas, for the games to go on."

I winced. The day before the opening ceremony, and Rio was going to be painted black. Who wanted to go to some of the most beautiful beaches in the world, much less the Olympics, if there was the possibility of a violent uprising six miles away?

But what choice did da Silva have? Several countries had announced they would pull their teams if they did not believe their athletes were safe. The general had to show that he was not letting the situation spin out of control; if he didn't, the Olympics would end before they started.

In my eyes, da Silva was up to the task. In the next fifteen minutes, the general outlined a plan that would double police presence outside and inside the favelas most likely to riot. He ordered six helicopters into the sky at dusk to assist teams of BOPE operators being lifted and dropped into hot spots.

"I also want a noticeable bump in the number of police assigned to Copacabana, Ipanema, Leblon, and all the beaches south to Barra da Tijuca," he said. "The world is coming to see Rio's finest, so let's make sure they get it. And no one talks to the press. Until further notice, I am the only spokesman. Clear?"

The police brass nodded, and he dismissed them.

When they'd all filed out, the general came over to me and Tavia.

"Is there anything I missed?" he asked.

"Sounds like you've got it all covered," I said. "The helicopters will help, but it's a blow to Rio's global image."

"Unless we stamp it out now," da Silva said. "They want to protest, they can do it peacefully. That's all we're saying. No rights get trampled if we—"

His cell phone rang. The general grabbed it and listened as he walked a short distance away.

"What?" da Silva demanded.

He listened again, and as he did, a vein at his temple began to bulge and quiver. Then, his face reddening, he barked, "We'll be right there."

He punched off his cell, looking shaken. "That was the medical examiner. Some test results came back on Luna Santos. He says they're frightening."

Chapter 59

IN THE PATHOLOGY department in the basement of Hospital Geral, Dr. Emilio Cardoso scratched at his belly while waiting for a computer file to open on a large screen on his office wall.

"There," Dr. Cardoso said after the screen jumped to two side-by-side images. "The cells on the right are from Luna Santos's liver. The cells on the left were taken two years ago from Henri Dijon."

Every cell looked like the shell of an alien insect with a coiled, snakelike body and multiple heads.

"Hydra," I said. My stomach reeled. I took an involuntary step back.

Tavia was also rattled. Our exposure to the deadly virus at the tail end of the World Cup had been a terrifying affair, one we did not want to repeat.

General da Silva's face was sweaty and stony. "Are you sure it's Hydra?"

"No doubt," Dr. Cardoso said. "A mutation of the virus killed Luna Santos before her blood was drained and before she was shot and burned. But the thing to notice is that in Dijon's liver cells, there are six heads. In the sample from Luna's liver, there are nine. It certainly makes poor Castro look like a prophet."

"Poor Castro?" I said, staring at the images with a foul taste in my mouth.

"Dr. Lucas Castro," Cardoso said. "He was the first in the world to diagnose Hydra. He saw a four-headed version in the upper Amazon when he was working for the World Health Organization. He was also the doctor who diagnosed the six-headed cases two years ago. Those two children and Dijon."

"We were there, Tavia and me," I said. "Didn't he want to quarantine one of the favelas?"

Dr. Cardoso nodded. "Castro feared that the outbreaks weren't over, that Hydra would return stronger and deadlier than ever. And no one listened. He got so upset about it, he quit his job at the Oswaldo Cruz Institute because no one there took his warning or his work seriously."

"I remember him," General da Silva said. "Where does he work now?"

"Here," Cardoso said. "Upstairs. I've been waiting for your permission to show these images to him."

General da Silva chewed on that a moment before saying, "Can't stick my head in the sand. Let's get Dr. Castro involved pronto."

We arrived at Dr. Castro's door a few moments later. Brazilian dance music played inside. The medical examiner knocked sharply.

"Yes, yes, just a moment," a man's voice called out, and the music was turned off. The door opened.

Tall, bearded, late thirties. The man's eyes flitted over us. "Can I help you?"

"Dr. Castro?" General da Silva said, and he identified himself as the chief of Olympic security. "We have something you need to see."

"Oh?"

"You discovered Hydra?" I asked.

A cloud came over the doctor's face. "If that's what this is about, I'd rather not discuss it. No one was interested after the last outbreak, so I—"

Castro stopped, gazed around at us, said, "Has it surfaced again?"

"A mutation of it," Dr. Cardoso said. "We'd like you to take a look at a tissue sample, tell us for sure."

"Now someone's going to listen to me?" Castro said bitterly. "Now you want my help?"

"Better late than never," the medical examiner said.

The doctor thought about that and then sighed. "Of course. Let me look. Where are these samples?"

"Down in pathology."

"Right here in Hospital Geral?" Castro said, surprised, as he finished locking his office door. "I hope to God safety measures have been taken."

"The tissue was recovered from a badly burned body," Dr. Cardoso said. "The heat would have killed any remaining live virus."

Dr. Castro relaxed, said, "If it was hot enough, that's right."

As we walked back to the pathology lab, we filled Castro in on Luna Santos and the discovery of her burned corpse.

"Barra da Tijuca?" he said. "That's far from the favelas."

"What's the significance?" da Silva said.

Castro said, "The outbreaks have always come in small clusters in dense populations, people living all over each other. Even in the early outbreak in the Amazon, the victims all lived within yards of one another in the jungle. So my thinking is, why does someone like this Luna and not one of the favela people get infected? And how? And are there others?"

Tavia said, "For all we know, Doctor, she visited a favela and came in contact with someone carrying the virus."

Dr. Cardoso said, "In that scenario, at least two people have been exposed to Hydra in Rio in the past few days."

"Yes, if your victim contracted Hydra from another human," Castro said as we reentered the pathology department. "But, you see, that's been the mystery with the disease right from the start. Where did it originate? Some filthy backwater of the Amazon? From a tick on a rat or a monkey? Or in bird shit? And how does it travel now? Airborne? Blood to blood?"

"Level with me, Doc," General da Silva said. "How contagious is it?"

"We don't know," Castro said. "The first outbreak in the jungle was controllable, occurring in a place where it could be surrounded and burned out. But the last time, do you remember? During the World Cup?"

"We were with Henri Dijon when he collapsed," I said.

Dr. Castro seemed impressed, said, "You're both lucky to be alive. Did you have symptoms?"

"No."

"Interesting. Strong constitutions. Extraordinary immune systems."

Tavia said, "I'm puzzled. Why weren't you brought in to help us two years ago, Doctor? You'd diagnosed the earlier cases. You were the only one who'd ever seen it firsthand."

The doctor's face clouded. "This is what happens when politics control science, Ms. Reynaldo. Because I challenged an idiot who worked for the mayor, because I argued for a quarantine of the favela where the children were infected, I was persona non grata.

"This is Brazil; once I'd been pushed aside, there was no way for the politicians to let me back in without admitting they'd been wrong. That would have humiliated them. Your lives were put at risk so that would not happen."

I thought back two years, seeing a dimension to the day of the World Cup final that I'd been blind to before. Rather than bringing in the expert, in order to save face, the politicians had left the decisions up to doctors with no experience of the disease. It worked out for Tavia and me, and I was grateful, but what had happened to Castro was unjust and reckless.

Cardoso turned on the screen again, showed the two different cells.

Cradling his elbow, tapping his lips, and transfixed by the images, Dr. Castro moved closer, whispered, "Nine heads."

"What does that mean?" General da Silva asked.

Castro didn't answer, but his face grew graver by the moment.

"Doctor?"

"I can't be sure," he said at last. "But I would think it means the virus that produces the nine heads, Hydra-9, if you will, is more deadly and contagious than Hydra-6, which was more deadly and contagious than Hydra-4."

"Is that true?" I asked. "The more heads on the cells, the deadlier the virus?"

"Without further examination of someone who's

contracted this mutation of the disease, I can't say for sure, Mr. Morgan," Castro said. "But it follows, doesn't it?"

General da Silva chewed on that before saying, "As a precaution, how do we treat something like this?"

The doctor's cutting side returned. "You don't, General. Why? Because my requests for grants to create a vaccine or an antiviral for it were denied repeatedly by the Cruz Institute and the government."

There was silence in the pathology department until da Silva said, "Give me best-case and worst-case scenarios."

Castro studied the images again, said, "You might have one or two victims and no more. Like the last time. That's best-case. Worst-case, Hydra-9 is highly communicable and already spreading and you face a public-health crisis of monumental proportions."

Chapter 60

"JESUS CHRIST," DA SILVA said. "Riots and a deadly virus outbreak. It's over. The Rio games are done."

"Not yet," I said. "Luna Santos died days ago and there hasn't been another case since. Is that how it works, Dr. Castro? The outbreak, I mean? Hydra comes on in spates of activity and then, as mysteriously as it surfaces, it goes into hiding and mutates to more deadly strains?"

Castro pondered that. "The Amazon outbreak was swift, from the original case to more than thirty in less than four days. During the World Cup, there were two deaths within moments of each other and then a third the following day."

"And after that nothing, in both cases," da Silva said, perking up. "So, given the virus's behavior before and the fact that it's been days since we found Santos, could we already be beyond the life cycle of the virus? Catastrophe averted?"

Castro hesitated and then said, "I see where you're going, but I can't say the outbreak is over for certain. Although I would call the growing amount of time since the initial case a very positive sign."

Da Silva beamed. "I can tell the president your opinion?"

"You can," Castro said, bowing his head. "You'll call me if there are other cases that flare up?"

"You'll be the first person we call, Doc," the general promised.

We all shook hands with the virologist and walked away with his phone number. Da Silva was on his cell already, returning his focus to favela pacification. In front of the hospital, a police officer on horseback was herding along a crowd of poor people seeking medical attention.

Something about the scene gave me pause, and then, out of the blue, I had an odd feeling, a vague inkling of something that I couldn't name or describe. Da Silva's car came around. Tavia and I hailed a cab and headed back to Private Rio.

"I can't stop thinking about Hydra-9," Tavia said. "The virus going viral, I mean. It's just too damn…"

"Petrifying," I said.

That odd feeling, that inkling, was still nagging at me. In my mind's eye, I saw the cop on horseback and the crowd of desperately poor people wanting help. I saw Luna Santos, her body drained of blood and scorched by fire. Then I saw the look on Dr. Castro's face when he first saw the images of Hydra-9-destroyed cells in the pathology lab. What was revealed in that expression?

The vision of Castro at that moment became sharper in my memory the more I thought about it. Finally, I recognized the doctor's expression for what it was, and the vague inkling became insight.

I opened my eyes, said, "Isn't it funny how sometimes it just takes a different perspective to see things clearly?"

"How's that?" Tavia said.

"I want to know more about Dr. Castro."

"Why?"

"Because I think I saw admiration in his eyes."

Chapter 61

CASTRO CLOSED THE door to his office and leaned his sweaty head against it. *Catastrophe averted.* Wasn't that what General da Silva had said?

The doctor wanted to laugh and cry because it was true. Catastrophe averted. The Olympics would go on, as would his detailed scheme.

Still, he couldn't help but think about the Private investigators, Morgan and Reynaldo. Had they seemed suspicious of him? Dr. Castro closed his eyes, replayed the entire discussion. No. Neither of them had so much as raised an eyebrow at him.

And he'd been careful, kept his separate lives separate, kept everything flying below the radar, and he would make sure it stayed that way for the next thirty hours. It was all he needed. It was all he would ever need.

A worrisome thought niggled: People wouldn't remember that he and Luna had danced at the samba club, would they? How would people even know that Luna had been at the club?

They wouldn't. He'd covered his tracks with Luna and with poor—

A knock came at his office door. Castro broke into

a sheen of cold sweat. Had they come back? Had he missed something?

With a trembling hand, the doctor opened the door and found one of his pretty little graduate students standing there. What was her name?

"Dr. Castro, have you seen Ricardo?"

Ricardo. That was better.

"No," he said. "Why?"

"No one's seen him in days," she said. "He hasn't been back to his apartment, and he's missing all his classes."

"That's troubling, but I wouldn't jump to conclusions. He could be off with a girl somewhere, sowing his wild oats or something."

Castro had wanted her to laugh. Instead, the thought seemed to crush her.

"Oh," she said. "Sure, I suppose."

Dr. Castro felt sorry for her, said, "If I hear from him, I'll have him call you."

"Please. Tell him Leah was looking for him."

"I'll do that, Leah, and again, I'm sure he's okay. Ricardo's always struck me as someone who can take care of himself."

"Unless he got caught up in the riots last night," she said.

Castro liked that idea. He looked concerned, said, "I'll call some friends in the police department, see if they know anything."

Leah said, "I can call the hospitals."

"There," Castro said. "We have it covered."

They traded cell numbers and she left.

The doctor closed the door again, feeling like things were closing in on him, that he should act sooner rather than later. He hadn't meant to leave un-

til long after dark, but he felt compelled to go now as
the city's traffic began to build.

Castro grabbed the few items he needed, put them
in his medical kit, and put that in a knapsack. With
nary a glance at the office where he'd worked all these
months, or at the hospital, or at the lines of poor
patients waiting to be seen, Castro left his past life
behind and set out into the teeming city, looking to
disappear.

Chapter 62

MOVING DOWN THE hall at Private Rio, talking on my cell, I told Cherie Wise that I would be at her suite by three thirty to watch the latest release from Favela Justice. Then I hung up and entered the lab.

Mo-bot and Sci had six big screens running as they helped Tavia look into the life and times of Dr. Lucas Castro. I scanned the various web pages and documents they'd already called up.

Dr. Castro seemed an all-star by anyone's estimation. Born in a small favela in northern Rio, orphaned young, Castro defied crushing odds and won a full scholarship to the federal university, where he excelled.

Castro studied medicine and virology, graduating with an MD and a PhD, credentials that won him a place at the prestigious Oswaldo Cruz Institute, arguably Brazil's finest medical-research facility. The doctor garnered high praise for his early research and then took a two-year leave of absence to work with the World Health Organization.

Castro worked in Uganda, Haiti, and in the Upper Amazon River Basin, where he was a member of the team that first encountered Hydra. A Brazilian physician named Sophia Martine was also on the team. Martine was a river doctor, moving up and down the Amazon's tributaries by boat and offering medical service to the poorest of the poor. She was the first to hear of a virus plaguing the primitive peoples of the rain forest.

"That's her," Tavia said, pointing to a picture of an attractive young woman doctoring a baby in a jungle setting. "They married soon after meeting. Castro returned to his job at the Cruz Institute. She gave up her river practice to work for a Rio-based NGO that gets medical care into the favelas."

"And where is she now?"

"Dead," Mo-bot said, calling up the death certificate.

It said *Sophia Martine Castro. Cause of death: Accidental. Massive blunt-force trauma.*

"Car accident?" I asked.

"I don't think so," Tavia said, pensive. "I think I remember this case."

She went to a keyboard, typed several words into Brazilian Google, and hit Enter. Scanning the list, she said, "It's her. I don't know why I didn't put the names together before."

A clipping from the newspaper *Folha de São Paulo* appeared on the screen with the same picture of Dr. Martine doctoring the baby.

"What's it say?" I asked.

Tavia said, "She was killed during a protest in a favela that was being demolished to make way for one of the World Cup stadiums. Eyewitnesses said she got too close to one of the bulldozers, walked toward it at an odd angle. The machine operator claimed he never saw her, ran right over her while razing the slum."

"That's brutal," Mo-bot said.

"Maybe brutal enough to threaten her husband's sanity," I said.

Arms crossed, Tavia said, "I still don't fully understand why you're suspicious of him."

"I don't either," I admitted. "Not fully. But there was that look of admiration. And what possible reason would someone have to shoot Luna Santos, drain her blood, and burn her?"

"Rage?"

"There's that explanation," I agreed. "It was all an expression of some deep homicidal anger we might never understand. Except Luna was infected and ravaged by Hydra-9 before she was shot and burned."

"Okay?" Sci said.

"What if the killer was trying to hide the infection rather than the gunshot wound? If so, the killer had to have known the infection was there. And the best person to make that sort of diagnosis is Dr. Lucas Castro."

Tavia said, "Maybe the best, but not the only."

"Granted," I said.

"Jack," Mo-bot said. "You haven't explained *why* Castro would shoot Luna and then burn her. And you don't have anything that links Castro to Luna. There's no reason why she'd go to him for a diagnosis only to have him flip out, kill her, and burn her."

"Unless *he* infected her," I said.

"Why would he do that?" Tavia asked. "How could he do that?"

"I don't know," I said, staring at the screens, seeing his birth certificate. "This may be nothing, but check his parents' death certificates. I'd like to know what they died of."

Mo-bot was already typing.

"What other Brazilian databases can you access that might give us another look at Dr. Castro?" I asked.

Tavia thought about that, went to the keyboard, and got into property and tax records. Castro currently worked at Hospital Geral and as a virology professor at the federal medical school. He rented a small apartment in Santa Teresa. In the secretary of state's files, she found Castro listed as principal of AV3 Research, which rented space in a light-industrial area of northwest Rio.

"Jack?" Mo-bot called. "I found Castro's parents' death certificates."

Tavia left her screen, went to Mo-bot's. As she read, her facial muscles tensed. "They died of dengue fever within a day of each other. Castro was six."

"So maybe Castro grows up obsessed with viruses because a virus took his parents," I said. "He spends his professional life obsessed with them. And somehow Luna crosses his path, and either she's infected and he realizes it, or he infects her and wants to cover it up."

Tavia's cell rang. She turned away, answered.

"But why Luna?" Mo-bot said. "Was she random?"

"Doesn't feel random to me. Their paths crossed for a reason."

"We just have to find out where," Sci said, nodding.

I thought about the manner of Sophia Martine Castro's death and what that might have done to her husband, tried to see it from his perspective. His wife was dead. Whom did he blame?

The construction worker? No.

The construction company? No again.

The authorities behind the building of the stadiums, the people his wife was protesting against when she died? Yes, that was the scenario that felt right.

But where did Luna fit in?

"Check Luna's husband, Antonio," I said. "Tell me if he was working for the World Cup organizing committee at the time of Sophia Martine's death."

My cell rang. Cherie Wise was calling. It was 3:28, two minutes before the latest update on her husband was to be delivered.

"Cherie," I said. "I apologize, I'm hung up in the lab at Private Rio."

"At Private Rio?" she shouted, sounding like she'd been drinking. "We have to watch this alone?"

"Stay on the phone with me," I said. "The girls are with you?"

"You said you'd be here, Jack," she snapped. "I thought I could count on you for that, at least."

Tavia came over, giving me a time-out signal.

"Hold on one second, Cherie," I said and pushed the mute button.

"That was Mariana Lopes," Tavia said. "If she's right, we've been played."

"What? By who?"

"Urso. The Bear."

Chapter 63

THAT AFTERNOON, THE digital controls of the brand-new subway system failed and went offline for three hours, snarling traffic from one end of Rio de Janeiro to the other just as the bulk of the international athletes were arriving.

Tavia and I were stuck in a cab heading back toward Alemão and Spirit. Favela Justice was late delivering the video clip of Andy Wise, and I was trying to figure out how we'd been so conned.

Mariana Lopes said that earlier in the day a woman named Claudia had overdosed on heroin and was brought to her clinic near the Alemão favela. Nurses administered an opiate antagonist and Claudia began to come out of it.

The television was on in an adjacent room, tuned to the coverage of the Wise trial and the billion-dollar penalty.

The junkie heard it in her stupor and said, "Estella says Urso's in on that shit, big-time. The American they took...like in that trial? Just show. About the money. So much—whoo—Estella gonna be able to quit her shitty life once and for good."

When Claudia fully awoke fifteen minutes later,

Lopes pressed her about what she'd said. But the junkie said she had no idea what Lopes was talking about.

Lopes said, "She stuck to that story until she walked out my door. But when you administer an opiate antagonist, many people react as if they've been given truth serum. You can't believe some of the confessions I've heard."

"Who's Estella?" Tavia asked.

"Claudia's sister," Lopes said. "And Urso's longtime girlfriend."

"You know where Estella lives?"

"I do," she'd said, and she'd told her how to get there.

Tavia said, "That's damn close to where we talked to Urso that first night."

As traffic finally began to move, my cell phone buzzed. The third Favela Justice video was coming in. Tavia downloaded it to her iPad and hit Play.

We got that scene again with Andrew Wise at the center of the screen, tied to the heavy chair, and everything around him cast in black. Wise looked defiantly at the camera, but you could see the ordeal was weighing heavily on him.

Rayssa appeared in the primitive mask, said, "You've seen the damning evidence. You've had the night to think on it. Now is your chance to vote. Use Twitter and hash tag WiseGuilty or hash tag PayTheBillion if you think Mr. Wise should pay the ransom. You have five hours. The results will be released this evening at nine."

Behind her, Wise shouted, "Don't I get a defense? Or is this a total kangaroo court you've got going here?"

That seemed to startle Rayssa, who looked back at him.

"I'll give you five minutes," she said.

That charged up the billionaire.

Wise stared at the camera, said, "Did my company, WE, build many of the Olympic and FIFA venues? We did. We were invited to enter a global competition with many other fine construction firms. We made detailed bids, and we won."

"You gouged the people of Brazil," Rayssa said.

"We offered Brazil the best deal they were going to get," Wise snapped. "The government could have turned our bid down, but it didn't. You want someone to blame, blame them. I am in business to make a profit. You may not like that idea, but there's our difference of opinion. And if you don't like it, you should have put together a bid yourself with zero profit built in."

Rayssa said, "Many of the documents we've shown the world are overage requests above and beyond your bid."

"Prices change over time for basic construction supplies like rebar and concrete," the billionaire said as if she were a naive fool. "We had a clause in the contract that said explicitly that WE could file for additional payments if supply costs exceeded a certain threshold. There is nothing shady about this. It's how business is conducted in the real world."

Wise fixed his attention on the camera again, said, "All this bullcrap about Favela Justice? Don't believe it. That's a cover game. They're not out to help the poor. They're just after my money. If you agree, vote hash tag WiseDecision and—"

The screen went to static for several long moments

before Rayssa came back on, saying, "Believe a billionaire's spin, or believe the cold hard facts Favela Justice has put before you. Voting is open now."

The screen went black. I immediately called the lab.

Sci answered, said, "That was a clumsy attempt at erasing part of the tape."

"Can you restore it?"

"Already done," Sci said. "It's coming your way now."

I waited, then heard Tavia's iPhone ding, alerting her to the file.

We opened it and saw a fuzzy image of Wise; it was like we were looking at him through snow. His voice crackling, he said, "Give them nothing."

The big guy in black wore a new samba mask as he stepped into view from Wise's left side, punched the billionaire in the face, and then gagged him.

Tavia nodded angrily. "I'll bet that was Urso."

"So who's Rayssa? Estella?"

Pointing at the steep hills of the favelas ahead and above us, she said, "I think the answer to that question is up there."

Chapter 64

THE WINTER SUN hung low over the western mountains, casting the Spirit favela in a slanted light that shadowed the walkways of the slum. The smells, sounds, and visuals were as vibrant and depressing as ever.

Like a buzzing hive, the favela teemed with a stinging energy all its own. But it was an existence lived so close to the margin and in such close quarters that it made me think that Favela Justice had a point.

What would have happened if the billions spent on World Cup and Olympic venues had instead been spent in places like this? New schools. Better homes. Sanitation and clean water, at the very least.

That was basic, wasn't it? Didn't we have an obligation to lift the lowest to an acceptable standard of living? Or was an existence in a shack with raw sewage running by the front stoop acceptable?

In my book it wasn't, and I said so to Tavia.

"You've got no argument from me," she said. "But what if Wise was right? What if this whole Favela Justice thing is a cover, a diversion for extreme extortion?"

"Then why go to the trouble of having this sham vote on Twitter? What's the point?"

"Maybe they want a two-for-one deal. Shame Wise *and* get his billion."

"Possible," I said. "But as bright a guy as Urso is, I can't see him orchestrating something like this. On such a grand scale. Or am I underestimating him?"

"I would never underestimate the Bear," Tavia said. "But I agree that it seems a stretch for a slum gangster to take down a billionaire."

"The Wise girls said Rayssa was in charge."

"Hold that thought," Tavia said and stopped to talk to a woman in a doorway. I caught every fifth word and the name Estella. At the mention of Estella, the woman got a sour look on her face but waved vaguely uphill and to the right.

"I've got a solid idea where she lives now," Tavia said. She led us up through the maze of the slum, passing two side alleys that ran along the contour of the steep hillside.

We took a right into the third contour passage up the hill. It was barely three feet across. We had to stand sideways when other people came our way. The smells of each shack simmered with those of every other off the alleyway, making an aerosol soup that was alluring one moment, putrid the next.

At a dark blue door with stars painted on it, Tavia stopped and knocked. A television played inside. The drape in the window fluttered.

"Who's there?" said a girl with a thin, reedy voice.

"My name is Tavia. I'm a friend of Urso."

"You don't look like a friend of Urso."

Tavia laughed, said, "He worked for me just last week, and I wanted to give him another job."

"Urso's not here. Try his house."

"We looked for him there already. Where's Estella?"

There was silence. Then: "Estella's not here. How do you know her?"

"Through Urso," Tavia said pleasantly. "Could you open the door? I promise I won't bite. I just want to talk."

After several moments, we heard a chain slide. The door opened a crack, revealing a beautiful girl who looked about eight years old. She stared at us suspiciously.

"What's your name?" Tavia asked, crouching down.

"Milena," she said.

"Milena. That's a beautiful name. I'm Tavia and this is Jack."

She looked at me with interest, said, "Americano?"

I nodded and smiled. "California."

She grinned, gave me the thumbs-up, said, "Estella loves California."

"Doesn't everyone?" I said.

"Is Estella your mommy?" Tavia asked.

Milena nodded.

"Where is she?"

"Work, I guess. She was gone when I got home from school."

"Where does Estella work?" I asked.

She shrugged, said, "I don't know, some place in Copacabana."

"What does she do there?"

"I told you," Milena said, annoyed. "Work."

Tavia said, "Do you remember the name of the place she works?"

"Sena-torn...or something."

"Sena-torn?"

"You know, like half man, half horse?"

Before I could respond, Tavia said, "Centaurus?"

Milena nodded. "That place."

Tavia dug in her pocket, held out fifty *reais*, said, "That's for you to buy yourself whatever you want, okay?"

Milena got wide-eyed, snatched the bill from Tavia's hand, clutched it to her chest, and said, "Thank you."

"Thank you," Tavia said. "Be safe, Milena."

With a last glance at me, Milena shut the door.

"What's Centaurus?" I asked.

Tavia hardened. "Arguably the most notorious place in all of Rio."

Chapter 65

CENTAURUS WAS ONE of the most storied brothels in the world.

Male celebrities of all nations have been caught exiting the bordello over the years, including, most recently, Justin Bieber, who tried to hide by running out with a sheet over his head. The paparazzi got the picture anyway.

"It's run by women and only women," Tavia said as we sat in the car. She gestured down the block to a nondescript building. Above the door there was a bas-relief of a centaur wearing a towel around its neck.

"The only men will be bartenders, the cashier, and those bouncers," Tavia went on, pointing to two bruisers in tuxedos. "You're a gringo, so everyone will try to hustle you. Even the bouncers. The whole place is designed to relieve you of whatever money you bring in there. Remember that. Everybody's got an angle."

"Scams?"

"A million. They'll try to bump you to upgrade a room, and then not give you a better room. They'll charge you double on the entry just because you're a gringo. They'll inflate the price on every item on the menu. That kind of stuff."

"But this place is legal, right?"

"As long as the proper bribes are maintained, businesses like Centaurus remain perfectly legal in Rio. The women, who are known as *garotas,* are all licensed and checked two to three times a week by a doctor."

"Why are you telling me all this?" I asked.

"Because I can't go inside. It's men only."

"Sexist lot, you Brazilians."

"When it comes to brothels, that's correct."

"How do you know all this if it's men only?"

Tavia hardened again. "A Centaurus girl got murdered a few years back when I was still with the national police. I had to interview most of the women who worked in there at the time. They told me how it works."

"Okay," I said. "I'll be in touch when I find Estella."

"If anyone asks, tell them you're an old friend of the centaur. And keep your robe on," she said.

"No strutting about naked?"

She laughed. "No strutting about even with your robe on."

"I've got my marching orders, then," I said. I kissed her and climbed out of the car.

Chapter 66

I DON'T KNOW what it is about me and bouncers. Anyone in a position of power outside a door sees me coming and reacts to some threatening vibe I must give off.

Sure enough, one look at me crossing the road in a jog, and the big boys closed ranks in front of the door, crossed their arms, and puffed out their chests.

The one on the right was built like a welterweight boxer, and tall. The one on the left was brick-shaped and no-necked. He gave me the hard eye as I walked up to them. They didn't say a thing, just stared at me sullenly.

"Is Centaurus not open?" I asked.

"Your first time?" the Brick asked.

I did as Tavia instructed, laughed, said, "The centaur is an old friend."

"Fifty *reais* entry fee," said the Boxer.

"C'mon, guys," I said wearily. "I've been coming for years. I pay my entry at the booth at the top of the ramp and tip you leaving."

"I don't recognize you," the Brick said. "And I've got a memory for faces."

"Funny, I don't recognize you either," I said, and

then I gestured to his partner. "This guy I remember. In fact, I think I tipped you big last time."

The welterweight studied me, and then nodded. "I remember that."

"There you go," I said to the Brick, who scowled and stood aside.

There was a similar attempt to fleece me at the cashier's window.

"First time?" the cashier asked hoarsely. He had a goiter or something on his neck and weird, buggy eyes that suggested a thyroid problem.

I told Bug-Eyes what I'd told the bouncers out front, and he still tried to tack forty on top of the actual one-hundred-*real* entry fee. I called him on it and handed him a hundred note.

He looked at me as if I were a lower form of life than he was, something I could not imagine. Unhappy, Bugs gave me a wristband and a locker key and motioned me through the glass door.

I went down the hall and took a left into a locker room, where several men were dressing. An older woman was keeping the place clean. Per Tavia's advice, I gave her a tip immediately. She smiled, showed me to my locker.

I was undressing when fingernails trailed across my back. I looked over my shoulder and found a dead ringer for the singer Nicole Scherzinger wearing a black cocktail dress and smiling brilliantly at me.

"Where are you from?" she asked in decent English.

"The States."

"Mmm," she said. "I love this place, the U. S. of A. What's your name?"

"Jack."

She looked me up and down. "You have the classic build, Jack."

I looked her up and down and said, "You too."

She laughed, said, "I am Vitoria. You like me? We go to room?"

Tavia had coached me on the full-court press. Some of the girls hung around the front hall trying to poach customers before they could climb the stairs to the nightclub, where most of the working ladies would be found.

"I'm going to look around," I said. "But thanks."

She pouted at me, ran her hand back through her long ebony hair, and said, "You don't think I'm beautiful?"

"No, I think you're breathtakingly beautiful."

"Good," she said, smiling brilliantly again. "We go, then? You'll never forget Vitoria. The whole rest of your life you'll close your eyes and think of me."

"I'm sure I will," I said. "But an old friend recommended Estella, and I came wanting to see her."

Vitoria's dark eyes widened. Her pert little nose scrunched up and she looked at me askance and said, "Whatever you're into, Jack."

Chapter 67

UNNERVED, I WATCHED Vitoria walk away fast and wondered what it was about Estella that had caused that reaction. Tavia had told me that Centaurus could provide a woman for every sexual perversion. Except for pedophilia; no girl there was under eighteen. That was strictly forbidden and checked constantly.

But other than that, anything goes, I thought, stripping off the last of my clothes and putting on one of the clean and folded terry-cloth robes stacked on tables. God only knew what Urso's woman was into or offering.

I slipped on some sanitized rubber clogs and left the locker room, following the sound of pulsing dance music and Tavia's directions to the top floor, where I entered a medium-size, L-shaped room with a bar, low mood lighting, and a cornucopia of attractive women. There were twenty men in robes and fifty ladies of all shapes and sizes dressed in lingerie. Every one of them was aggressive.

I hadn't taken ten steps into the room when women started to swarm me from all angles. They surrounded me, smiling, looking dazzling and appreciative, asking me questions and touching me lightly. The women behind me started whispering in my ears, pressing themselves against me as they described their skills and specialties. I wondered if this was how Ulysses felt strapped to the mast of his ship, listening to the Sirens' song.

After twenty seconds of this—well, maybe thirty—a few of them started taking liberties with my terry-cloth robe, and I called a halt to the action.

"Please, ladies," I said, raising my hands. "You're all lovely, truly, but I'm looking for Estella this evening."

Suddenly there was a lot more room around me and the spectacular smiles were all turning, as if they'd sniffed something unsavory about me.

"Is she here?" I asked.

A vivacious redhead rolled her eyes, said, "She's over in the corner, Mr. Freaky Man. But she looks tied up to me."

I followed her gaze and saw a pleased and very heavyset Chinese guy sitting on one of the plush couches and pouring himself a healthy shot from a bottle of Johnnie Walker Red he'd had chilling in an ice bucket. He swayed slightly, obviously hammered. He drank half the whiskey in two gulps.

Then he leered at the gorgeous brunette woman in black lingerie sitting beside him and started to rub his free hand all over her very pregnant belly.

Chapter 68

GROSSED OUT?

I was.

It was about as creepy a thing as I have ever witnessed, and my initial reaction was to recoil, turn, and walk away as fast as Vitoria had. The fact that the women who'd surrounded me were now looking at me as if I were a lower form of life than Bug-Eyes only made matters worse.

I was about to pull out my cell and call Tavia, get her take on how best to handle the situation, when I glanced into the corner and saw from Estella's blank, faraway expression that she was suffering.

Without another thought, I walked over to them and said, "Estella?"

She blinked, sat up, and looked at me quizzically. The Chinese man's drunk eyes were trying to focus and doing a poor job.

"Wait your turn," he slurred.

I ignored him, said, "I'll pay you twice what he's paying you, plus tip."

Estella smiled.

The Chinese guy got belligerent, said, "She's with me, gringo."

"Not the way I understand it," I said. "Have you had your wristband checked with Bug-Eyes?"

Estella smiled even more at me and tried to get up. The Chinese guy put out a pudgy arm to hold her in her seat, said, "You stay where you are, bitch."

Why do some people have to do things the hard way? I curled my left hand into a fist with the first knuckle of my middle finger exposed and smashed it tight behind his jaw about an inch below his right ear. He made a soft squeal of pain, let go of Estella, and slumped against the couch, looking like he was about to be violently sick on his terry-cloth robe.

I held out my hand. "Estella? Shall we?"

Urso's girlfriend grinned ear to ear, stood, and took my hand. She paraded me through the room, ignoring the disgusted, sidelong glances of the other women, and led me through a maze of hallways to an empty room with a bed, a shower, and mirrors on the walls and ceiling.

She shut the door, said, "Shower together?"

"That's not necessary," I said, showing her my Private badge.

Estella rolled her eyes. "Haven't you been paid this month? C'mon, I had a real customer up there."

"I'm not a cop. I'm looking for your husband, Urso."

She wasn't expecting that. Frightened, she looked to the door, said, "The Bear's not my husband."

"But I'm betting he's the father of that baby in your belly."

"What's he done?"

"You tell me."

"No," she said, trying to get by me. "I don't know nothing."

I blocked the way, said, "Your sister, Claudia, says you do."

"Claudia's a junkie." Estella sneered. "No one believes her. You let me out of here now or I start screaming you're trying to kill my baby."

"And I'll start screaming that you're part of a conspiracy to kidnap and torture one of the world's richest men. You'll be having your baby in prison, and who knows where Milena will end up."

That got to her. "You leave my baby and Milena out of this. And I've got nothing to do with whatever that Urso's up to."

"But you know he's involved in Wise's kidnapping."

Estella held her belly, stared at it like it revealed terrible secrets.

"We can keep you safe," I said.

"No, you can't," Estella said in a lost voice.

"Yes, we can, and if you help us, there will be money in it for you."

Shaking, Estella sat down on the bed. "Money?"

"A lot of it."

Hugging herself, she said, "Like what? Fifty thousand *reais*? A hundred?"

"I was thinking three million U.S. dollars would be a fair reward if what you tell me leads to Mr. Wise's rescue. You'll be able to leave this place, start over somewhere else, make a life for Milena and your baby."

She was looking at me in disbelief. "Three million. No way."

"Urso's asked for a billion, or haven't you been watching the television? Three million's a bargain."

Estella shook her head. "A billion? Is he stupid or something?"

"You tell me."

"No. It's got to be that crazy know-it-all college bitch filling his head with all this bullshit."

"Rayssa?"

"Her name's not Rayssa. It's Amelia."

Chapter 69

AMELIA? MARIANA LOPES'S adopted daughter? Friend of the Wise girls?

So much of it made sense, and yet so much didn't. Amelia Lopes had been with Alicia and Natalie at the beginning of their trip to Rio. She would have had time to learn their identities and set up the kidnapping.

But the girls said they'd told no one their real names. And wouldn't they have recognized Amelia's voice as Rayssa's?

A sad thought started to worm and grow in my brain.

"They're going to kill Urso for this, aren't they?" Estella moaned. "They'll just shoot my Bear on sight for this, and my kids will be left without a father."

Before I could think about any of it, there was a knock at the door.

"*Tempo,*" a woman said. My forty minutes was up.

I sat on the bed next to Estella and said, "If we're to have any hope of keeping Urso alive, we need to get you out of here."

That frightened her. "It is not allowed. I must stay to the end of my shift."

"This can't wait. There are some people who want to talk to you."

"*Polícia?*"

"Yes."

"They can't be trusted."

"And Amelia can?"

Another knock. "*Tempo!*"

I wanted to ask more questions and thought about buying more time, but then I decided we needed to leave. Now.

"If you want that reward money, you'll have to come with me. Go get dressed in your street clothes. Meet me by the locker room."

"They'll stop us," she said.

"They're not stopping me."

Estella looked unconvinced but said, "Okay."

We left the depressing little room. She went to change, and I did too. I waited and waited until I thought she might have chickened out or run for it. But just as I was about to go looking for her, she appeared near the locker room, dressed in a shapeless black cotton maternity dress and looking more frightened than ever.

"Just follow me and let me handle it," I said.

I threw Bug-Eyes one hundred *reais*, said, "Keep the change."

He spotted Estella, said, "Where do you think you're going?"

Estella rubbed her belly mournfully. "I'm sick. My friend drives me home."

"Don't work like that."

"It does today," I said.

His hand shifted under the desk. I knew he was going for a gun, so I lunged forward, reached through the window hole, grabbed him by his collared shirt, and yanked. His knees cracked against the desk. His face smashed against the window, and he crumpled.

A woman started screaming. I glanced back into the brothel and saw Vitoria raising hell.

Taking Estella by the arm, I said, "We've got to go, fast."

We went through the glass door, took a hard left on a rug of synthetic grass, and headed down on a slight slant toward the entrance. I'd hoped to reach it before the bouncers came in, but no such luck.

When we were halfway down the ramp, the Brick and the Boxer came through the doors. The Brick carried a police baton. The Boxer had a sap.

Chapter 70

I PUSHED ESTELLA back as the Boxer moved into range. I sprang at him, blocked his arm before he could clobber me, and kneed him hard in the gut.

The Boxer made a *puhhh* sound and crashed. I spun toward the Brick. His overhand baton strike just missed my head but smashed hard against my left shoulder. My arm felt jolted electrically and went numb.

When he raised his arm back to strike me again, I punched him in the triceps with my good hand. It threw him off balance. He slashed the baton at me. I dodged it and punched him in the windpipe. He staggered, dropped the baton, and went to his knees, choking.

"C'mon," I said, picking up the baton and holding out my hand to Estella.

Estella was wide-eyed as she stepped around the bodies of the fallen bouncers. I pushed open the front door and saw a third bouncer charging me. I cracked the baton off his forehead and knocked him senseless.

Tavia came screeching up to the curb. I put Estella in the back, got in front.

"How'd it go?" Tavia asked, throwing the car in gear.

"I feel like I just escaped some perverse level of hell, but I think we've got the break we—"

Boom! The rear window shattered.

Tavia stomped on the gas. I twisted in my seat.

Through the blown-out window I saw a bleeding Bug-Eyes running down the street after us, trying to get another shot.

Chapter 71

THE MOON WAS but a sliver low in the eastern sky. The small jungle clearing in the shadow of the Dois Irmãos Mountains was barely lit by the glow of Leblon and Ipanema far below. Amelia Lopes stood for a long minute listening to the sounds of the rain forest, the peeping of tree frogs, the sawing of crickets, the rustle of birds on the roost. There was balance there. It was all so natural.

Then she heard a distant car horn and looked out over the glittering lights of the superwealthy to the favelas, seeing everything she considered unnatural about Rio and the world in one long, sweeping glance.

The megarich. The megapoor. You couldn't find a country or city on earth that displayed the income gap as glaringly as Rio de Janeiro did. The city went from ultrachic to squalor in a matter of miles. These brutal facts and more had caused Amelia Lopes to start thinking of herself as Rayssa.

Rayssa the warrior. Rayssa the revolutionary.

She wore the name like armor. As Amelia, she was rather passive, risk-averse, and incapable of violence. As Rayssa, she was visionary, audacious, cruel, and, if need be, deadly.

A billion dollars, she thought as she climbed toward the cluster of shacks in the trees at the top of the clearing. She went to the smallest hut, the one where Andrew Wise was being held. *Think of what good a billion dollars could do in Rio's favelas. Think of what forces for good would be unleashed.*

Fervent now, she nodded to one of Urso's men standing guard. He pulled open the door. Wise was sitting in the chair, his hooded head lolling on his chest. But when Rayssa stepped inside, the tycoon must have heard her because he raised his head groggily.

"Water," he said.

Rayssa ignored the request. "Thought you might want to know the vote count with two hours to go."

"I don't care. I want water. I want food."

"For hash tags WiseGuilty and PayTheBillion, total stands at twenty-three million and counting. For hash tag WiseDecision, it's eleven point two million," Rayssa said, and she turned to go.

The tycoon called after her, "Please. It's inhumane."

That stopped her. She looked over her shoulder, spitting mad, and said, "Welcome to hungry and thirsty, Mr. Wise, the plights of the poorest poor."

She left him then, and closed the door. She told the guard to feed and water the prisoner in an hour or so. Give him some time to come to his senses.

The generator kicked to life, masking the jungle sounds with a constant thrum. Rayssa was barely aware of it as she returned to the largest shack, the one with all the satellite dishes on the roof. She entered and found the pickpocket Alou at his keyboard and screens.

For a moment, she gazed at the boy genius in wonder. So young and so brilliant, but because he was
born in the slums, this society would have thrown him
away. How fortunate he was to have found a bed in
Mariana's orphanage. How fortunate he was to have
played with a computer at such a young age. How
smart Rayssa had been to encourage—

Her cell phone rang. She frowned when she saw it
was her mother calling.

"Mom?"

"You actually picked up," Mariana Lopes said in a
disapproving tone.

"I've been busy," Amelia said. "Wrapping up the
fieldwork. I told you."

"A mother longs for her daughter's voice every
once in a while."

No matter how much kindness and empathy she
dispensed in the course of a day, Amelia's mother was
always putting guilt trips on her daughter.

"You don't have time for me now?" Mariana said.
"I understand."

Rayssa would have hung up, but Amelia was sens-
ing that Rayssa's existence was coming to an end. And
for the first time, she realized the dire consequences of
her actions.

"I have ten minutes, Mom," she said. "Let me get
somewhere I can talk."

Chapter 72

"CAN YOU HEAR me, Mom?" Amelia Lopes said.

We'd put Amelia on speaker. Mariana Lopes looked at Sci and Mo-bot, who were trying to track Amelia's location, and then at Tavia and me. Tavia nodded.

"Loud and clear, dear," Mariana said, but there was a tremor in her voice. She was still shocked by the fact that her daughter was the ringleader of the Favela Justice plot. She had refused to believe it until Estella, Urso's woman, told her what she knew: that Amelia met, slept with, and brainwashed the Bear after he was driven from Alemão favela.

"She made him believe that the way we live is a crime," Estella said. "She made him believe that not fighting the situation was a worse crime."

This evidently sounded like something Amelia would say because Mariana's shoulders slumped and she wept, and then she agreed to help us.

She got more confident the longer the conversation with her daughter went on. They chatted about challenges at the orphanage. They talked about Mariana's hip, which had been bothering her enough that she was considering hip-replacement surgery, and about when Amelia might be finished with her field research and able to come back to Rio to see her.

"Soon," Amelia said. "After the Olympics are over. When it's less hectic."

Mariana looked over at us. I made a spinning motion with my finger and she tried to talk about Amelia's field research some more.

But after two minutes in that vein, Amelia said, "Mom, I've got to go now."

"Oh," Mariana said, growing nervous. "Of course. Call me tomorrow?"

"If I can," Amelia said. "Mom?"

"Yes, dear?"

"Are you proud of me? Of the way I've lived my life?"

Mariana looked at us. Tavia nodded and I twirled my finger again.

"Mom?"

"Of course I'm proud of you," Mariana said, tears welling in her eyes. "You're a woman of great learning, conviction, and kindness."

We heard a sniff over the speaker. "Thanks, Mom. I needed to hear that."

"Are you okay, Amelia?"

"I'm fine," her daughter said, and sniffed again. "Love you."

"I love you too."

The line went dead. Mariana began to weep again.

"Did you get her?" I asked as Tavia moved to comfort Mariana.

"Wait a sec," Mo-bot said, not picking up her head.

Sci didn't look up either. They both pounded at their keyboards and then suddenly, virtually in unison, they stopped.

"Got her," Mo-bot said with a satisfied grin.

Sci said, "Give the software a minute or two and we'll have a position for you within ten feet of where she was standing."

"You did fine," Tavia was saying to the orphanage director when I walked over beside them.

"I feel like Judas Iscariot," Mariana said.

I said, "What you did was noble. A mother looking out for her child."

Mariana glanced up. "Don't kill her. Please? She's my only child."

I frowned, said, "Senhora Lopes, we are not assassins. We will not intentionally harm your daughter. But she is a kidnapper, a murderer, and a terrorist. She'll be brought to—"

"There she is," Sci said.

"Throwing it on the screen now," Mo-bot said.

At the far end of the conference room, Google Earth appeared showing a satellite view of Rio de Janeiro. A red pin blinked off the north flank of the Two Brothers Mountains.

Sci manipulated the image, zoomed in, and tilted the perspective so we could see that Amelia had been in the jungle five or six hundred yards east of the Rocinha favela and close to the bottom of a cliff that went up two thousand feet to the top of the second mountain.

Sci zoomed in again, and a blurred view of the slope below the cliff appeared. Mo-bot used filters to clear the image, and we saw the pin blinking at the upper end of a long narrow clearing just off the spine of the slope. Near the pin, in the trees up the hill and closer to the cliff, there were several shacks.

"If that's where they've got Wise, it's going to be

a bitch getting in there quietly," Tavia said. "If we go in on foot we'll have to go through Rocinha or Vidigal, and that will raise all sorts of alarms. They'll no doubt have sentries, people watching the trails to and from the favelas. And they're probably in the trees all around the clearing."

"You could go in by helicopter," Sci said.

"We'd lose the element of surprise," Tavia said. "And depending on how fanatical Amelia has turned her followers, we could be in for a firefight. But it's the lesser of two evils. We really don't have a third choice."

Looking at the sheer faces of the Two Brothers, I flashed back twenty-four months and said, "Maybe we do."

Chapter 73

DR. LUCAS CASTRO waited until dark before he went to get his car from the parking garage. He took several detours to make sure he wasn't being followed and finally pulled into the light-industrial complex around eight fifteen.

Less than twenty-three hours now, Castro thought as he drove through the complex. *It will be worth the sacrifice. It will change everything.*

The doctor pulled around the corner and hit the brakes. There was a small red Fiat Palio parked in front of his lab. He couldn't see anyone inside.

A voice in his head screamed: *Back out. Turn around. Get lost.*

But Castro needed to get into his lab and retrieve the pack.

He drove closer and was parking when a head popped up in the red Fiat. A young woman blinked and squinted in his headlights.

He knew her!

Leah? Yes, Leah, that was her name. Ricardo's friend from school. Why was she here? How in God's name had she come to be here?

Castro had no choice now. He had to find out what she knew.

The doctor climbed from the car, leaving the head-lights on, came around, and stood in the beams. She recognized Castro then. Her mouth opened in confusion.

"Leah?" he said, smiling. "Is that you?"

After a moment's hesitation, she rolled down the window. "Dr. Castro? What are you doing here?"

"You've found where Ricardo's been hiding," he said cheerfully. "C'mon in, I know he'll be happy to see you."

She brightened. "Ricardo's here? Inside?"

"Finishing up some work. He'll be done in an hour."

"Why didn't you tell me this the other day?" she asked.

"Ricardo asked me not to," Castro said. "He was swept up in our research and didn't want to be interrupted. Great minds are like that. Don't take it personally. The important thing is you're here now. Let's go inside."

He turned and fumbled with the key at the door. He heard the window roll up, the car door open, and then the crunch of her weight on gravel.

"Ricardo is supersmart, isn't he?" she said.

Castro felt the lock click open and looked over his shoulder, seeing her smiling, relieved, anticipating Ricardo. Young love. *It can turn suspicion into eagerness, can't it?*

He opened the door, reached in, and flipped on the lights, revealing the empty office.

"Ricardo sleeps in the main lab most nights," he said, stepping inside. "We've got experiments that require twenty-four-hour monitoring, but I'm here for the night. Why don't the two of you go out, catch up?"

"That would be nice," Leah said, coming in behind him.

He turned, held his car remote in his hand, turned the headlights off. She went past him into the room, and he shut the outer door.

"Hold on," he said as she moved to the inner door. "If he's done his job, he's locked it from the inside."

Leah tried the knob, said, "He's done his job."

"Good man," Castro said, smiling. "I sensed right away he was special. How did you figure out Ricardo was working here?"

"Oh," Leah said. "The police found his scooter not far from here, and then I had a friend who works for TIM Cellular ping his last known location before his phone died. And he was right there, outside your door."

So someone else knows about Ricardo and now Leah being at my door, Castro thought. Did it matter? Not after tomorrow. Before then? Yes, it mattered very much.

He opened the inner door, stepped down into the warehouse space with the clean room in the middle.

"Wow," Leah said, coming in behind him. "That's impressive."

"Isn't it?" Castro said. "Ricardo came up with a few of the ideas."

"Where is he?"

"Inside the clean room, I suspect. He can't hear us because it's soundproofed. Do you want me to call him out? Or do you want to go inside and surprise him?"

"I'll go in."

"You have to wear a hazmat suit and a visor."

"That's okay. This will be fun."

The doctor smiled. "I can't wait to see the look on his face when he sees you."

Chapter 74

RICARDO'S BLOODLESS FROZEN face looked up at Leah as she struggled, jerked, choked, and kicked to break the death grip Dr. Castro had around her neck. But Castro's hands and gauntlets held tight.

From inside her hazmat visor, Leah made noises that sounded like she was screaming underwater. Each time she opened her mouth, the force behind the protest was weaker. Each time, the plea was fainter.

Her third effort was barely a whimper. Then she sagged. Castro had to struggle to keep her from pitching over into the lift-top freezer. She'd been gazing into it in disbelief and horror when Castro began to strangle her. He held on long after she'd lost consciousness, made sure she was good and dead.

When he finally released Leah and removed her visor, her eyes were wide open, dull, and bloodshot. Her tongue lolled out of her mouth and had turned bluish. He felt for a pulse at her neck and found none.

He stripped her out of the suit, hoisted her up by her torso, and got her to the lip of the freezer.

He stared in at Ricardo, said sadly, "The two of you together at last."

Castro dumped her in so she landed facedown on

Ricardo. He arranged Leah's arms and head so their lips almost met. He recalled an image of his late wife, Sophia, in the prow of a long canoe on some remote backwater of the Amazon, smiling at him out of the deepest love.

Soon, he thought. *Soon I will set off to find you.*

Castro's breath had gone shallow. He saw auras at the perimeter of his vision, purple and ice blue. His heart raced, and he felt hollow and dizzy; the pain in his skull was like hammer strikes coming from the inside.

The doctor knew what was happening, and he slammed the freezer shut. He turned around and lay down on the floor of the lab, knowing a migraine was about to incapacitate him. *Not now,* he thought fearfully. *Not now.*

"Breathe," Castro whispered. "Lots of time. No urgency. No loss. Breathe. Lots of time. No urgency. No loss."

He repeated Sophia's four-line chant, the only method that had ever given him relief or comfort from the migraines he'd suffered since medical school.

Breathe. Lots of time. No urgency. No loss.

Castro repeated his wife's prescription again and again, a monotone chant to calm himself. Minutes became an hour that way; he simply breathed with no concept of time or urgency or loss. Gradually, slowly, the hammer strikes and the flashes of lightning in his skull became weaker and fainter until the doctor slipped away into a deep, dreamless sleep.

Chapter 75

THE HELICOPTER ROARED a hundred feet over the water and two hundred yards off Ipanema Beach. Although this was the dead of winter in the Southern Hemisphere, the beaches were jammed and people were partying. Then again, it was the night before the Olympics opened, and despite the recent violence in the favelas and the traffic snarls, hundreds of thousands of fans and athletes had come to Rio for the games.

Tavia sat in the jump seat beside me, wearing black and body armor and carrying night-vision goggles. I was similarly attired and having a radio-headset conversation with General da Silva, who'd agreed to put Lieutenant Acosta and a BOPE contingent at our disposal.

At the moment, they were landing on a rooftop helipad in Leblon and would begin a straight ascent up the mountain toward the jungle clearing where we believed Andy Wise was being held.

The rest of us had other plans.

Two minutes later, the chopper landed on the highway at the south end of São Conrado beach. Two men were waiting. They threw long black duffel bags into the hold and climbed in.

Few words were spoken before the helicopter lifted off again and spiraled north. We left São Conrado, rose up over the mountainous jungle between Rocinha and Vidigal favelas. The pilot cut the running lights and soon we were hovering over the south end of the Two Brothers.

We landed on the western mountain and got out, pulling the two duffel bags and other gear out after us. Crouching there, we ducked our heads to the wind blast as the helicopter lifted off and flew away south.

Tavia and I turned on headlamps and watched as the two men opened the duffels and removed titanium poles, struts, wires, and the dark fabric of a pair of large tandem gliders. They had them ready for flight in under ten minutes.

We lifted and moved the gliders to the cliff. This was where the idea that had sounded great on paper started to look incredibly bad in reality.

"Jack?" Tavia said. "You okay?"

"I'm beginning to think we're insane," I said, checking the sound-suppressed Glock .40 on loan from BOPE in a chest holster and the three full magazines beside it.

"I think it's a brilliant idea," she replied. "We land silent, reconnoiter the place, and wait for the BOPE to ride in and save the day."

She quickly got into a harness behind the pilot, looking over his right shoulder. She'd taken off her headlamp and was fussing to get her night-vision goggles positioned correctly, and I finally decided I couldn't back out. It had been my idea, after all.

Harnessed behind my pilot, I asked him, "Sure you can do this?"

He reached up, switched on his goggles, and chuckled. "Look at that, will ya? Piece of cake."

I'd kept my night-vision turned off. I couldn't stomach seeing that first big step into the void. Tavia and her pilot ran off the side of the cliff and disappeared into the blackness without a peep.

"Let's do this before I chicken out or puke," I said.

We took four big steps before the bottom dropped out, and we fell away into an inky darkness.

Chapter 76

WE FELL TEN feet.

Twenty feet.

At thirty I thought we were headed for a quick ending, but an updraft caught us and, with a ripping and straining noise from the wing, we banked away on the wind like surfers arcing on a wave.

"First step's a bitch, isn't it?" the pilot said.

"I thought I was going to swallow my windpipe," I said, shaking from an adrenaline rush so strong that it was several moments before I could find the switch on the side of the goggles and flip the night-vision on.

That familiar ghostly green world appeared, but it was a world I'd seen before only from the noisy cockpit of a helicopter, with a shield blocking me from the wind and constant radio chatter in my ears. We picked up speed. The wind bit at our faces and goggles and whistled in our ears as we flew through a narrow canyon between the mountains, two miles long and barely five hundred yards wide.

For almost fifteen hundred feet below us, there was nothing but khaki-colored air and then the deep jade forest canopy. The vegetation seemed to undulate like a tranquil sea. Ahead, framed in the far mouth of the canyon, the lights of Ipanema, Copacabana, and Leblon burned an emerald fire.

My pilot had us eighty yards out from and almost parallel to the rim of the canyon. Tavia soared with her pilot a hundred yards ahead and one hundred feet lower than us. The pilots had said it was the safest way to go as we hugged the contour of the mountain.

"ETA?" General da Silva's voice crackled in my earpiece.

"Four minutes? Five?" I said.

"Mark that," the general said. "Diversionary fire will commence downslope at twenty-one hundred hours fourteen minutes. Full BOPE support at twenty-one hundred hours twenty-six minutes."

That gave us only twelve minutes to figure out where Wise was.

"Can you delay support until twenty-one thirty-two?" I asked.

After a pause, da Silva said, "Agreed, Jack. You'll have eighteen minutes to find him."

We banked away from the cliff wall and zigzagged into a long, gradual descent toward the mouth of the canyon. Two minutes later we flew out of the gap. The lights of Leblon were so bright, I turned the goggles off. We'd lost nine hundred feet in altitude by the time we banked after Tavia's glider.

Far below us, raucous, celebrating crowds were partying on the mosaic walkways along the beaches, and vendors were doing a booming business. No one looked up that I could see. We were like big black bats, invisible against the night sky.

"Two minutes out, General," I said.

We turned and flew west now, straight toward the

lower end of that jungle clearing. I drew my Glock from my chest holster.

Tavia's pilot stalled slightly to let us pass and land first. I flipped the night-vision goggles on. We dropped under five hundred feet.

Shooting began in the trees far downslope of the clearing, a short-burst followed by four or five random shots and then nothing.

Three hundred and fifty feet. Two fifty. There were men with weapons and flashlights running downhill toward the shooting. We flew right over them, no more than seventy feet above their heads. They never looked up, just dashed on into the trees.

My pilot pulled a release, and our legs dropped. He stalled the glider hard. We floated toward the ground. We reached our feet out like night birds in search of a roost and landed with barely a sound.

Tavia and her pilot landed just as quietly about twenty yards away.

"We're down," I said, getting myself free of the harness.

"Eighteen minutes," the general said.

"Understood."

The glider pilots knew to go to the tree line and wait there in cover until the BOPE forces landed. Tavia and I split up. She took the right flank of the clearing and I had the left.

The Glocks out and ready, we snaked fast through the trees to within fifty yards of the shacks. I switched the goggles to infrared mode. The wavering heat glow of three people showed inside the near shack's walls. Two people were in the shack closer to Tavia. Armed men, five of them, were arrayed across the front of both buildings.

"Tavia, stay put, cover me, I'm going to go in there, see if I figure out which one's holding Wise."

"Sitting tight," she replied.

I slipped around and got higher up the mountain than the shacks. Then I dropped in behind them, sneaking the last twenty yards to a lit open window at the back of the larger shack.

I turned off the goggles, eased up, peeked inside, and saw a kid in front of several computer screens. I recognized him—the pickpocket who'd taken Cherie Wise's purse. Beyond him, an armed man stood in the doorway. Where was the third person I'd seen in the infrared?

The middle computer screen in front of the boy came on and showed Andrew Wise sitting in that familiar chair, blinking at the lights.

The billionaire looked haggard and drawn, but his eyes still had a spark.

Wearing that primitive mask, Amelia Lopes appeared beside him.

Chapter 77

"WELCOME TO THE Favela Justice show," Amelia said, facing the camera. "We had sixty-three million votes in that short time. Isn't that incredible? Sixty-three million. And the hash tags? Top three on Twitter for the last six hours. The size of the vote speaks volumes about the interest people have in the plight of the poor. So what was the outcome?"

Amelia turned the mask this way and that, as if considering the results.

"Before we give you the final tally," she said, "let's review the highlights of the case against Andrew Wise."

For the next few minutes, she did just that. The billionaire said nothing.

When she finished, she said, "What do you think the numbers are going to be, Senhor Wise?"

"I have no idea," Wise said. "They don't matter."

"They don't matter? Poor people don't matter?"

"I didn't say that," Wise said.

"The world just heard you say that," Amelia said, turning back to the camera. "Sixty-three million votes. Final tally in the case against Andrew Wise. For hash tag WiseGuilty: twenty-nine million. For hash tag PayTheBillion: eleven million.

"But hash tag WiseDecision? Only twenty-three million votes in favor of the accused and now convicted Mr. Wise."

She paused, then turned her thumb up, then turned it down. "Forty million people thought Mr. Wise should pay the billion-dollar penalty. But is a billion enough when a man has so many billions? Shouldn't we exact some greater punishment for his deeds?"

Amelia reached around behind her and came up with a pistol. "Shouldn't Andrew Wise pay for his greed in a much more permanent way?"

She aimed the pistol at Wise's head, said, "Any last words?"

Wise looked frightened for the first time. He glanced at her and said, "Forty million people said I should pay a billion dollars to the poor. I get that, but they never said a thing about killing—"

He stopped his defense at the sound of a helicopter coming hard.

Chapter 78

I HEARD THE BOPE's helicopter coming too. So did one of Urso's men, who roared out an alarm. Things started going downhill fast from there.

The armed guy went to the pickpocket, said, "We're going, Alou!"

Then he looked through the window and saw me, tried to swing his gun my way. I shot him twice in the chest and then aimed at the boy.

"Where are they?"

Terrified, he pointed toward the second shack.

"Stay there," I said and I was turning to run that way when I saw movement beyond the boy and caught a fleeting glimpse of someone running out the front door carrying something that turned my blood cold.

Bolting to my right, I shouted, "Abort the landing, General! Repeat, abort the landing! They've got a—"

A man holding a machine gun appeared, started firing wildly in my direction. Tracers ripped past me like shooting stars as I sprinted around the corner of the shack.

The helicopter was close now. I could see the bays

open, crowded with men in SWAT gear, even as more gunfire erupted. They weren't aborting.

I heard several shots.

"I'm engaged," Tavia said.

"Shoot Urso! He's got a rocket grenade!"

I came around the front of the shack. Caught in the spotlight, the Bear was on one knee and already aiming. Tavia shot and I shot, and we both hit Urso, but not before he triggered the surface-to-air missile.

With a thud, the rocket fired and flame blew out the back of the launcher. The recoil tore it from Urso's grasp and he began to crumple as a thin plume of fire trailed the missile into the crowded hold of the police chopper. The warhead exploded in a boom and a brilliant flash that engulfed the bay.

The bird made a metallic groan that I knew all too well. The helicopter listed, shuddered, and tumbled from the sky. It struck ground and cartwheeled across the slope into a tree before rupturing in a churning ball of blinding fire.

For a second I was so shocked I just stood there. Then I charged the second shack, hearing shooting to my right and bullets behind me.

When I hit the front porch, I fired two shots to my right and then threw my shoulder into the door. The door frame splintered. I hit it again and it gave way. I stepped into a short passage that led to a black curtain rimmed in bright light.

"Hear them coming?" I heard Wise say. "You can't win."

"No, rich man," Amelia said. "It's you who can't win. It's you who won't win. No matter what happens to me, I want you to know who helped me. I want you to know the tragedy of your fucking life."

I stepped through the drape, accidentally kicking over the tripod and camera as I aimed the Glock at Amelia Lopes from eight feet away. Amelia had dropped the mask. She had the pistol to Wise's head and was whispering something in his ear.

"Drop the gun!" I said as she started to turn. "Now!"

"No," she said, a split second before the gunshots that ended it all.

Chapter 79

I WALKED OUT of the shack minutes later feeling like a zombie. The air stank of burned fuel. Several helicopters circled overhead, beaming multiple spotlights on the clearing and the carnage left in the downed chopper's wake.

There was a deep gash in the mountainside where the police helicopter had hit first. Where it had struck the slope again and again during the cartwheels, the ground looked speared and slashed like so many dots and dashes. Crash debris littered the tree line.

The chopper left a trail into the jungle that was also unmistakable. The trees and all the vegetation there had been lopped off above twenty feet, leaving bare, scorched trunks that looked like spent and broken matchsticks set upright in black sand.

I stared at that gaping scar of the battle dumbly, wondering at the meaning of it all, and then fear seized my throat like a constricting snake.

I triggered my microphone, said hoarsely, "Tavia?"

I spotted a flashlight still burning on the ground, grabbed it, and began to run, praying for her voice to come back to me.

"Tavia? Answer?"

I sprinted across the slope, telling myself everything was fine, that her radio must have gone out.

"General da Silva?" I said.

"You're done, Jack. You've cost the lives of ten men."

"I called for an abort. It was ignored! Tell the helicopters above me to train their spotlights where the chopper went into the jungle. Now."

After a long pause, da Silva said, "Done."

"Tavia!" I yelled. "Tavia, answer me!"

The acrid stench of burned helicopter fuel was everywhere, a caustic fog that singed my nostrils and lungs. Throwing my arm across my mouth and nose, I scrambled lower and diagonally across the slope so the cut and burned trees were right there below me.

The helicopters circling above had gotten their orders from da Silva. Six wide and powerful spotlight beams played on the debris field. A long chunk of helicopter blade stuck out of the side of one tree like a giant machete. A strut hung off another like a Christmas ornament.

Some fifty yards from where the chopper had slashed into the jungle, what remained of the fuselage still burned and threw up a foul, black smoke. Here and there, I saw what might be body parts.

"Tavia?" I called. "Are you there?"

No answer.

Tears began to well in my eyes, and I brushed them away hard and went closer. One of the choppers above me adjusted its beam, revealing a scorched tree at the far lower edge of the crash path. The tree had been split almost lengthwise, with the front piece gone and the rest of the trunk sticking up like a church spire half sheared off.

At the base of that tree, Tavia lay facedown.

I ran to her, begging God to let her be alive.

But when I reached her side and started to turn her over, I knew by the slack in her neck that it was broken and she was gone.

Chapter 80

Friday, August 5, 2016
2:00 a.m.
Seventeen Hours Before the Olympic Games Open

LIEUTENANT BRUNO ACOSTA led me into Private Rio's offices. The entire staff was there waiting, anxious and somber. I'd texted them all and asked them to assemble for some difficult news. Cherie Wise and her daughters were there as well, all of them clearly frantic with worry.

The second they saw Lieutenant Acosta, they all sprang to their feet.

"What's happened?" Cherie cried. "No one will tell us what happened after the camera died."

Acosta bowed his head. "I'm sorry, Mrs. Wise, to be the bearer of tragic news, but...I'm so sorry..."

The billionaire's wife stared at the police lieutenant in disbelief and growing horror. "No," she said. "No, that's..."

Cherie began to waver on her feet. Natalie grabbed her arm, held her up, whimpering, "Mom? Please say it's not..."

"It's not right." Alicia sobbed and held tight to her mother.

Cherie sagged down into a chair, jaw slack, eyes fixed on a future that looked black and void. I moved, and she focused on me.

"You said you'd save him," she said in a devastated voice. "You and Tavia assured me he would not die."

Before I could reply, Lieutenant Acosta held his palm up to her and said, "Mr. Morgan put his life on the line to save your husband, Mrs. Wise. Octavia Reynaldo gave her life trying to save your husband."

Gasps went up all around the room. Cherie looked even more distraught. Seeing that and the shock on the faces of the good people of Private Rio threw me back into utter misery and it took every bit of strength I had not to break down.

"No," Natalie said, holding her stomach and bursting into tears. "No. No."

Her sister put her face in her hands and continued weeping.

"It wasn't…" Alicia choked. "He wasn't…Rayssa said…"

Lieutenant Acosta stepped toward her, said, "Ms. Wise?"

Alicia raised her head, peered at him with tortured eyes.

Natalie looked at her sister in terror. "No."

Alicia's jaw quivered and her skin flushed before she glared at Natalie and shrieked, "It's all about money! That's what you told me! She was just going to scare him and take his money."

"That's what she told me!" Natalie screamed back.

In the stunned silence that followed, I watched their poor mother. I saw every tic and tragic bit of Cherie's terrible path to understanding.

She gaped at them in bewilderment. "You knew? You were a part of…"

"Mom," Alicia said in a terrified voice. "Amelia showed us how Dad's company screwed the poor people of Brazil. She told us we could begin to right that, that Dad deserved some punishment, and it would help the poor."

Natalie said, "Mom, she made it sound like a good thing, a rebalancing."

Cherie looked at her daughters like they were alien creatures.

"You betrayed your father because he made too much money?" she said. "You played judge and jury with your own dad? Sent him to his death?"

"No!" Natalie cried. "It wasn't like that."

Cherie lunged up and out of her chair. She slapped Natalie and backhanded Alicia. Lieutenant Acosta stepped in and restrained her. She went hysterical in his arms.

"It's over," she wept. "Everything is over."

"Cherie, it's not over."

Cherie Wise didn't hear and sobbed in grief and loss.

"Cherie, baby doll, I'm right here."

A Private nurse pushed in a wheelchair bearing Andrew Wise. The billionaire sported a whopper of a bandage around his head and looked as weak as a newborn colt.

Cherie raised her head, saw her husband alive, and fainted dead away.

Chapter 81

AFTER MO-BOT GAVE her smelling salts, Cherie gazed at her husband in wonder and confusion. "You're alive."

"Thanks to Jack's skills," Wise said, holding her hand. "He shot her through the right side of her chest, spun her away from me before she pulled the trigger. Her bullet cut a bloody groove across my forehead."

Cherie started to cry. "Why did you do this? Why did you torture me?"

For the first time, the billionaire turned his attention to his daughters, who wilted helplessly under his unblinking appraisal.

"Before she died, Amelia told me I'd been betrayed by my own girls. She said she wanted that to be my last thought."

Natalie looked ready to disintegrate and Alicia began to weep. "What have we done? Oh my God, what have we done? She said it was all about money."

The billionaire watched them without emotion, as if he were studying some interesting object in nature.

"Maybe you didn't know Rayssa planned to shoot me," Wise said at last. "So I forgive you for that."

Natalie trembled, said, "Dad?"

"I've had some time to think," he said, more to his wife than his daughters. "Amelia Lopes was right. I made too big a profit. It is time to give back. So I forgive the girls for that as well."

Alicia tried to go to him, but Lieutenant Acosta stopped her, spun her around, and started putting handcuffs on her. "Alicia Wise, you are under arrest for conspiracy to kidnap and murder."

"No," she whined. "We didn't kill anyone."

"You participated in the murder of two of my people," I said angrily. "Or have you forgotten the two bodyguards who died in the fake kidnapping?"

"We didn't know that's what was going to happen!" Natalie said as Acosta put her in cuffs as well. "Amelia kept us in the dark, said it would be better."

Cherie had gotten enough strength to hold on to her husband as Acosta prepared to take their daughters away.

"Dad?" Natalie said. "You said you forgave us. Won't you help us?"

"I'll pay for your attorneys," he said. "But I will testify against you."

"So will I," Cherie said, and she cried harder.

"Get them good lawyers," Lieutenant Acosta said. "With all the media attention, they're both going to wind up in prison. There's no way around that now."

Chapter 82

DR. CASTRO CAME awake slowly, groggily. He was still in the hazmat suit, lying on his back on the floor of his lab. How long had he been...

Castro bolted upright, feeling claustrophobic, and gazed around wildly until he saw the clock on the wall: 7:01 a.m. He'd been asleep—what, almost ten hours? At least that.

He had to move, now, leave this lab forever. Castro got to his feet, opened the lid of the freezer, and saw that Leah's clothes had ice on them and that her strangled expression had frozen in place.

He shut the freezer, went to the refrigerator. He opened it and looked at all the vials and bags of blood, virus and mutation, virus and mutation, the whole history of Hydra-9's development from the very beginning laid out on shelves, oldest on the bottom, state-of-the-art up top.

Castro took bags of Luna's contaminated blood and used a funnel to make the transfer into a lightweight titanium cylinder, then he screwed on a pressurized fitting with a short, stout piece of hose dangling off it. He did the same thing with bags of

Ricardo's blood and then wiped down both cylinders with a bleach solution.

At 7:40 a.m., the doctor looked around, feeling like he'd forgotten something. But he couldn't put his finger on it, decided it was nothing of real consequence, and left the lab.

After he stripped off the hazmat suit, Castro took the cylinders to his workbench and a green-gray North Face Cinder 55 internal-frame backpack that he'd bought online at Moosejaw.com. The Cinder 55 had 3,356 cubic inches of space inside and thick, rugged outer walls of abrasion-resistant nylon. Serious mountain climbers used these packs to lug gear to and from base camps.

The backpack was almost full already, but there was still room for the blood cylinders, a bota bag of wine, water, and dried meat and fruit. His last lunch. His last supper.

He put a rain jacket on top of his supplies and equipment, toggled shut the main compartment, and then turned the top flap over. He unzipped the top flap pocket, slid in a nine-millimeter pistol with two full clips, and cinched the pack tight.

Hoisting it onto his back, he guessed the weight at forty-five pounds, and he made adjustments to the shoulder straps and waist belt so it rode snugly above his hips, centered along his spine. He was satisfied with the Cinder 55 and the way he'd packed it.

And he was more than satisfied with the items inside it and all the details that had gone into their design and construction. Things were coming together now. Preparation was about to meet opportunity.

Dr. Castro took a shower. He shaved and dressed in dull gray pants with a belt that featured a figure-eight buckle that was really the handle of a three-inch dagger that slid and locked into a hidden sheath. He'd taken it in trade for stitching up the son of a gangster but had never had any use for it until now.

After putting on a gray work shirt with collar and cuffs, Castro set a gray ball cap on his head and eased on a pair of wraparound sunglasses. He picked up the pack, threw it over one shoulder, took one last look at his laboratory, and left, locking the place up tight.

After engaging the dead bolts on the outer door, he put the pack in the trunk of his car. With the keys he'd taken from Leah, he opened her car, started it, and drove it several blocks away. He left her cell phone on and placed it under the seat.

Castro ran back, got in his car, and pulled away. It was 8:15 a.m. He was behind his original timetable by fifteen minutes.

Chapter 83

SOMEONE KNOCKED SHARPLY at the door to my suite. I opened my eyes a crack, feeling more rested than I had in days. Then the night before and the heartache returned, and I realized that for a long time to come, sleep would be my only refuge from the nightmare of being awake.

Tavia, my lover, my friend, was gone. The woman who might have become my wife was gone. It felt like someone had torn something out of me by the roots.

The knock again.

"Coming," I said. I threw on a robe, went to the door, and peered through the peephole.

Justine Smith stood there, and my heart instantly felt better.

I opened the door, smiled wanly as she said, "Oh, Jack, I'm so sorry."

"Yeah," I said, and held out my arms. She came into them and the door swung shut.

"I know how much Tavia meant to you," Justine said. "I got on a plane as soon as I heard, came straight here from the airport."

All the emotions I'd kept bottled inside broke

through, and I held on to one of the few women I've loved in life while I went to pieces over the loss of another. Justine held on and on, exuding deep and sincere empathy, rubbing my back while I mourned.

When it was out of me, I felt wrung out and embarrassed.

Justine put her hand on my cheek, gazed into my tortured eyes, and said, "I am here for you."

I reached and held her hand there, said, "You're a good friend, the best."

"Keep remembering that."

"I could never forget," I said, and I hugged her just for being there.

Then my cell phone rang. Justine pulled back, smiling sympathetically.

"Let it ring," I said. "Hungry?"

"Famished," she said. "Let's order room service and talk about Tavia?"

The old me would have dismissed that out of hand. My inability to open up was what had ultimately done in my romantic relationship with Justine. But I had to talk about Tavia. I had to tell someone about the love I'd lost.

"I'd like that," I said.

"Good," she said. "I'll order. You get showered and dressed."

I gave her a mock salute and headed to the bathroom, thinking once again how great Justine was. Goddamn it, even though I'd blown it with her and even though she was with someone else now, Justine still had the purest heart of anyone I'd ever met. Just having her to rely on made the burden of Tavia's death seem almost bearable.

I climbed out of the shower and was dressing when my cell phone began to ring again. I looked at the caller ID and answered.

"General da Silva?"

"There's a good chance I will be fired today," he said stiffly. "Getting a police helicopter and several men shot out of the sky in full view of many of the Olympic venues evidently does not sit well with the president."

"I imagine it wouldn't," I said.

"If I am relieved of command, you'll continue on?"

"In any role the government wants," I promised.

"I appreciate it, and I can't say how sorry I am about Tavia. She was one of a kind, a special person, and the only woman I have ever truly feared."

I laughed at that, said, "She could be fierce at times. That's one of the things I loved about her." Then my laugh turned wistful and died.

"I'll be in touch once I know," da Silva said.

"I'll eat and then get to work."

He hung up. Mo-bot called a minute later.

"You sleep?" she asked.

"I was going to ask you the same thing."

"On the couch here at Private Rio," she said.

"Seven and a half solid hours here."

"That's a blessing. How are you? I mean…"

"It's tolerable as long as I don't think about it, meaning about every minute or so I get stabbed in the gut. But Justine's here."

"That's a help. Jack, you poor thing. Listen, I finally tracked down the articles of incorporation for Dr. Castro's business. You'll never guess what the company was organized to do."

"Infectious-disease research?"

"How'd you guess that?"

"The way things are going, I just imagined the worst-case scenario and threw it out there."

Chapter 84

DR. CASTRO DROVE southwest through Rio, using every little trick he knew to avoid the strangling traffic, but then it started to rain and that mucked up everything and he was stuck again in the midst of bumper-to-bumper vehicles. To pass the time, he tuned to an all-news radio station and listened intently to the description of the government raid on the Favela Justice terrorists.

Billionaire Andrew Wise had been rescued, and Amelia Lopes, aka Rayssa, was dead, along with a dozen of her followers, including a notorious gangster named Urso who'd used a rocket launcher to take down a BOPE helicopter. Several people had died in the crash, among them Octavia Reynaldo, head of Private Rio.

Wise had gone out in front of cameras and microphones and announced his intention to spend the rest of his life figuring out how to better the lives of the poorest of the poor. A reporter asked if his daughters were in custody, and he'd said they were under arrest.

Amelia Lopes and the Wise twins, Castro thought. *Kindred spirits. I would have liked to have known them.* Daughter of a saint, product of poverty, Lopes saw the

inequities and acted. Guilty rich girls confronted with
the inequities of life joined her. It made sense to him,
and in many ways he agreed with their goals.

But Amelia Lopes had thought about the gap
between rich and poor in entirely economic terms,
the benefits and losses, the income, the greed, the
want. To Castro, the biggest gap was in health care.
The richest had access to the best medical care
and a sanitary environment conducive to long human life. The poorest had feces flowing past their
doors, pestilence, and recurrent plagues. The richest
couldn't see that a simple rise in the living standards
of the poor would lead to fewer crippling diseases
and fewer early deaths.

Why? Because the rich were ignorant of what it
was like to live at the mercy of a parasite, a disease, or
a virus. *So they have to be taught,* the doctor thought as
traffic began to ease and he picked up speed. *They have
to be shown.*

Forty minutes behind schedule, at eleven a.m., Dr.
Castro finally drove into Laranjeiras, a largely residential neighborhood in south Rio with a funky street
vibe. Little cafés, nice parks, lots of vendors. And the
base station for the cog railway that climbed to the top
of Corcovado Mountain.

The rain lightened to a drizzle. Castro went past
the rail station, slowed along a high wall, and then
turned through a pair of iron gates into a cobblestoned
courtyard in front of the shambles of a palace built
in the early 1800s by the dethroned king of Portugal's
doctor. The palace must have been grand and glamorous once.

Squatters lived there now; the limestone walls
were slick with moss, and the wooden shutters hung

off their hinges and moldered. Castro had seen the palace many times. The building had been one of his wife's favorites. Sophie always thought it should have been in a movie, that it was the perfect place for a vampire to await sundown. Castro sat there a moment after he parked, swearing he could see Sophie right there, entranced by the decrepit building.

Then he shook the memory off and got out, confident that this was the perfect place to leave his car. After dark, the squatters would strip it, take it apart, and sell the pieces. Nothing would go to waste.

Castro got the backpack out of the trunk, threw his keys inside, and shut it. He felt eyes watching him, looked up three stories, and saw a boy looking down at him through the lightly falling rain. The kid was shirtless and eating something, but he was also clearly watching the doctor.

That pleased Castro as he walked back through the gates. If the kid saw him toss the keys in the trunk, the car would be gone within the hour. He walked away, heading west and uphill past the Museum of Native Art and onto Rua Cosme Velho, a twisting, climbing road.

The rain stopped and behind it came a breeze from the northeast, from the equator, bringing equatorial heat to Rio. Castro reached the entrance to the sports complex at the College of St. Vincent de Paul, where he had been doing a weekly clinic for athletes the past six months. The security guard recognized him, asked him what was in the pack.

"Sand, mostly," Castro replied. "I'm going climbing in the Andes in December and getting into shape. Walking everywhere I can with this on."

The guard looked at him like he was kind of nuts

but nodded and let him pass through. Castro headed to the athletic department building.

But when he got there, he cut back to his right, out of sight of the guard, and made his way across a practice field and around grandstands to the rear corner of the college grounds.

Castro went to a heavy iron gate, pulled the cotter pin that held the latch tight, and opened the gate, praying that the squealing it made would not attract attention. He exited, shut the gate, and breathed a sigh of relief.

The doctor was in the dripping, steaming jungle now, safe from all prying eyes. He just had to be careful and stick to a route he'd plotted for months. He had a brutal series of climbs and traverses ahead of him. There were other ways, some of them probably easier, but Castro had chosen this approach because from above he would be invisible, and because he wanted to suffer.

Chapter 85

JUSTINE AND I climbed from a taxi outside a long steel building in a light-industrial complex in Rio's Estação District.

Lieutenant Acosta pulled in behind us and got out. For an early Friday afternoon, the entire complex seemed empty. Then again, the president had declared the opening day of the Olympics a national holiday in Brazil.

We went to the door of AV3 Research and knocked. No one answered.

"Think you have enough cause to enter?" I asked.

"We're in Brazil," Lieutenant Acosta said. "I'll invent a cause, say I was doing a well-being check on Castro. If we find nothing, we're good and we back out."

We tried to force the door, with no luck. It was reinforced steel and triple dead-bolted. Acosta called a locksmith. After we'd waited for forty minutes in the lieutenant's car to get out of the suddenly oppressive heat, the locksmith had the door swinging open.

The outer office wasn't much—file cabinets, an old desk. But we found the second door and had the locksmith pick it. It was 1:25 p.m. when we finally gained access to Castro's inner sanctum, turned on the lights, and saw the clean room.

We walked around it, finding the entrance, but looking first through glass windows into a spotless, elaborate, and meticulously arranged laboratory.

"I'm not going in there," Justine said.

"I'll go," I said.

"I will too," Acosta said.

"We don't know what we're dealing with, Jack," Justine said.

"We'll have a look around outside first," I said. "Get a clue."

We walked through the workshop, finding a metal band saw, a bender, and lengths of titanium rods and flats. Jars of titanium screws and bolts. A small welding setup. Cargo netting. Various gas canisters of different sizes.

"Someone's building and looking to save weight," I said.

"For what?" Acosta asked.

"I can't figure it out. Maybe he left a design or something."

I began opening drawers, finding the usual tools but also calipers, a guide to stress testing, stout metal fittings, and lengths of high-pressure hose. In a bottom drawer I found something odd: a short length of black hose clamped to what looked like an airbrush.

"What's that for?" Acosta asked.

"No idea," I said. I set it aside and moved on toward a second bench that smelled like airplane glue and featured tiny wood clamps, fine-toothed saws, and scalpels. There were thumbtacks and little bits of paper stuck to the wall above the bench. Something had been torn down.

On top of the bench were two airbrushes and a can of hose glue. I opened drawers and found sheets of balsa wood, cardboard tubes, and what looked like little plastic fins. What the hell was he building?

"We haven't seen anything that says he's a threat," Justine said.

"If it's anywhere, it's in there," I said, gesturing to the laboratory.

"I'll wait here," she said.

Acosta and I went through the zipped door into a kind of anteroom. Hanging on one wall was a protocol list with a diagram that we followed to suit up safely. The hoods and gauntlets went on last.

"Part of me thinks this is nuts, Jack," Lieutenant Acosta said.

"I think that part of you is right," I said, getting used to the way he sounded over the little motorized HEPA filter that cleaned the air we were breathing.

I bent down, unzipped another door, and climbed into an air lock with an exhaust fan and ductwork leading to a large air-scrubbing device overhead. Near the exhaust fan there was a showerhead with a sign next to it: *2% bleach*.

Lieutenant Acosta climbed in after me and peered through the porthole window on the opposite door. "So there are infectious diseases in there?"

"Strong enough to require a Clorox bath afterward," I said, and I shivered before unzipping the third door and stepping out into the lab.

I was struck again by how regimented the room seemed. Everything had a place and everything was in its place.

I spotted Justine looking in through the small window in the far wall and gave her the thumbs-up before walking past a row of glass cages and seeing wood chips and rodent feces in the bottom. Above the glass enclosures there were unplugged electronic monitors. What did they measure?

I walked over to the refrigerator. Acosta circled the other way, looking at the scientific apparatus near a lift-top freezer.

I opened the fridge and felt my breath catch.

Hundreds of vials of blood hung in racks inside. They were labeled in code on the side of the trays: 1-1:7v, 1-1:7m, 1-1:8v, 1-1:8m...

What did any of that mean? I had no idea. I picked up an IV bag of blood lying on the lower shelf.

I turned it over in my hand and read what was written there.

LSantos-1—H:9v Contraido: 7.30.16.

"Lieutenant?" I called. "You better come see this."

"Not before you see this, Jack," Acosta said.

Still holding the IV bag, I shut the fridge door and saw Acosta holding up the freezer top and pointing inside.

Chapter 86

I STARED IN at the frozen couple. Their lips—his gray and hers blue—barely touched. On the young woman's back, there was a rectangular piece of freezer paper. Someone had scrawled across it in big block letters: *Enfin os ricos estão atormentados.*

"What's it mean?" I asked.

"You can translate it two ways," Acosta said. "'For once the rich are tormented,' or 'For once the rich are plagued.'"

Oh Jesus, I thought, and closed my eyes. It was real, then. The weird gut sense I'd had being around Castro the first time had been true.

"What'd you find?" Lieutenant Acosta said.

I showed him the bag of blood and the label. "Luna Santos-1—Hydra-9 virus. I don't know what *contraído* means."

"'Contracted,'" Acosta said. "As in disease."

Contracted July 30, 2016, then. "That was the day Luna died," I said. "Castro was using this secret lab to develop a deadly virus, using humans as his guinea pigs, and..."

I turned back to the freezer, leaned way in, and studied the color of the dead couple's skin.

"This wasn't just a lab," I said. "It was a propagation operation too."

"Meaning what?"

"We know he drained Luna of blood. Judging by the extreme pallor, the male victim has been drained of blood too. But there's only one blood bag in the fridge, and not enough in the vials to make up for the difference. We're talking liters of infected blood. We need experts in here, and we need to find Castro."

"You really think he plans on..." Acosta looked sick.

"Based on this place? I think he's been planning for a long, long time."

I glanced at the clock. It was a quarter to five, two hours and...

I knew it all then, fought a queasy, liquid feeling, said, "We need to get out of here. Now. I think I know where he's going to attack."

We shut the freezer, put the IV bag holding Luna Santos's infected blood back in the fridge, and returned to the air lock, where we took bleach showers and shed the white suits.

"What is it?" Justine asked.

"Bad," I said, punching in General da Silva's number.

"You still have your job?" I asked when he answered.

"Holding on by the skin of my teeth."

"Then this is going to be tough to hear, General, but Acosta and I think Lucas Castro is going to release a plague at the opening ceremony."

Chapter 87

THE SUN HAD broken through the clouds, and the heat from Bahia just kept rising. The heat and the north wind had come as a surprise to Dr. Castro. It did not help him, but it could be dealt with. And he believed that the winds would change again before sunset, turn back out of the southeast.

But now, it was just plain stupid hot. Dr. Castro stopped, wiped his brow, and shrugged off the heavy backpack. He drank and ate a piece of jerky before setting off again, climbing higher through the jungle toward the base of a long charcoal-colored cliff.

The faint path to the cliff was steep, but the doctor kept at it, pulling himself up over roots and through brush, slippery fern beds, and stands of wild bamboo, trying to distance himself from the apartment buildings below.

Two o'clock had come and gone before he reached an even fainter trail inside the tree line below the cliff. He had found the path in his scouting trips and used a machete to trim out the rough spots.

The doctor studied the damp earth there and saw no tracks. He'd learned that most people wanting to follow the contour of the mountain took a heavily used trail some two hundred vertical feet below. In his experience only the odd rock climber or two came this far up, and even they rarely used this trail.

He'd met a few over the past two months. One of them had used a Cinder 55 backpack as a cargo bag for ropes and such. An American. Billy White from Fort Collins, Colorado. He'd recommended the pack.

Good guy, Dr. Castro thought. *Nice guy.*

The faint path ahead continued through the jungle, and he had to be sure of his footing, keeping his weight and balance shifted toward the steep slope to his left. One false step and he'd go down hard. Very hard. And tumble and then hit hard again.

The north breeze ebbed. The rain forest turned even more oppressively hot. Insects were buzzing, birds were calling, and somewhere a monkey chattered. But no human voices. Not even a distant car horn.

It suited Castro. He did not want to run into anyone today. He wished to be like a virus: Alone. Mutating. Incubating. Not existing in people's minds until their friends started dying all around them.

Dr. Castro pushed on into one of the mountain's deep and densely forested side canyons. For all intents and purposes, he was invisible.

Alone. Moving. Mutating. Incubating.

Castro imagined he was becoming like Hydra-9. In the shimmering heat he was hyperaware of everything. He felt part of nature now, the buzzing and sawing, the building and destruction, all of it unfolding in an imperfect but inevitable process.

One species becomes dominant, and then, with something as insignificant as a twist in the strand of a virus, the same species is laid low, making way for some better, stronger, and smarter creature.

Great good will come of this, he thought. *The population is out of control. The rich are out of control. This will be a check. This will create some balance.*

"Hey there, Doc."

Dr. Castro startled at the soft voice, almost tripped off the wrong side of the trail, but he managed to grab onto a vine. He looked up and saw Billy White sitting on a rock about fifteen feet above him, tanned, bare-chested, ripped, Petzl helmet and a pack next to him, chewing on an energy bar.

Chapter 88

"BILLY," CASTRO SAID. He coughed. "I didn't see you there."

White wiped off sweat below his short blond dreadlocks and flashed the doctor an aw-shucks smile. "Just taking a rest. I'm playing mule, hauling out a bunch of gear from the last time we were in here climbing."

The American stood and ambled like a goat down over the loose rocks between them. "Frickin' hot, isn't it? Hey, that's the pack!"

"Yes."

"Didn't know it came in that color."

"I dyed it like that," Castro said.

"Nice," the climber said. "I'd bow-hunt with something like that back home in Colorado. At least that's what I was thinking. Where'd you get it?"

"Moosejaw.com," the doctor said.

"I've got the two smaller ones, but I've never seen the big boy. Want to take a rest, let me look inside?"

"I'd rather not," Castro said. "I'm trying to make the top of the mountain before dark. I'll have a ride waiting up there."

"Yeah?" Billy said. "You know the way?"

"I've done it before."

"Lead on, then," he said. "I'm always up for a virgin climb."

The doctor didn't know what to do. He did not want Billy White with him. He wanted Billy White to go downhill and out of sight.

"I was sort of hoping to do this alone," Castro said. "Kind of a solo thing."

"I get it and no worries," White said. "I hunt for the same kind of solitude."

The doctor smiled. "I appreciate it. Well, be seeing you, Billy."

Before Castro had fully turned to set off down the trail again, he felt the weight come off his shoulders.

"Jesus, Doc, you got that sucker packed to the gills," White said. "What the hell's in here?"

He'd grabbed the bottom of the pack and hoisted it.

"Sand," Castro said, upset. "I'm training. Thinking of climbing Everest someday."

"Yeah?" White said, letting go of the bag. It dropped and there were clanking noises as the weight returned to the doctor's shoulders and hips.

"Don't sound like sand to me," White said. "Really, Doc, what's in there?"

The American said all this good-naturedly, but Dr. Castro felt like he had no choice in the matter now. With his body still turned three-quarters away from the American, he released the chest strap and then the hip belt.

"Since you're so interested, I'll show you," Castro said. "Help me?"

White grinned and grabbed the pack with two hands.

"Careful," the doctor said. "I have sensitive scientific equipment in there."

"I didn't think it was sand," White said, crouching down, unsnapping the flaps, and admiring the hardware. "You doing an experiment?"

"Something like that," Castro said.

"What's your hypothesis?" White asked, lifting the flap to look into the main compartment.

"You a scientist as well as a climber?" Castro asked, feeling increasingly nervous about White rummaging around in his pack.

"This is a nice feature, the top compartment on the flap," White said thoughtfully. "Awful bottom-heavy, though. Doc, hasn't anybody taught you to put the heaviest stuff highest?"

The American started to unzip the top pocket, and Castro knew he'd see the pistol and extra ammunition. He reached over, picked up a chunk of jagged granite, and swung it like a hammer at the American's skull.

White must have sensed something because he jerked to his left just before the sharp rock struck and took a hard but glancing blow high on the side of his dreadlocked head. The American lurched to his right and fell on his side, clutching at his bleeding head and groaning. "What the fuck! What the fuck!"

Finish it, Castro thought, and he took two steps and then stood over White with one boot on each side of him so the American climber's upper body and head were in range.

The doctor started to raise the rock to smash it down on White's head and be done with it. The American swung a fist and hit him in the balls.

The doctor hunched up, dropped the rock, and almost puked. White lurched up and punched him in the face. Castro fell backward, almost slipping off the flat and into the rock piles below.

He was stunned but aware of White getting to his feet. Blood gushed down the side of the American's face, which had turned primal.

"What the fuck's in that pack, Doc?" White asked, taking a step toward Castro and kicking him hard in the ham of his left leg. "Tell me what's in that pack you want to kill me to keep me from seeing!"

The American cocked his boot as if to kick him again. Before he could, Castro stuck a three-inch dagger through the side of the calf of his opposite leg.

White howled in agony and danced back before going down on the rocks. He lay there, screaming and panting, then tried to reach the figure-eight handle of the dagger.

The American saw Castro get to his feet and come for him. White's face turned purple with fury, and he made insane little grunting noises before he grabbed the handle and wrenched the bloody dagger from his calf.

"C'mon, Doc," White said, swinging it at Castro. "I'll fucking kill you now. What you got in that pack?"

The doctor reached into the open top pocket of the Cinder 55, pulled out the pistol, and shot the American dead at point-blank range.

Chapter 89

THE INTERNATIONAL BROADCAST facility for the Olympic Games was a ten-story temporary structure built at the far south end of Copacabana Beach, where it commanded a gorgeous view of the white-sand shore and, across the waves, Pão de Açúcar.

Huge glass windows dominated the north side of the building, where NBC and other television networks had their sets. Behind them was one of the most sophisticated broadcast facilities on earth.

Every image, every video clip, and every blip of the live feeds coming from various Olympic events would pass through the facility on its way to editing studios and satellites that would beam coverage of the games around the world.

For that reason alone, shortly after the World Cup, Mo-bot had recommended that General da Silva set up a temporary Olympic security command right behind the broadcast center and tie it into every feed. He'd agreed, and she'd been in on the design from the beginning.

There was a floor-to-ceiling, wall-to-wall curved screen at the front of the command center, a large, windowless, and high-ceilinged single-room affair with tiers of workstations facing the big screen.

On the narrow left side, live video feeds from around Rio played. The narrow right side of the screen featured feeds from security cameras at various intersections and venues around the city. The vast majority of the screen, however, was dominated by a real-time satellite image of Rio de Janeiro, another of Maureen's suggestions.

General da Silva was standing next to Jack in front of the screen, shaking his head.

"I can't do it, Jack," the general said. "I can't pull the plug on the opening ceremony with less than five hours to go. It would destroy Rio's reputation, humiliate—"

"How good is Rio's reputation going to be if you don't pull the plug and Castro gets some bioweapon inside Maracanã Stadium? What do you think will happen to you if your president and all her invited dignitaries are exposed, and the world learns you could have stopped it?"

Da Silva looked like he was a man trying not to drown. After several moments he said, "We are not stopping the opening ceremony."

"General," I said.

He waved me off. "As of now, I am banning the use of all cars, taxis, motorcycles, and bicycles within three miles of the stadium. As of now, I am calling in army units to seal off the area and enforce the vehicle ban. Access will be limited to residents, ticket holders, accredited media, vendors, and athletes. Period.

"Dr. Castro's picture will be sent to the phone of every police officer, every soldier, every Olympic volunteer, and every municipal employee in Rio, including the bus drivers. We'll give it to the media as well. That doctor is not getting anywhere near Maracanã Stadium. The people of Rio are going to hunt him down for us."

Chapter 90

I HAD TO hand it to General da Silva. In a very short time his ham-fisted tactics had done a lot to ease my concern over the opening ceremony going forward.

Looking at that real-time satellite image in the command center, I could see that the streets for miles around Maracanã Stadium were now devoid of all vehicles except for the trucks of credentialed vendors, the buses ferrying volunteers, athletes, and coaches, and the strings of Mercedes-Benz limousines bearing foreign and International Olympic Committee dignitaries. Thousands of people on foot streamed toward the stadium.

Security got tighter within a fifteen-block radius of the Maracanã. Brazilian army tanks were already parked in every major intersection. BOPE and Brazilian army special forces units had closed off some streets, funneling all pedestrians through checkpoints where their identification, tickets, and credentials would be reviewed three times before they reached the stadium. Every single person involved in Olympic security had a picture of Dr. Castro on his or her cell phone, and the media had plastered his photo everywhere, telling everyone he was dangerous and that anyone who spotted him should call the police.

So far, there'd been no sightings.

Had da Silva's drastic measures scared Castro off? It was possible, but I wasn't betting on it as the digital clock in the security command center rolled toward zero hour.

"Jack, I'm going to the stadium at six p.m.," the general said.

I understood. Da Silva wanted to be there if Castro somehow got his deadly virus in. The general was a proud man. He wouldn't have it said that he had foreknowledge of a deadly threat and chose to ride it out in safety six miles away.

"I'll go with you," I said.

Justine and Mo-bot turned around at their workstations.

"That's not a good idea," Justine said.

"No, it's a necessary one," I said.

"Well, I won't be going with you."

"And neither will I," Mo-bot said. "I draw the line at willingly exposing myself to a deadly virus."

"I get it," I said. "But I don't have a choice in the matter, do I?"

"Sure you do," Justine said, irritated.

"How's that?"

"You *have* a choice," she said. "But as usual, Jack, you just plow ahead, never thinking of the consequences."

"I have thought of the consequences," I shot back. "The consequences of not going, especially what that would do to Private's reputation."

"And how is Private going to look after the untimely death of its leader and driving force?"

Before I could reply to that, an excited Lieutenant Acosta came toward us with a wide-eyed and shabbily dressed boy who looked about eleven years old.

Acosta said, "This young man has a very interesting tale to tell."

Chapter 91

FELIX MARTINS LIVED with his mother and brothers and sisters in Rio's Laranjeiras, squatters on the third floor of a moldering palace that once belonged to the king of Portugal's physician. Toward midday, Felix had heard a car roll into the courtyard parking area, and he went to look.

The car took the last available space. A man in gray work clothes got out, retrieved a large gray-green backpack from the trunk, and then threw his keys inside the trunk and shut it.

"Did you see his face?" I asked.

"I recognized him from the pictures on the television right away," Felix told us. "I went straight to the police station."

"Is the car still there?" Justine asked.

Felix knit his brow, seemed conflicted, but then shook his head and said the car had been stolen around one o'clock that afternoon.

Acosta said, "You know who stole it?"

The boy chewed his lip. "It was almost like he wanted it stolen."

"Maybe he did," I said. "Who's got it?"

"I dunno," he said. "Some friend of my mother's. Ask her."

Acosta said, "I will. When was the last time you saw him?"

"When he went out the gate."

"Which way did he turn?" I asked.

Felix thought about that and said, "Right."

Mo-bot found the decrepit palace and put it up on the big screen, giving us the aerial view. You could see the courtyard and wall plainly. Maureen highlighted the area on the satellite feed and then pulled back to show the winding road heading north until it dead-ended in the steep and choked jungle of the Tijuca National Park.

Mo-bot highlighted Maracanã Stadium, which was north-northwest of the end of the road, and we requested the distance between the two spots.

"Four point two miles as the crow flies," she said.

"Not on foot," I said. "Look at the brutal terrain that he's got to cross to get there. Up and down several thousand vertical feet here, here, and here. In some places I'd bet it's steep enough for ropes."

"Difficult, but not impossible for a fanatic," said General da Silva. He gestured to the northern edge of the forest. "But look where he can exit the jungle. Somewhere above São Francisco Xavier Metrô station, not three-quarters of a mile from Maracanã Stadium."

It did look tempting from a strategic perspective, but something about it still didn't seem right to me.

"Could a man cross that kind of terrain in six or seven hours?"

"If he was fit and knew the paths," Lieutenant Acosta said. "I'm sure."

The general said, "I'm moving more police all along that front where he'd come out. In the meantime, we'll try to spot him from the air."

Chapter 92

WHEN DR. CASTRO judged he was about one hundred feet below the summit of the mountain he'd been climbing the better part of the day, he turned around and sat on a rock outcropping beneath an umbrella-shaped tree that hid him from above. The weight of the pack came off his back and he stifled a groan at the effort it had taken to get here.

Since Dr. Castro had reached the head of the canyon on the west flank of the mountain, the path had been nearly straight uphill. It had been back-breaking work to stay balanced with the pack while grabbing onto roots and small saplings and thorny brush, hoisting himself higher, foot by grueling foot.

But Castro had welcomed the pain and drove himself unmercifully toward the top.

Twice on the way up, he'd had to cross a winding switchbacked road. The doctor had hidden behind the guardrails until the roads were clear, and then sprinted to the other side. The sun was low over the mountains by then, casting the final part of his ascent in shadows, which suited him. He sat for a few minutes to slow his breath and slamming heart.

He heard a helicopter. He'd been hearing them off

and on all day, and now he peered out through the vegetation, seeing several of them to his northeast, flying low and in formation over the jungle. Then he spotted a closer one, making a loop around the summit above him.

Castro slid deeper into the dark shadows as the helicopter passed and faded away. He heard a loudspeaker announcing that in honor of the national holiday, the area was closing at five o'clock.

By ten past, the shadows were deepening and he hadn't heard a car go by on the road below him in a good twelve minutes. But the doctor had done his homework and knew better. At 5:20 p.m. one last car left the summit. It carried two guards, who stopped to lock a series of gates on the switchback road as they descended.

Feeling refreshed, Castro tightened down the straps on the pack and started climbing to the summit of Corcovado Mountain as the sun drifted lower and into a haze brought on by the heat. The doctor soon stopped by a fence that surrounded the observation terraces below the statue of Christ the Redeemer.

Bathed in a gold and copper light, the Redeemer was the iconic symbol of Rio and now the Olympic Games. The doctor felt, however, that the Christ had been hijacked to hawk Coca-Cola and Visa and the goods of other multinationals. He did not look up at the statue. He stayed on task.

Castro knew there were only three people left on the summit of Corcovado now. Two worked for NBC, a producer and a cameraman there to provide a long-lensed look at Rio by night. They'd be picked up later by helicopter.

The third person was Corcovado's trusted watchman Pietro Gonzalez. Dr. Castro stood there patiently in the shadows until the watchman appeared on his rounds. Castro whistled softly to Gonzalez, whose daughter and son had died of Hydra the day before the World Cup final.

Gonzalez stopped and signaled to Castro to wait. The doctor heard another helicopter circling, filming footage of the statue for the global audience.

How many would watch the opening ceremony? Castro had heard as many as a billion people.

That would do it, he thought. *A billion people will get the message shoved right down their throats.*

Finally Pietro gestured to him to hurry. Castro came up and over the rail, followed the security guard to a door on the back of the pedestal that supported the statue of the Redeemer.

Pietro had a key ready; he twisted it in the lock and pulled the door open.

Castro said, "Thank you, my friend."

"For my babies and your wife, and all of the oppressed," Pietro said, handing the doctor a headlamp and a small jar of gray makeup.

Chapter 93

"WE'VE GOT ABOUT ten minutes of usable light left," General da Silva said, grunting in frustration from the copilot's seat of a Brazilian army 36 AS350 helicopter, a nimble four-seater with a cruising speed of a hundred and fifty miles an hour.

Lieutenant Acosta and I rode in the back. We'd spent the better part of an hour flying over the most likely routes Dr. Castro could have taken through the mountainous jungle between Laranjeiras and Estação.

The pilot had flown us right above the rain-forest canopy, where we did our best to peer through the dense vegetation, hoping to catch a glimpse of the doctor and his backpack. In most places the cover was too thick to see anything. Even in those areas where it thinned, the winter jungle was as much gray pastels as greens. If he was wearing gray, he'd be all but invisible down there.

"Take us to the stadium," da Silva said finally, and he called in for an update on the police presence in the streets between Maracanã and the jungle.

As the sun sank below the western mountains, it turned the sky an intense magenta color that was breathtaking.

My cell phone rang. I tucked it in under the headphones and said, "Jack Morgan."

"It's Sci, Jack. I'm with the forensics team at Castro's lab."

"Go ahead."

"Did you see all the thumbtacks with the little corners of paper left above one of the workbenches?"

"Yes."

"I found the papers in a dumpster behind the lab,"
Sci said. "Some are weather maps of Rio that show
wind speed and direction. The rest are printouts of
wind data going back ten years, all in the month of
August."

"And I'm interested in this why?" I said as we
swung over the lines of opening-ceremony ticket
holders still trying to clear security and get inside.

"Because of what else I found," Sci said. "Balsa
wood, stout cardboard tubes, and sheets of aluminum
with finlike shapes cut from them."

"What do you mean, finlike?"

"Like the kind that stabilizes a model rocket," Sci
said.

"Like a kid's hobby thing?"

"Exactly, except some of the discarded cardboard
tubes I found were five inches in diameter and four
feet long."

We were coming in for a landing and it all started
to hit me. Historical wind direction and speed. A huge
model rocket. Capable of carrying...

"Jack?" Sci said as the helicopter landed.

"What's the prevailing wind direction and speed in
Rio in August?"

"Southeast at eight to ten miles an hour."

"Which means he was thinking about trajectory,

which means he doesn't have to be here at the stadium to…"

"Correct," Sci said. "He could be a mile or more away."

"Well done," I said, and hung up.

The second the pilot signaled it was safe to get out, I did and told da Silva and Acosta about my conversation with Kloppenberg.

"A rocket?" the general cried.

"The wind's southeast right now, eight miles an hour," I said, glancing that way and seeing the silhouette of the closest mountain. "He could be up there, just waiting for the right time to launch."

Da Silva thought about that and looked ready to throw a fit.

"How the hell are we going to defend against something like that?"

"I have no idea," I said.

Chapter 94

AFTER THE DOOR had closed and Pietro had thrown the bolt, Dr. Castro stood there in the pitch-dark cavity of the statue, taking a moment to be grateful for having gotten this far.

Then he flipped the headlamp on, fitted it to his head, and checked his watch. Right on schedule. He paused to smear his face, neck, and hands with the gray makeup.

He started the eight-story climb up a narrow iron staircase anchored into the inner wall of the Christ. He took his time, not wanting to bump the pack or make any noise that the two NBC workers might hear and report.

At 5:44 p.m., Dr. Castro reached the top of the staircase. He was inside the chest of the Christ, right at the junction of the two outstretched arms. Dropping the pack on the catwalk, Castro took a minute's rest and then carried the pack into the hollow interior of the Redeemer's right arm and the folds of his sleeve.

When the doctor started, the ceiling of the passage was more than eight feet high. But by the time he reached the elbow, it had dropped to less than five feet.

It featured in the crook of the arm a large hatch that workmen used to maintain the statue exterior.

He checked his watch. It was 5:52.

Dr. Castro knew he should wait, knew he should focus on assembling a few things, but now that he was actually here, with the hatch right there, unexpected excitement seized him and he gave in to impulse. He threw the lever that unlocked it and felt the hatch door ease.

Heart pounding, Castro gently pushed on the hatch and felt it go up. Wind came whooshing in. So did blazing light, which concerned him.

He shouldn't risk a look. Not yet. But then he realized the winds had shifted, gone southeasterly, eight or nine miles an hour, which was exactly what he wanted. He needed that wind direction and speed if this was to happen tonight. Now everything was perfect, and everything he'd planned for two years was about to move from dream to reality.

That made him feel blessed, powerful, and, well, righteous. He was doing this for Sophie and the Gonzalez kids. He was doing this for every other man, woman, and child who'd died needlessly of poverty.

Castro pushed the hatch up another inch and then another. He peeked out, seeing just the lights and the top of the arm. When he'd raised the door eight inches, he could see down to the terraces and spotted the NBC guys with their backs to him, drinking beer and watching the network coverage on an iPad.

They had no idea he was there. That emboldened Castro. He pushed over the door and laid it carefully on the Christ's upper arm. Then he stuck his gray hat, gray face, and gray shoulders up out of the gray elbow of the Redeemer.

The sun was a ball of fire in the haze, and the sky to his west was an incredible dun-red color that seized his attention for several moments. Off to his east, several hundred yards, yet another helicopter circled the summit, but he wasn't concerned.

All of Rio lay below the doctor now. The lights were going on, twinkling like so many jewels and charms. But Castro was interested only in that part of the Marvelous City that lay past the outstretched right hand of the Christ, five miles off, below a circling blimp.

Maracanã Stadium was lit up like the ultimate gem, no doubt already filled with a crowd of the people wealthy and powerful enough to afford one of only forty-five thousand tickets to the opening ceremony. They had to be eagerly counting down the minutes until the big night began.

I know I am, Dr. Castro thought before ducking down inside the arm and getting to work.

Chapter 95

"YOU CAN'T GET some kind of radar in here?" Lieutenant Acosta asked. "At least so we know something's been launched?"

"On this short notice?" General da Silva shot back. "Impossible."

We were standing in the parking lot of the stadium, watching the thousands of people still pressing to get inside and looking off into the breeze, to the southwest toward the closest mountains.

"Then you better go tell your president," I said. "You've got twenty minutes until the ceremony starts. Let her decide. But she better be quick about it."

The Olympic security chief struggled, then swore in Portuguese and hurried off.

Lieutenant Acosta got a phone call and listened while I stared at the sky, which had gone from fire red to fading charcoal ashes. I didn't know what to do. Common sense said to grab one of the hazmat suits from the helicopter and wear it all night. But part of me wanted to be defiant, to show that I would not be controlled by a threat.

"We had a second sighting of Dr. Castro in Laranjeiras," Acosta said, pocketing his phone. "The security guard at the College of St. Vincent de Paul saw him carrying a heavy backpack toward the back of the campus. He said Castro went through a gate there and disappeared into the forest."

"Where's the college?" I asked. "Show me on a map."

He pulled out his iPhone and called up the map, showed me.

I studied it, said, "That's the wrong way."

"What?"

My phone rang. Caller ID said it was Mo-bot.

I ignored her call, said, "If Castro goes out that gate on foot he's heading due west, not north-northwest toward Maracanã."

"What's due west of the college?"

Before I could futz with the screen, my phone rang again.

"Here," I said, handing him his phone and answering mine. "Things are kind of intense at the moment, Mo-bot."

"They're about to get more intense," she said. "I've got him. He made a mistake and I've got him. Or at least where he was about fifty minutes ago."

Lieutenant Acosta glanced up from the map on his phone with a puzzled look and said, "Due west; he's up on Corcovado Mountain."

"On Corcovado Mountain?" I said into my phone.

"How did you know that?" Mo-bot said, sounding deflated.

"An educated guess based on where he entered the jungle."

"Oh," she said, happy again. "Well, believe it or not, I've got video of him sticking his gray self up out of Christ's right arm. I'm sending it to you now."

I didn't wait for it, just started running toward the helicopter.

No pilot.

Acosta had followed me. "What's going on?" he demanded as I wrenched open the army chopper's front door.

"Castro's going to launch his rocket off the Redeemer."

Chapter 96

IN THE HEADLAMP beam, Dr. Castro gazed at his masterpiece reassembled on the inner floor of the Redeemer's right arm. The Hydra-9 and propellant canisters fit snugly into the payload hammock. The hoses were all tight. So were the airbrush connections.

He'd paired his phone via Bluetooth to a small joystick in his shirt pocket. He'd also linked the phone through apps and a local cellular service to a GoPro Hero camera and to the GPS navigator on board the workhorse of his delivery system: a Freefly Alta drone.

Castro had bought the Freefly drone on the Internet for $8,495. It was worth every penny. With a fold-up design, collapsible struts, and five propellers, the drone could carry a payload of fifteen pounds for more than ten miles.

The doctor's delivery system weighed in at a little over ten pounds, and the Freefly didn't need to carry it more than five miles. Castro felt confident knowing he had more than enough fuel and power to reach the stadium and get the job done right.

He folded the struts and props so he could get the drone up through the hatch and carefully set it on the

Christ's right arm. The doctor glanced down at the two NBC employees more than one hundred feet below him.

One of them was taking a piss off the side of the terrace.

The other one was still looking at his iPad and said, "It's starting."

Perfect, Dr. Castro thought as he snapped the drone's arms quietly into place. *We'll be fashionably late, coming to the show with the last of the stragglers, making it a full house.*

Castro gave the Freefly a command through his phone. The battery-driven motors started up. The propellers slowly turned.

The doctor reached around to arrange the hoses and airbrushes one last time. Taking a deep breath, he said, *"Boa viagem."*

Castro got the joystick control. He increased the power until the propellers were a blur and watched with delight as the drone lifted off with its precious load.

When the Freefly was ten feet overhead, the doctor used the joystick to send the drone north and at an angle to the southeast wind. With the black-mesh hammock, the nine hoses, and the airbrushes dangling below the drone, he thought it looked kind of like a jellyfish as it left the spotlights for the darkness.

"Hey!" someone yelled.

Dr. Castro twisted and looked down, saw the two from NBC looking up at him. He had a moment of panic, but then decided to ignore them.

There was no way they could get inside the statue in the fifteen or twenty minutes it would take for the drone to fly the five miles. There was no way to stop him until it was too late. But just in case, Castro picked up his phone and called up another feature on the drone's navigation app.

"Hey, what the hell are you doing up there?" one of the men shouted.

The doctor wanted to watch the screen of his phone, wanted to stay glued to the feed from the GoPro, seeing the lights of Maracanã Stadium out there in the distance already.

But he turned his head and looked down.

The cameraman had aimed his lens up at Castro. The producer was on a phone talking excitedly.

It doesn't matter, Castro thought. *Nothing matters any—*

He heard the thumping of a helicopter in the darkness to his west but couldn't make out running lights. It was circling and coming closer.

Dr. Castro didn't try to duck down or hide. He was done hiding.

Using the joystick, flying the drone, the doctor felt totally at peace with his decisions, no fear now, no regrets now.

None at all.

Chapter 97

"SON OF A bitch, there he is," said Lieutenant Acosta, who sat beside me in the copilot's seat of the police helicopter looking through high-powered binoculars.

"You have eyes on him?" da Silva demanded over the radio.

"Affirmative, General," Acosta said. "Right where Mo-bot spotted him."

"Where's the rocket?"

"I don't see any rocket."

"Then get closer, goddamn it, and throw your lights on him. And put on your radar and the camera, Jack. I want to see what you're seeing."

The Brazilian military helicopter had a millimeter-wave radar system and optical and infrared cameras mounted below the nose.

I turned them on and immediately heard *blip!*

I took my eyes off the statue and glanced at the screen. *Blip! Blip!* It was small, moving slowly right along the tops of the trees. It vanished then, and I figured it for a big bird of some kind.

"I can't see any rocket," Lieutenant Acosta said, drawing me off the radar screen.

"Has he already launched it?" General da Silva asked.

"No, we would have seen it take off," I said, picking up speed, turning on the spotlight beam, and flying straight at Christ the Redeemer.   •

I slowed the chopper and hovered one hundred feet from the outstretched arms of the Christ. Even with the gray outfit and the matching paint on his face, you couldn't miss Castro's head, shoulders, and torso sticking up out of the arm.

He wasn't looking our way. His head was down. His hands were busy.

"What's he doing?" I asked.

Pistol drawn and in his lap, Acosta peered through the binoculars. "He's looking at a large iPhone on the arm in front of him, and he's using a control of some sort with a joystick."

I thought of the blips back there on the radar. Small. Slow speed. Right at the treetops. I felt sick.

"It's not a rocket," I said. "He's flying a drone."

"Shoot him," General da Silva said over our headsets.

"General?"

"Put a bullet in his head," da Silva said. "Then get control of that goddamned drone."

I had a handful of reasons why I thought that killing Castro wasn't the best idea. I angled the spotlight directly on the doctor before handing the microphone to Lieutenant Acosta. "Call him by name. Tell him to bring the drone back and surrender."

Acosta said, "Dr. Castro, this is the federal police. Bring back the drone or you will be shot."

The doctor stared at us blankly, then he nodded and put the joystick down. He touched the screen of his phone with his left hand at the same time he reached below the hatch rim with his right.

Castro came up with a pistol, aimed it at us, and fired three quick times.

All three bullets went through the windshield.

Acosta roared out in pain, "I'm hit!"

Chapter 98

DR. CASTRO SAW the bullets strike the windshield and watched the cop in the passenger seat jerk on impact. He swung his gun toward the pilot, but the chopper pulled away hard. He shot at the rear rotor as it retreated but missed.

Castro glanced at the image from the GoPro on his phone screen; the stadium was much closer. Distance to target: 2.9 miles. ETA: eleven minutes.

He looked up, hoping to see the helicopter heading toward a hospital, but it wasn't. The chopper was taking a wide loop around the statue, too far for him to shoot. Could he keep them at bay, circling for eleven minutes?

Castro believed he could, though he was certain he would die soon, and not from Hydra-9. He'd shot at a military police helicopter. The men in the helicopter somehow knew about the virus.

They would try to kill him to get control of the drone. But the doctor knew that was an impossibility. There was nothing they could do now to stop it. The statue was locked. They might try to land on the other arm, but no. Who would get out? Not the cop with the bullet in him. And not the pilot.

The helicopter was to Castro's right now, some two hundred yards, searchlight off. It changed direction and closed the distance at an angle slightly to his rear, back toward the Christ's head.

The doctor grabbed the joystick control and flung it into space, then he twisted around, swung the pistol toward the chopper, and started firing.

Chapter 99

CASTRO FIRED FIVE times. All five bullets missed the mark, though one hit the helicopter's landing strut and another the lower fuselage. The doctor thumbed the latch that dropped the clip. He groped for another.

"Kill him," I said.

"I can't," Acosta said.

One of the doctor's first shots had hit the lieutenant in the right shoulder. He was trying to support his quivering arm with his left hand enough so that he could get a decent sight picture on Castro.

"Gimme the gun," I said.

The lieutenant handed it to me.

I set it in my lap, reached up, and undid the slide window.

Air rushed in. I took the control stick with my right hand and pushed the gun out the window with my left. I spun the chopper one hundred and eighty degrees and saw Castro lift his head and his gun, grinning like a madman.

The instant I had a sight picture, I shot, shot, and then shot again.

Chapter 100

THE FIRST BULLET went right by Dr. Castro's left ear.

Before he could return fire, the second slug hit him squarely just below the sternum. He bucked at the impact; it was like he'd been punched in the gut, except this punch was as hot as lava. Castro managed to squeeze off one round.

The pilot shot a third time and hit Castro high in the right chest.

The doctor was flung against the hatch frame. He swooned in shock and pain. The pistol slipped from his fingers, bounced off the statue's arm, and fell to the terrace below.

Castro was dazed, but not confused. The doctor knew who he was and wanted to show the police that it didn't matter what they did; he'd already won.

Castro held up the phone and with a bloody smile waved it at the helicopter and the men inside. Then he dropped it inside the arm.

It is done, he thought happily as he slumped toward death.

It is irreversible.

It is…good.

Chapter 101

WE WATCHED CASTRO sag against the hatch, drop the phone into the arm of the Christ, and die.

General da Silva saw him die too, said, "Now get control of that drone."

"We can't get control," Acosta said. "He's put it on autopilot. That's why he waved his phone at us before he died."

I hadn't understood then, but now I agreed. If Castro had gone to this extreme, he must have had backups.

Swinging the helicopter away from the statue and accelerating north, I said, "General, evacuate that stadium."

"The opening ceremony's already started," da Silva said indignantly.

"That drone's flying right at you and forty-five thousand other people with more than a billion people watching. Your call."

"Find the drone," he said. "Knock it out of the sky."

"It's a pretty big sky, General," Acosta said with a grunt as he got his belt around his upper arm and pulled the tourniquet tight.

"Actually, it's not," I said, and I took the helicopter up to one hundred and sixty miles an hour. "We know where it's going. We'll just get there first."

"I'm going to have the cellular towers shut down, Jack," da Silva said.

"What? Why?"

"That phone controls it. We'll cut the link."

"Don't do it," I said. "If you cut the link, it could go off anywhere, and we'll never get a crack at intercepting it."

I didn't wait for a reply, said into the headset, "Mobot, are you there?"

"In the security center, Jack."

"Patch me through to Sci," I said as we closed on the stadium, which was glowing brilliantly.

"I'm sitting right beside her, Jack," Kloppenberg said.

"We have a drone on autopilot heading toward the stadium with Hydra-9-infected blood on board. We have to figure out how to stop it."

After a moment, Sci said, "How will it be dispersed?"

"I'm not sure," I said as I dropped our airspeed over the parking lots of Maracanã and turned the chopper around. We hovered there, looking back toward the Redeemer.

Sci said, "If the drone's navigation is on autopilot, it's heading to a specific location. Which means that the triggering device of the delivery system has to be location-specific as well. Once the drone hits a certain GPS spot, the virus is released."

"So if we stop it from getting to the stadium, there will be no release?"

"Unless he put redundancies in place."

"Such as?" I asked.

"Maybe if it crashes, it goes off?"

"Great," I said, gaining altitude and turning back toward the stadium.

I flew right over the top of Maracanã and hovered there about three hundred feet up. Below us, athletes from more than one hundred countries were surrounded by troops of samba dancers shaking their stuff on raised stages. "They're pointing at us," Acosta said, looking out his window. "They think it's part of the show."

I didn't care. I was scanning the horizon back toward the mountains. Where was it? A minute ticked by.

General da Silva said, "You've upset the organizers by hovering up there."

"I don't give a damn," I said, still peering back to the southeast.

Where was the drone? Had it crashed? Had something gone wrong? Was the drone down? Was Hydra-9 already killing somewhere outside the—

Blip! Blip!

Glancing at the millimeter-wave radar readout, I said, "Here it comes. Six hundred and fifty yards out."

I pushed the stick forward and we flew toward the drone.

"What do you want me to do?" Acosta said.

"Pray," I said.

"What are you going to do?"

I thought of Sci warning me not to knock it down. I thought of the location-specificity in the triggering device. I thought of the helicopter I was flying.

In the next instant I saw our only chance.

Chapter 102

"THERE IT IS," Acosta said when our spotlight caught the drone, which was three hundred and fifty feet away and puttering along at fifteen miles an hour. "Looks like an octopus or something."

"Tanks, hoses, and airbrushes," I said. "The dispersal system. I'm going to try to hook it with the front of my strut."

I turned the screen to camera view. It was a fisheye lens and showed both landing struts at a curved angle.

I had three windows to look out—two in the door and one down by my ankles that gave me a solid view in front of the left strut. I swung the helicopter gingerly in behind the drone, which got caught in our rotor wash and dropped altitude fast.

I backed off and for a second I thought I'd blown it and knocked it out of the sky. But then the drone began to climb again.

I decided I couldn't do this with finesse. I was going to have to swoop in, dive at it, and, hopefully, hook it.

We were three hundred yards from the stadium

when I made a nifty move with the control stick, came in at a steep angle, and missed snagging the drone by inches.

"It's almost here!" General da Silva cried as I spiraled up and away from the drone, getting in position for one last try.

"Jack told you to evacuate the stadium, General," Lieutenant Acosta said. "You wouldn't listen to him."

I ignored all of it, searched for the drone, and spotted it ten yards from entering the airspace right above the stadium and dropping altitude fast. I hit the throttle and dove the chopper once more, tilting the bird almost on its side so I could watch the strut knife right at the drone.

I missed again.

But a foot peg on the strut support about two feet back hooked the mesh hammock.

The drone now dangled upside down below the hammock with its five propellers spinning wildly.

"Got it," I said, and I pulled away from the stadium.

Ten voices started hooting and cheering in my headphones.

"Well done, Jack!" General da Silva roared.

"Perfectly executed," Sci said.

"Almost perfectly," I said, exhaling long and low. "But we'll take it. Any idea where we should bring the virus?"

"Take it to Castro's lab," Sci said. "The clean room is still up. It can be contained and dealt with there."

Before da Silva could comment, Justine's voice came over my headset.

"Jack, I'm looking at your camera feed. I can see

the drone hanging there, and there's something flashing green in that hammock thing."

I looked down and through the lower door window and saw a small digital readout blinking in bright green: *00:60, 00:59, 00:58, 00:57…*

Chapter 103

"JACK, IT'S A TIMER!" Justine said. "It's going off in—"

"Fifty-four seconds," I said, gritting my teeth, gaining altitude, and wondering what in God's name I was going to do.

In far less than a minute, Castro's biological weapon of mass destruction was going to trigger about three feet below me. The tanks were full of Hydra-9 virus. Those hoses and airbrushes were going to let loose a mist of death over Rio de Janeiro.

"Jack," Lieutenant Acosta said, truly frightened. "Are we going to—"

I swung the helicopter in a tight three-hundred-and-sixty-degree turn, scanning, looking, trying to figure out where to go.

"Forty-five seconds, forty-four..." Justine said.

I ignored her, and when the chopper's nose came around to the east-northeast, I saw the cruise ships docked around the Pier Mauá and others moored in a small cove of Guanabara Bay toward the commercial piers at Caju.

"Thirty-eight," Justine said. "Thirty-seven, thirty-six..."

"Hold on," I said and accelerated the helicopter straight at that cove.

"Twenty-five, twenty-four…"

We roared over throngs of people partying in the streets of Gamboa, celebrating Rio and the Olympic Games, blissfully unaware of the danger flying above them.

"Eighteen, seventeen, sixteen…"

I dropped altitude fast as I came over the crowded central bus station. The spire of Santo Cristo church flashed by.

"Ten, nine, eight…"

"Hold on!" I shouted at Acosta as we flew fifty feet over traffic-jammed Kubitschek Avenue and the sea wall that holds back the bay.

"Six, five, four…"

We barely cleared the top of a cruise ship moored there.

"Three…"

I drove the stick down.

"Two…"

We dropped like a stone the final thirty feet.

The last thing I remember before impact was the inky surface of the bay coming up fast and Justine saying, "One…"

Chapter 104

"JACK?"

I heard someone call my name from far down a long, dark tunnel.

"Jack, can you hear me?"

I recognized the voice as Justine's, took a deep breath that hurt like hell, and forced open my eyes. At first it was all blurry and nothing made sense. Then things came more into focus.

I was lying in a hospital bed, surrounded by monitors. Justine sat in a chair next to me. She was holding my left hand with both of her hands and grinning at me with watery eyes.

"Welcome back to the living," Justine said. "God answered our prayers."

My head swam. "How long have I..."

"Four days," she said, taking away one hand to wipe away her tears. "In addition to a broken sternum, you sustained a head injury in the crash. You had some brain bleeding and swelling. They kept you in a medically induced coma until they could drill holes in your skull to relieve the pressure. That was two days ago."

"What a difference two days make," I said, and

laughed, which made my chest hurt and started a clanging in my head.

I must have moaned because Justine stood up from the chair all worried and said, "You shouldn't move a lot."

"I just figured that out," I said. "Is there anything they can do for the ax-in-my-skull feeling?"

A nurse bustled in. "He's awake! When?"

"Five minutes ago," Justine said. "And he's amazingly alert. Knows me. Logical. Coherent."

The nurse looked up at the clock and brightened. "I win, then. We had a pool going on how long it would be for you to wake up once we took you off the sedatives. I got it by eighteen minutes."

"Glad to be of service," I said.

"His head hurts," Justine said.

"I imagine so," the nurse said. "I'll get the doctor."

My eyes drifted shut, and I fell into a dreamless sleep until the neurosurgeon shook me awake. Justine was still there, and she made phone calls while the doctor examined me.

He seemed satisfied with my progress and told me he'd give me something to take the edge off the pain. I wanted to kiss him.

Shortly after I was given the drugs, some of the fire in my chest and the pounding in my head ebbed. I started to drift off again.

Seymour Kloppenberg and Maureen Roth came in and woke me up again. Sci grinned and bobbed his head. Mo-bot burst into tears.

Fussing over my sheets, she blubbered, "We were all so worried."

"You shouldn't have been. My head's the hardest part of me," I said.

"Not anymore," Sci said. "It's the holiest part of you."

"Funny," I said.

"That was a brilliant move, in case no one's told you yet."

I blinked in confusion. "What was?"

"Crash-landing that helicopter and Castro's virus into salt water."

"It was the only thing I could think of. Did the device go off?"

"It did," Sci said. "But Castro developed Hydra-9 as an airborne pathogen. The saline and the pollution in the bay killed the virus, probably on contact. There's no evidence of it anywhere in the cove, anyway, and they've been testing around the clock."

"That's our superhero at work," Justine said with a wry smile.

"I am no superhero," I said. "Lots of people helped stop Castro, and none more important than Maureen."

"Oh, c'mon." Mo-bot tittered. "My part was luck."

"You thought to look," I said.

"No, I happened to glance at the NBC raw feeds and in came footage of the Redeemer shot just before dark when there was this weird reddish color in the western sky. I thought it was dramatic, so I blew it up on the big screen in the command center. One second the statue's right arm was flat, and the next second it was like it had biceps—you know, a big bump that wasn't there before?"

"But you saw the bump, and you magnified the image enough to see it was Castro standing in the hatch," I said.

"Well, yes, I did do that," Mo-bot said.

"Thank God you did," I said. "Even though we figured Castro had gone up Corcovado Mountain, we never would have located him inside the statue in time to save forty-five thousand people from a deadly virus. This one's all you, Maureen Roth. *You* saved the day."

Mo-bot beamed and laughed, said, "I'll take some of the credit, but you did all the crazy stuff to stop him and his drone."

"Acosta was a big part of it too," I said. "He took a bullet. How is he?"

They sobered. Justine said, "Bruno died on impact, Jack."

I'd been growing stronger by the minute until then. I sagged and felt shitty.

Acosta was dead. Tavia was dead. I was involved in both tragedies. I was a contributing factor in both deaths. I'd survived them both and felt the guilt of that like a heavy blanket around me.

"Bruno was a great cop," I said. "Smart. Tough. As brave as they come. But I couldn't figure out any other way to handle the virus than to crash."

"You did the right thing," said General da Silva, who'd just come into the hospital room. "Acosta would have said the same. He died a hero and a martyr for every single person in that stadium and for every single person who might have contracted the virus afterward. You two prevented a national calamity, Jack. I know the president wishes to thank you personally when you're up to it."

That was nice, but losing Tavia and Acosta in the process of keeping the Olympic Games safe was a bitter pill to swallow, one I was sure I'd be tasting in the back of my throat for years.

Wanting to change the subject, I said, "How are the games going?"

The general smiled and opened his hands wide. "Since the opening ceremony, my marvelous Rio has been showing its true colors. The games have been a nonstop party so far. The greatest the world has ever seen."

"I'd expect nothing less," I said.

"The doctors said you'll be able to leave in maybe two days," da Silva said. "So any event you want to go to after that, you'll have the best seats in the house. Next Sunday night is the men's hundred-meter. Fastest-man-on-earth race."

I'd seen the finals in London and almost turned him down, but then said, "Get me four tickets."

"Done."

I gestured to Sci, Mo-bot, and Justine. "You're coming with me."

Roth clapped and Sci seemed pleased.

"Sure you don't want me back in L.A., looking after things?" Justine said.

"I kind of need you here."

She smiled, held my hand again, and said, "I'll stay in Rio as long as you want me here."

Chapter 105

THEY LET ME out of the hospital two days later. I could walk, but the pain drugs and the holes in the head and the broken ribs ruled out my driving or doing anything strenuous for the foreseeable future.

General da Silva arranged for us to stay in his sister's two-bedroom rental in Ipanema while I convalesced. Justine and Mo-bot took turns taking care of me. We watched the Olympics and really got into the rowing and the indoor bicycle racing for some reason. Very exciting stuff.

Justine spent a lot of time on the phone with Emilio Cruz, her boyfriend. Cruz works in my L.A. office. I could tell there was some friction over her not returning until the games were over.

"You can leave anytime," I told her. "I'm feeling better."

"I'll leave when I believe you can take care of yourself," she said.

"You sure?"

"Jack, yes, I'm sure," Justine said, pushing back her hair. "I almost lost you. I...don't think I could have...I just have to make sure you're okay."

Her eyes welled with tears and she looked away,

embarrassed. My heart almost broke because I realized she still carried a torch for me, as I did for her.

"Thank you," I said, swallowing at the emotion in my throat. "But I don't want to upset you and Cruz."

"I thought Emilio and I were good," she said, sniffing and wiping at her eyes. "But if our relationship can't stand this stress, then it wasn't meant to be."

Justine touched me with her loyalty and with her acknowledgment of the thing that still lived between us, whatever it was. I couldn't think about that for long. It seemed like I was insulting Tavia somehow.

So for the first time in a long time I started talking. About everything.

Over the course of days, I told Justine all about Tavia and broke down several times in the process. I felt as if I'd really opened up, held nothing back, and as a result we'd never been closer.

"You've come a long way," Justine said early Sunday afternoon, nine days after the crash, as she helped me into a sport-fishing charter boat I'd hired out of the Botafogo Bay marina. "It's good you're not keeping it all bottled up the way you usually do."

"Think I've earned a spot on *Dr. Phil*?"

"Uh, no, but you're making progress," she said, smiling with concern. "Sure you don't want me to come along?"

"This is something I need to do alone."

"I'll be waiting right here for you when you come back."

"What am I? Forrest Gump?"

Justine laughed, said, "Forrest is a lot faster."

"I think my grandmother's faster at the moment," I said and settled into my seat and put Tavia's ashes on the deck between my legs. "At least go have lunch or an açaí berry smoothie or something."

"Açaí berry smoothie it is. Those things are addictive, aren't they?"

"Massively," I said as the captain started his engines.

"There's really no one else?" Justine asked.

I shook my head, said, "She was an orphan."

The mate threw off the lines.

As the captain chugged us out of the marina, I watched Justine at the end of the dock watching me until we lost sight of each other.

We picked up speed and headed toward the harbor mouth. Sugarloaf Mountain loomed to our right, looking as impossible and breathtaking as ever.

For a moment I thought about the climbers Tavia and I and General da Silva had rescued off the cliffs the day before the World Cup final. It seemed like several lifetimes ago.

When we were more than a mile offshore, the captain slowed his engines and looked to me. I gazed around at the relative position of Sugarloaf, Copacabana, and the lighthouse toward Devil Beach.

I nodded. It looked right.

The captain cut his engines. I picked up the urn and fought my way to my feet and to the side of the boat.

For a moment I looked around again, wanting to be sure, swallowing at the ball of emotion that swelled in my throat.

I unscrewed the lid of the urn and, whispering hoarsely, said, "So here you are, Tavia, right where you wanted to be, a part of Rio forever."

I had to stop for several moments and breathe not to cry.

"I loved you, Tavia. I miss you, and I always will."

Then, with shaking hands, I spread her ashes on the water.

There was little wind and they floated on the surface for a few minutes before drifting off into the glinting light toward Copacabana.

I sat down, feeling hollow and alone, before nodding to the captain.

When we reached Botafogo Bay, I got up and stood in the bow, shading my eyes and peering toward the marina.

Justine, my friend, my very best friend in the world, was right there on the dock, smiling and waiting for me.

Acknowledgments

Our gratitude goes out to the Cariocas, the welcoming people of Rio de Janeiro, who went out of their way to teach us both sides of their "Marvelous City," the glamorous and the rich as well as the destitute and the poor.

Our exceptional guide, João Carlos Desales, showed us the tapestry of life inside some of the world's most desperate slums, and then did the same for us in some of the world's wealthiest neighborhoods. This book could not have been written without him.

We were also helped by Lais Tammela Souza and Rosangela Farias, who led us to Rio's stunning physical landmarks and pointed out little-known facts that later became part of the book.

Lieutenant Marco Veiga of the Rio de Janeiro State Military Police helped us understand the BOPE and the favelas from a law-enforcement perspective. Oca dos Curumins, also known as "Tia Bete," runs an after-school program inside the Alemän favela, and gave us social insights into the dynamics of Rio's teeming slums.

Dr. Raquel Souza at Hospital Federal dos Servidores do Estado worked with us on tropical diseases and how they spread in Brazil. Lucia Montanarella of the Rio Olympic Authority was gracious with her time in explaining the various venues of the 2016

Olympic Games. Raquel Aguiar with the Oswaldo Cruz Institute was a big help.

We are also grateful to the nameless people of the Alemän, Marabel, and Vidigal favelas who made us feel welcome, the folks we met at the FIFA World Cup Final, and so many other Cariocas who shared with us their unique city and lifestyle.

About the Authors

JAMES PATTERSON received the Literarian Award for Outstanding Service to the American Literary Community at the 2015 National Book Awards. He holds the Guinness World Record for the most #1 *New York Times* bestsellers, and his books have sold more than 350 million copies worldwide. He has donated more than one million books to students and soldiers and funds over four hundred Teacher Education Scholarships at twenty-four colleges and universities. He has also donated millions to independent bookstores and school libraries.

MARK SULLIVAN is the solo author of thirteen thrillers, including *Thief,* and the coauthor of five Private novels with James Patterson. He lives in Bozeman, Montana, with his family, and loves to travel.

BOOKS BY JAMES PATTERSON

FEATURING ALEX CROSS

Cross the Line • *Cross Justice* • *Hope to Die* • *Cross My Heart* • *Alex Cross, Run* • *Merry Christmas, Alex Cross* • *Kill Alex Cross* • *Cross Fire* • *I, Alex Cross* • *Alex Cross's* Trial (with Richard DiLallo) • *Cross Country* • *Double Cross* • *Cross* (also published as *Alex Cross*) • *Mary, Mary* • *London Bridges* • *The Big Bad Wolf* • *Four Blind Mice* • *Violets Are Blue* • *Roses Are Red* • *Pop Goes the Weasel* • *Cat & Mouse* • *Jack & Jill* • *Kiss the Girls* • *Along Came a Spider*

THE WOMEN'S MURDER CLUB

16th Seduction (with Maxine Paetro) • *15th Affair* (with Maxine Paetro) • *14th Deadly Sin* (with Maxine Paetro) • *Unlucky 13* (with Maxine Paetro) • *12th of Never* (with Maxine Paetro) • *11th Hour* (with Maxine Paetro) • *10th Anniversary* (with Maxine Paetro) • *The 9th Judgment* (with Maxine Paetro) • *The 8th Confession* (with Maxine Paetro) • *7th Heaven* (with Maxine Paetro) • *The 6th Target* (with Maxine Paetro) • *The 5th Horseman* (with Maxine Paetro) • *4th of July* (with Maxine Paetro) • *3rd Degree* (with Andrew Gross) • *2nd Chance* (with Andrew Gross) • *1st to Die*

FEATURING MICHAEL BENNETT

Haunted (with James O. Born) • *Bullseye* (with Michael Ledwidge) • *Alert* (with Michael Ledwidge) • *Burn* (with Michael Ledwidge) • *Gone* (with Michael Ledwidge) • *I, Michael Bennett* (with Michael Ledwidge) • *Tick Tock* (with Michael Ledwidge) • *Worst Case* (with Michael

Ledwidge) • *Run for Your Life* (with Michael Ledwidge) •
Step on a Crack (with Michael Ledwidge)

THE PRIVATE NOVELS

Missing (with Kathryn Fox) • *The Games* (with Mark
Sullivan) • *Private Paris* (with Mark Sullivan) • *Private
Vegas* (with Maxine Paetro) • *Private India: City on Fire*
(with Ashwin Sanghi) • *Private Down Under* (with Michael
White) • *Private L.A.* (with Mark Sullivan) • *Private Berlin*
(with Mark Sullivan) • *Private London* (with Mark
Pearson) • *Private Games* (with Mark Sullivan) • *Private:
#1 Suspect* (with Maxine Paetro) • *Private* (with Maxine
Paetro)

NYPD RED NOVELS

NYPD Red 4 (with Marshall Karp) • *NYPD Red 3* (with
Marshall Karp) • *NYPD Red 2* (with Marshall Karp) •
NYPD Red (with Marshall Karp)

SUMMER NOVELS

Second Honeymoon (with Howard Roughan) • *Now You
See Her* (with Michael Ledwidge) • *Swimsuit* (with Maxine
Paetro) • *Sail* (with Howard Roughan) • *Beach Road* (with
Peter de Jonge) • *Lifeguard* (with Andrew Gross) •
Honeymoon (with Howard Roughan) • *The Beach House*
(with Peter de Jonge)

STAND-ALONE BOOKS

The Family Lawyer (with Robert Rotstein, Christopher
Charles, Rachel Howzell Hall) • *The Store* (with Richard
DiLallo) • *The Moores Are Missing* (with Loren D.
Estleman, Sam Hawken, Ed Chatterton) • *Triple Threat*
(with Max DiLallo, Andrew Bourelle) • *Murder Games*

(with Howard Roughan) • *Penguins of America* (with Jack Patterson with Florence Yue) • *Two from the Heart* (with Frank Constantini, Emily Raymond, Brian Sitts) • *The Black Book* (with David Ellis) • *Humans, Bow Down* (with Emily Raymond) • *Never Never* (with Candice Fox) • *Woman of God* (with Maxine Paetro) • *Filthy Rich* (with John Connolly and Timothy Malloy) • *The Murder House* (with David Ellis) • *Truth or Die* (with Howard Roughan) • *Miracle at Augusta* (with Peter de Jonge) • *Invisible* (with David Ellis) • *First Love* (with Emily Raymond) • *Mistress* (with David Ellis) • *Zoo* (with Michael Ledwidge) • *Guilty Wives* (with David Ellis) • *The Christmas Wedding* (with Richard DiLallo) • *Kill Me If You Can* (with Marshall Karp) • *Toys* (with Neil McMahon) • *Don't Blink* (with Howard Roughan) • *The Postcard Killers* (with Liza Marklund) • *The Murder of King Tut* (with Martin Dugard) • *Against Medical Advice* (with Hal Friedman) • *Sundays at Tiffany's* (with Gabrielle Charbonnet) • *You've Been Warned* (with Howard Roughan) • *The Quickie* (with Michael Ledwidge) • *Judge & Jury* (with Andrew Gross) • *Sam's Letters to Jennifer* • *The Lake House* • *The Jester* (with Andrew Gross) • *Suzanne's Diary for Nicholas* • *Cradle and All* • *When the Wind Blows* • *Miracle on the 17th Green* (with Peter de Jonge) • *Hide & Seek* • *The Midnight Club* • *Black Friday* (originally published as *Black Market*) • *See How They Run* • *Season of the Machete* • *The Thomas Berryman Number*

BOOK**SHOTS**

The Medical Examiner (with Maxine Paetro) • *Black Dress Affair* (with Susan DiLallo) • *The Killer's Wife* (with Max DiLallo) • *Scott Free* (with Rob Hart) • *The Dolls* (with Kecia Bal) • *Detective Cross* • *Nooners* (with Tim Arnold) • *Stealing Gulfstreams* (with Max DiLallo) • *Diary of a Succubus* (with Derek Nikitas) • *Night Sniper* (with Christopher Charles) • *Juror #3* (with Nancy Allen) • *The*

Shut-In (with Duane Swierczynski) • *French Twist* (with Richard DiLallo) • *Malicious* (with James O. Born) • *Hidden* (with James O. Born) • *The House Husband* (with Duane Swierczynski) • *The Christmas Mystery* (with Richard DiLallo) • *Black & Blue* (with Candice Fox) • *Come and Get Us* (with Shan Serafin) • *Private: The Royals* (with Rees Jones) • *Taking the Titanic* (with Scott Slaven) • *Killer Chef* (with Jeffrey J. Keyes) • *French Kiss* (with Richard DiLallo) • *$10,000,000 Marriage Proposal* (with Hilary Liftin) • *Hunted* (with Andrew Holmes) • *113 Minutes* (with Max DiLallo) • *Chase* (with Michael Ledwidge) • *Let's Play Make-Believe* (with James O. Born) • *The Trial* (with Maxine Paetro) • *Little Black Dress* (with Emily Raymond) • *Cross Kill* • *Zoo II* (with Max DiLallo)

Sabotage: An Under Covers Story by Jessica Linden • *Love Me Tender* by Laurie Horowitz • *Bedding the Highlander* by Sabrina York • *The Wedding Florist* by T.J. Kline • *A Wedding in Maine* by Jen McLaughlin • *Radiant* by Elizabeth Hayley • *Hot Winter Nights* by Codi Gray • *Bodyguard* by Jessica Linden • *Dazzling* by Elizabeth Hayley • *The Mating Season* by Laurie Horowitz • *Sacking the Quarterback* by Samantha Towle • *Learning to Ride* by Erin Knightley • *The McCullagh Inn in Maine* by Jen McLaughlin

FOR READERS OF ALL AGES

Maximum Ride

Maximum Ride Forever • *Nevermore: The Final Maximum Ride Adventure* • *Angel: A Maximum Ride Novel* • *Fang: A Maximum Ride Novel* • *Max: A Maximum Ride Novel* • *The*

Final Warning: A Maximum Ride Novel • *Saving the World and Other Extreme Sports: A Maximum Ride Novel* • *School's Out—Forever: A Maximum Ride Novel* • *The Angel Experiment: A Maximum Ride Novel*

Daniel X

Daniel X: Lights Out (with Chris Grabenstein) • *Daniel X: Armageddon* (with Chris Grabenstein) • *Daniel X: Game Over* (with Ned Rust) • *Daniel X: Demons and Druids* (with Adam Sadler) • *Daniel X: Watch the Skies* (with Ned Rust) • *The Dangerous Days of Daniel X* (with Michael Ledwidge)

Witch & Wizard

Witch & Wizard: The Lost (with Emily Raymond) • *Witch & Wizard: The Kiss* (with Jill Dembowski) • *Witch & Wizard: The Fire* (with Jill Dembowski) • *Witch & Wizard: The Gift* (with Ned Rust) • *Witch & Wizard* (with Gabrielle Charbonnet)

Confessions

Confessions: The Murder of an Angel (with Maxine Paetro) • *Confessions: The Paris Mysteries* (with Maxine Paetro) • *Confessions: The Private School Murders* (with Maxine Paetro) • *Confessions of a Murder Suspect* (with Maxine Paetro)

Middle School

Middle School: Escape to Australia (with Martin Chatterton, illustrated by Daniel Griffo) • *Middle School: Dog's Best Friend* (with Chris Tebbetts, illustrated by Jomike Tejido) • *Middle School: Just My Rotten Luck* (with Chris Tebbetts, illustrated by Laura Park) • *Middle School: Save Rafe!* (with Chris Tebbetts, illustrated by Laura Park) • *Middle School: Ultimate Showdown* (with Julia Bergen, illustrated by Alec Longstreth) • *Middle School: How I Survived Bullies, Broccoli, and Snake Hill* (with Chris Tebbetts, illustrated by Laura Park) • *Middle School: My Brother Is a Big, Fat Liar* (with Lisa Papademetriou, illustrated by Neil Swaab) • *Middle School: Get Me Out of Here!* (with Chris Tebbetts, illustrated by Laura Park) • *Middle School, The Worst Years of My Life* (with Chris Tebbetts, illustrated by Laura Park)

I Funny

I Funny: School of Laughs (with Chris Grabenstein, illustrated by Jomike Tejido • *I Funny TV* (with Chris Grabenstein, illustrated by Laura Park) • *I Totally Funniest: A Middle School Story* (with Chris Grabenstein, illustrated by Laura Park) • *I Even Funnier: A Middle School Story* (with Chris Grabenstein, illustrated by Laura Park) • *I Funny: A Middle School Story* (with Chris Grabenstein, illustrated by Laura Park)

Treasure Hunters

Treasure Hunters: Peril at the Top of the World (with Chris Grabenstein, illustrated by Juliana Neufeld) • *Treasure Hunters: Secret of the Forbidden City* (with Chris Grabenstein, illustrated by Juliana Neufeld) • *Treasure Hunters: Danger Down the Nile* (with Chris Grabenstein, illustrated by Juliana Neufeld) • *Treasure Hunters* (with Chris Grabenstein, illustrated by Juliana Neufeld)

OTHER BOOKS FOR READERS OF ALL AGES

Give Thank You a Try (with Bill O'Reilly) • *Expelled* (with Emily Raymond) • *The Candies Save Christmas* (illustrated by Andy Elkerton) • *Big Words for Little Geniuses* (with Susan Patterson, illustrated by Hsinping Pan) • *Laugh Out Loud* (with Chris Grabenstein) • *Pottymouth and Stoopid* (with Chris Grabenstein) • *Crazy House* (with Gabrielle Charbonnet) • *House of Robots: Robot Revolution* (with Chris Grabenstein, illustrated by Juliana Neufeld) • *Word of Mouse* (with Chris Grabenstein, illustrated by Joe Sutphin) • *Give Please a Chance* (with Bill O'Reilly) • *Jacky Ha-Ha* (with Chris Grabenstein, illustrated by Kerascoët) • *House of Robots:*

Robots Go Wild! (with Chris Grabenstein, illustrated by Juliana Neufeld) • *Public School Superhero* (with Chris Tebbetts, illustrated by Cory Thomas) • *House of Robots* (with Chris Grabenstein, illustrated by Juliana Neufeld) • *Homeroom Diaries* (with Lisa Papademetriou, illustrated by Keino) • *Med Head* (with Hal Friedman) • *santaKid* (illustrated by Michael Garland)

For previews and information about the author, visit JamesPatterson.com or find him on Facebook or at your app store.

JAMES
PATTERSON
RECOMMENDS

JAMES PATTERSON

PRIVATE

NEW YORK · LOS ANGELES · LONDON · PARIS

& MAXINE PAETRO

PRIVATE

I've always been a curious person. It's one of the many reasons why I'm a writer. Something I always asked myself was: "What happens if a 'one percenter' gets into trouble?" The answer: Jack Morgan and PRIVATE. On Jack Morgan's agenda in his debut outing is investigating a multimillion-dollar NFL gambling scandal and solving a series of schoolgirl slayings. Then, the unthinkable—his former lover turned best friend's wife is murdered. One thing you should know about Jack is that beneath his Lamborghini-driving, red-carpet-event-attending surface, he's a very smart guy. And he takes no prisoners. Just wait till you get to the end of PRIVATE. You'll see what I mean.

JACK MORGAN
IS WANTED
FOR MURDER

THE WORLD'S #1 BESTSELLING WRITER

JAMES PATTERSON

PRIVATE
#1 Suspect

& MAXINE PAETRO

PRIVATE L.A.

If you've ever wondered what celebrity power couples do behind closed doors, you can stop all of your conjecturing—the answers are all in PRIVATE L.A. America's most popular celebrity couple has made an exit…from their lives. No one knows where they went or why, and it's up to Jack and his Private team to breach the walls of security and hordes of paparazzi to find the power couple. But when has anything good ever come from a pile of secrets buried under miles of genius PR? Jack's about to find that out, up close and personal, and he's in for the shock of his life. Because in the city of big dreams, nothing is what it seems. Especially if I'm involved.

PRIVATE UNCOVERS A
SHOCKING PAST AND A
LETHAL CONSPIRACY—
IN MODERN-DAY BERLIN
THE WORLD'S #1 BESTSELLING WRITER
JAMES PATTERSON
PRIVATE
BERLIN
MARK SULLIVAN

PRIVATE BERLIN

Every now and then, I find myself wanting a big change in scenery. Don't get me wrong. Jack Morgan and the Private team are great fun, but sometimes a little taste of the foreign makes life a bit more exciting. And by "exciting," I really mean dangerous. At Private's German headquarters, Chris Schneider—superstar agent—has gone rogue. He's the keeper of quite a few pieces of sensitive information, but one in particular could have earth-shattering consequences. Hang on tight and don't blink. This one is a rollercoaster of tension that'll leave you reeling.

JAMES PATTERSON
BOOKSHOTS

I'd like to recommend a new reading experience to you. It's called BookShots.

BookShots are a whole new format of books—they're 100% story-driven, no filler, no fluff, and always under $5.00.

And, at 150 pages, they can make reading more convenient. They can be read in an evening, on a commute, while exercising, even during breaks at work on a cell phone.

So welcome to BookShots and the reading revolution.

You can learn more at Bookshots.com.

All my best,

James Patterson

STORIES AT THE SPEED OF LIFE
JAMES PATTERSON
BOOKSHOTS
A MICHAEL BENNETT STORY
CHASE
WITH
MICHAEL LEDWIDGE

CHASE

A good-looking, well-dressed man plunges to his death from the roof of a chic Manhattan hotel. It looks like a suicide, except the victim has someone else's fingerprints—someone who's already dead. Now, Michael Bennett, our favorite detective with the NYPD, must head to the nation's capital, where he pokes at secrets that powerful people don't want revealed, uncovering a plot he never could have dreamed up.

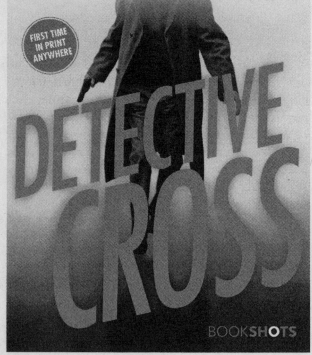

JAMES PATTERSON

DETECTIVE CROSS

BOOKSHOTS

DETECTIVE CROSS

When an anonymous caller has promised to set off deadly bombs in Washington, DC, Alex Cross is the only person the MPDC can trust to track down the terrorist. But is it a cruel hoax or the real deal? I decided to put Cross on this case because he's been duped by a false alarm before. But when he and his wife, Bree Stone, uncover the chilling truth, it may be too late...

JAMES PATTERSON

WITH
MAXINE PAETRO

WOMEN'S MURDER CLUB
THE MEDICAL EXAMINER

BOOK**SHOTS**

THE MEDICAL EXAMINER

My favorite Women's Murder Club stories are the ones where the whole gang has to work together—which is exactly what happens in this one. The premise? Two bodies arrive at the morgue, but one is still breathing. Here, you'll see Claire Washburn in her element as a medical examiner, and you'll watch Cindy Thomas find the hard-hitting truths as a journalist. And when the case gets even more twisted, it becomes the perfect nightmare for the Women's Murder Club.

JAMES PATTERSON

WITH
KECIA BAL
MasterClass Winner

THE DOLLS

Looks can kill

BOOK**SHOTS**

THE DOLLS

This is a story I wrote with the winner of the contest I ran with Master Class. (If you're looking to become a fiction writer, I recommend checking out my class.) It's a sexy thriller about artificial intelligence—it's current, creepy, and feels all too real. The book stars investigative reporter Lila Wallace, who thinks she's covering the technology beat but gets in way over her head when she discovers that wealthy, tech-savvy men are being murdered under mysterious circumstances. This one might keep you up all night.

BOOK**SHOTS**

THERE'S A REVOLUTION IN READING—IT'S CALLED BOOKSHOTS.

BookShots are a whole new kind of book—100% story-driven, no fluff, always under $5, and written and co-written by James Patterson himself.

At 150 pages or fewer, BookShots can be read in a night, on a commute, even on your cell phone during breaks at work.

FOR SPECIAL OFFERS AND THE FULL LIST OF BOOKSHOT TITLES, PLEASE GO TO: WWW.BOOKSHOTS.COM